Safe Under the Willow

Shannon Bibby

Shannon Bibby

Published by Shannon Bibby Printed by CreateSpace, An Amazon.com Company

ISBN-13: 978-1517199746
ISBN-10: 1517199743

Cover Art: Amanda McCann used with permission from the artist created by CreateSpace Cover Creator

Author photograph by Toni Martin; Used with permission from the artist

Thank You Willow, Autumn Dickinson; Used with permission from the artist

Disclaimer

While this novel is classified as fiction, some of the events within were based on the author's experiences and viewpoint. In those cases, names and identifying details have been changed to protect the privacy of the individuals involved.

Shannon Bibby

Dedication

This book is dedicated to all victims and survivors of domestic violence. I pray you all have the courage to find *your voice*.

B.B. – Thank you for loving me 'as is' in the hardest of times and getting us to the good times. You will always have my heart forever and always

A.D. - Without your relentless motivation and encouragement, I don't think this book would have ever been written. Thank you for always being my angel of inspiration.

J.S. - As you rest, I pray I bring a smile to your face when I see you in Heaven. All my love Silent Strength.

B.C. - Your unconditional everything will never leave my heart. As our adventures continue, may our RR always be bold and in His Truth

Our Lord & Savior, Jesus Christ. - Without You, my life would be filled of darkness. Thank you for showing me Your everlasting Light.
May every knee bend on that glorious day!

2 Corinthians 1:3-4
Blessed be the God and Father of our Lord Jesus Christ, the Father of mercies and God of all comfort; who comforts us in all our affliction, that we may be able to comfort those who are in any affliction, through the comfort with which we ourselves are comforted by God.

To my children:

May you always have the courage to follow God's will

Love,

Mommy

Shannon Bibby

Table of Contents

Safe Under the Willow

Prologue

Thank You Willow

Nested beneath your branches

Obscured from the outside world

With shaking hands and dampened cheeks

Sits a scared and lonely girl

Frightened to go back home

For fear of what waits

What should be her haven

Is filled with anger and hate

Bruises and bumps

Lies and excuses

Everyone at his hand

Ultimately loses

Enraged emotion

Rapidly beating heart

Treading lightly

For fear he'll start

Another beer

Another scream

She begs relentlessly

To let her be

Shannon Bibby

Her mom's words fall flat
Just before her body
Limp and lifeless
Beaten and bloody
That's when the girl ran
Seeking refuge under your veil
Your branches comforting her
Serving a protective shell
In the wind she hears
His voice calling so gruff
Quiet is she ever
Until he gave up
You chased away the demon
You chased away the pain
For a moment she was free
Til tomorrow the same

Chapter 1

The Phantom Returns

Flickers of light bounced through the window and off our yellow kitchen wall; amazing how light can travel so fully; so effortless. He's home. I knew she was going to be made the villain. She always was especially when he was made a fool in front of other patrons of the bar. Other times it was as though he felt it necessary to blame her for his hatred of life.

"Go on now; you don't want Daddy to see you up so late."

"Yes Mama," I replied.

Ten years old and I had to share a bedroom with my four year old sister. I ran up and buried my small frame under the shabby blue bedspread, trying to remain quiet and unknown so I didn't wake Chloe. "I hate him," I thought. A door slammed and the thunder of his voice rocked me to my very core. I felt terrified; yes terror, but also anger. The fighting escalated; I could hear my mother being thrown into one of the last lamps in our home; I laid quiet, stricken. The sound of her body made a thud against the unsteady stand the lamp was on. I heard the blast of the thick base of the lamp shatter. Darkness deafened the house of pain.

Rather than safe in slumber and dreaming of swinging and bopping up and down on the seesaw, I heard my mother sobbing and my father say, "Take that you no good bitch!"

Hearing him stagger up the stairs and evidently missing a step when I heard the pounding of his knee hit the thinly carpeted step and he yelled, "You'll pay for that."

Ninety seconds ticked by. I knew my father had passed out from the reverberation of his snore. I tipped toed down the stairs delicately so I wouldn't wake the drunken beast. I saw my mother still lying on our worn out brown carpeted floor. Mom looked up and gave me a troubled smile.

"I'm okay, Sweetheart; Daddy just got upset."

With all the anger built up inside me, I had a hard time not screaming at her. I knew Mom got enough of that from my father.

Instead, I regained my composure and said, "Mama, Daddy gets angry all the time. I know how he treats you. I see it, Mom. I'm only ten, but I'm not stupid. Why can't we leave Mama? Please, please, just pack us up and leave!"

I pleaded with her. I didn't understand how my mom could live a daily life of abuse and pain. What good did he do for us? He only brought heartache. He couldn't even keep a job most of the time. Frustrated, but feeling sorry for my mom, I helped her up off the floor. We began picking up the pieces of our cream colored lamp.

"I'll get the super-glue," Mom said.

Mom spent a small fortune on glue. The clerk at the dollar

store had asked her once why she bought so much glue. He seemed to imply huffing, but Mom was quick to intervene and shake her head no, then told him her young children are always breaking things. The clerk seemed to be happy with her answer and it ended their short conversation. I'm sure by the recycled clothes from the local thrift store we were dressed in, our outward appearance looked worn and ragged. We were poor, I understand that, but to be quick to judge that just because we were poor we were addicts made me want to defend what little honor we had.

I heard a car horn blazing at me and realized I was actually in my comfortable SUV at the light and it had turned green.

"Back to reality Jillian," I said to myself.

I stepped on the gas and as I glanced at my gauges, I saw my fuel light had come on. I decided to wait to fill up my tank on my way home since I was only two miles from work. I pulled into Buckingham Nursing Home, parking in my usual space. It was a beautiful warm morning which made me want to turn around and head back home. I envisioned the light breeze kissing my cheeks as I lay in the plush grass beneath my willow. Instead, I made my way to the time clock and a friend stopped me.

"Hey Jillian, how's it going?" I smiled and told Hailey I was doing good as I slid my badge. I've been employed by Buckingham for eight years as their Medical Records Coordinator and I couldn't have asked for a better job. It wasn't a position that demanded care to the residents, but rather a role that was filled with paperwork and following federal and state regulations. And I loved it.

"Mr. Hopkins passed away early this morning. I bet you have a huge chart to close." Hailey replied.

My heart sunk but I couldn't let Hailey know. I let out a small groan and being sarcastic said, "That's just what I wanted to hear to start out my week." We chuckled and I walked to my office, forgetting my routine morning coffee.

I held a soft spot in my heart for Mr. Hopkins. The gentleness of his voice, the wisdom that he spoke and the love for his family poured out in every conversation. He was a gray haired man with a distinctive mole above his upper lip, thin, tall and once attractive man had made a regrettable sinner's life for himself and his family.

I sat down in my comfortably cushioned executive chair and began to collect my thoughts creating a game plan for my days tasks. Bumping the picture of my children, I turned on my computer to let it boot up so that I could check my work e-mail. The unit was being sluggish and I started to get annoyed. These four walls seemed to suffocate me at times, even though I love my job. Instead of waiting the five minutes to pass, I made my way to the nurse's station where the commotion of nurses and doctors practiced their skills.

"Hey Betty, I heard Mr. Hopkins passed away. Let me know when you have everything completed so I can take the chart off your hands," I said with a small smile.

Once a resident, usually elderly, at the nursing home was discharged from our facility, I had to take their medical chart and break it down into a specific order. The chart itself contained nurses' notes, physician orders, therapy documentation and many other pertinent forms. Our corporate boss decided the order with my help a few years ago. The physician would then sign any orders that were missed during their stay. Once the chart was signed it was to be filed away in storage for the next ten years.

Betty was the daylight charge nurse and nice enough, though I had to push her on occasion to make sure I got all the records I needed on time. Betty was constantly doing paperwork and running from resident to resident making sure everything was going smoothly. She is a perfectionist yet never on time.

"Okay Jillian, I should have it to you by two."

I headed back to my office filled with gray filing cabinets of information containing these poor soul's lives who resided in the nursing home. Usually, older and without a lot of family, they stayed due to being unable to care for themselves. So, Buckingham becomes a permanent residence for many of them.

In my office, the white walls attempted to brighten up my space with a window looking to the woods. Deer munch on the foliage in the summer and I leave apples as a treat to my wildlife friends every week. Other than an occasional spotting of a deer or squirrel, the office was bleak without any wall hangings. The metal that intruded my space made me sad in instances like this. Losing a man like Mr. Hopkins made my heart ache.

"Man, I hope my kids don't send me to a nursing home," I said aloud.

As I sat back down I glanced over our census. We were at our fullest capacity, with a maximum number of residents living at our nursing home at one hundred and twenty. Now that Mr. Hopkins passed I'm sure we would get a new admission due to having an available bed. This means one thing for me - more paperwork. It's endless in this job, but for some insane reason I am good at being the medical records coordinator. I was proud of myself and my work. I took pride in what I did. If I didn't… no one would. I refused to be a duplicate of my father, unable to hold down a job. That's why I give all of my efforts on a daily basis to do things right, to do work that is worthy.

I started my daily routine and pulled out all the purged records for Mr. Hopkins. He was a resident at the nursing home for seven years which meant his chart needed to be thinned of older documents that wasn't needed for everyday use. Poor man had little family and only received visits from them about twice a year. His wife passed away eight years ago. Then, when he fell and broke his hip, his children refused to welcome him in either of their homes. I felt pity for him knowing that no one truly cared for him in his last seven years. An alcoholic all of his life, he put his family through the same torture I once had with my own family. I can't say I blame his son and daughter. I know how I keep the distance between my own father and me. I just wish they could have found peace with their past and could have forgiven their father. Unfortunately, for all parties, it wasn't the case.

Glancing through the paperwork, my mind started to escape me.

I had the pleasure of knowing the man Mr. Hopkins has been over the last seven years- not the same man his children knew. I think to myself, what if I were one of Mr. Hopkins's children? I could quite possibly feel the same way they did towards their father. The difference is that I wouldn't have had the same influences that I did with my own mother and father. Not that my life with them was any better; just different people. For instance, the pastor that helped me find God. Pastor Brenda aided me to understand that forgiveness was the Christian way of life. For me, it was learning to lay down the anger I felt toward my father and love him as he is. That didn't mean I had to welcome him in my home as an adult and allow his sinful ways into my family's life.

"You're just a seven year old kid, Jillian. You don't know anything about life. Get to your room you ungrateful bitch!" my dad roared as I defended my mom.

Here goes another fight. I can't stand back and watch him. I HAVE to stop it.

Tears streaming down my face I said, "No, asshole, go drink another beer with your buddies!"

With that comment I felt a quick blow to my mouth. My mom gasped as blood started gushing out as I screamed, "I HATE you!" The weight of my words was felt by the breadth of his fist as it made contact with my jaw. My mother stood speechless, fearing the gasp she let escape her lips. The taste of copper flooded my mouth. I could feel the warmth of the blood—blood that I shared with the man that just struck me—move down my chin in rapid succession before making its mark on what would later be a permanent reminder on our cheap carpet. My entire person was shaking, not with fear, but with absolute hatred for the sorry excuse of a man that stood before me. "I HATE YOU!" I roared. My throat was sore from the intense strain of exalting those three words that held so much power. *How could my mother just stand there and let him hit me?*

I ran upstairs to rinse my mouth out. I heard my dad bellowing at my mom. I knew I had to act fast so I could take my sister, Chloe, and my two younger brothers, Chris and Andrew, upstairs to get them away from the violence. Running down the stairs I called them.

"Come on guys, let's go upstairs and play."

They heeded my request and darted upstairs. I told them to stay in the bedroom and I closed the hollow white door. As I started down the steps, the third stair squeaked in our poorly constructed duplex. The house filled my heart of sorrow and the stale air reeked of beer and cigarette smoke.

"Please don't call her a bitch anymore, Chris. You know she's our daughter. Can't you treat her with a little respect?" my mother pleaded him.

"Why in the hell should I treat Jillian with any respect? That child has always defied me. She has no respect for me so I have no respect for her. PERIOD, Carol. Now, get me a beer," he demanded.

From the distance I heard the hand me down refrigerator door open and close. I decided to stay on the third step to monitor the situation from afar.

"Here's your beer, honey. I just want to ask you not to hit her anymore. Jillian is so frail; I don't want Children and Youth Services knocking on our door. You know I am petrified of losing our kids. Your mom threatens us all the time with that."

"To hell with my mother," my father interrupted, "she didn't do much better with me. Don't worry; I will make sure my mother stops calling Children and Youth. They are *my* kids, not hers. *I* decide what's best for them."

Okay, so no fighting with my mom tonight. Thank goodness. I guess he took his anger out on me tonight instead. I tried my best to turn around without making that squeaking sound again. I heard a

11

tiny move of the boards and quickly yet quietly went to my bedroom. I had the kids in the boys' room so I finally had my bedroom to myself. I silently thanked God because I needed the privacy. I started sobbing and sat down on my bed. The springs were old and worn out, so of course another creaking sound. I didn't care at the time, I just wished for a normal life. I felt broken inside. Happiness was never going to be an option while I lived at home.

One day after school, I happened to watch an after school special. The family was so loving and nurturing. Smiles rounded the table as they sat down to dinner discussing their day. "So, that's what a family is supposed to do," I thought to myself. "Happiness does exist; just not in my world."

That night I made a promise to myself that I vowed to keep as long as I was on this earth.

"I promise myself to never marry a man like my dad or even date a guy that shows any qualities he has. I refuse to live like this forever. I want happiness and love!"

The knock at the door jolted me back, causing me to collide the chair into the filing cabinet drawer that I erroneously left ajar.

It was Hailey again, who was one of my closest friends at the nursing home.

Hailey laughed and said, "Sorry to have startled you! You look knee deep in paperwork. I thought you could use a break and get some coffee from the break room. Interested?"

"Sure," I smiled and grateful for the disruption of my flashback.

I really have to stop drifting off into my past like that while I am at work. I promise to try harder. It's so hard though when I knew Mr. Hopkins so well and he reminded me so much of my past. I put those events to rest twenty years ago. It frustrates me to know they are all surfacing again.

As we walked down the hall and made the second left to the break room, Hailey stopped me when no one was around.

"Okay girl, I know you and you know me. You neglected to get your ritual morning coffee. I know something is bothering you so spill it."

For whatever reason, I never told Hailey about certain things about my past. Hailey waited for a response as a million thoughts sped through my mind searching for the words I wanted to say without telling her the truth. I never told her about my childhood. We never got to that point in our alliance. In fact, I have only one true friend that I have ever confided in about my childhood. I'm not the type to put my business out there. It's mine, and it's personal.

I never wanted people to judge me or look at me differently if they knew the truth. Pity was never what I sought. I especially don't want that from Hailey, but maybe an understanding that my life before Nick wasn't glamorous wouldn't be so bad. Would it? Hailey Graham wasn't the kind of friend to beat around the bush. When she had something to say, out it went. I respected her for always being honest and not the type to spread gossip. She valued qualities like integrity as I did. She has always been a great friend to me and I cherish our friendship. Only issue was the mere thought of telling my story made my insides shiver.

I knew I had to say something so I said, "Just upset about Mr. Hopkins passing. No matter his history, I liked the old man."

"Awe Jillian, you know he had cancer and wasn't going to live much longer. You really shouldn't get attached to residents so easily. You know how much you hurt when they're gone. It's not good Jill, not good."

I could tell Hailey knew I was lying, but the kindness in her eyes said she also understood there was something I didn't want to be pushed on so she respected my privacy. Considering we were at work, I didn't think it was the appropriate time to have the conversation about who I used to be. I suppose I can talk to her about the truth when we go out to dinner next Saturday night. Maybe.

"Here's your coffee, two creams, just like you like it." Hailey cheerfully said as she extended her arm to supply me with my much needed turbo juice.

"Thanks, Hailey," I stated trying to smile as she slipped me a wink.

Hailey was always full of sunshine like I usually was and quick to catch a fake smile. Her personality is full of hope and joy. She is able to read peoples body language like I learned to do as a young child. It's kind of ironic how similar we are. We each have wonderful husbands and each blessed with two beautiful children. We are lucky in life. It just took me a little longer to get to this point than Hailey. As far as I have gathered, she has always had happiness. Determined and strong-willed with a great head on her shoulders. It's like looking in the mirror seeing my reflection in another person's body. We each have long straight auburn hair and deep secretive brown eyes. Our build is both slender and athletic. I wear light rimless glasses while she has contacts. My nose is a bit crooked, unlike Hailey's. My high cheek bones are accented nicely with my pink colored blush and my long lashes touch my glasses at times when I push them up too far. According to my husband, I have the most perfect, kissable lips a woman can have. Sometimes I wonder if he just says things to indulge the girly desires I hide deep in my heart. But I know he means well. My bust is definitely smaller than Hailey's and I have always secretly envied that of her. We are both well respected individuals with love in our hearts and faith in our pockets.

"Okay chic, I have to get back to work. Thanks for the coffee. I'll catch you on break."

"Sounds great Jillian, have fun!" With a quick wave, Hailey

was off to her own office.

She is the Social Service Director who is a phenomenal people person and makes sure her documentation is beyond pristine. She knows all the fastidious things to say at the appropriate time. She amazes me how well she handles the grieving or irate family members that enter our building on a regular basis.

Walking back in a daze, which looked to be my running theme for the day, the people scurrying around me caring for the residents and tending to the helpless physicians all seemed to blur together. My thoughts go back to my childhood. It bothered me to think of it. I moved past it. I learned from it and applied my life lessons to my world today. Why bombard me now? As I keep asking myself why, I found my way back to my desk. Two missed calls. Back to work ordering uniforms, creating a new policy for the Director of Nursing, calling physicians and helping the billing office check on some billing codes. I figured I better leave Mr. Hopkins chart on the back burner so I can get some work done. Just as I was about to call another physician's office to update their soon to expire license, my thoughts return to the flashbacks I've been having.

I wish I could understand why all the memories have been conjuring up. Part of me knew the reason, yet wasn't ready to deal with it. The conversation I had with Mr. Hopkins came to mind but I quickly shoved it aside. Twenty years ago things were different - I was different. Nick Davenport fixed everything for me. I was safe now. Life didn't have all the drama and nonsense I was used to back then. He was the angel that raised me out of the burning flames. He showed me what happiness was all about. Before Nick, I felt like I was sliding into second base while the umpire called me out before the ball hit the glove. Defeat at every attempt at normalcy, at any chance to get my life on track. I envisioned my father being the umpire, his smile parting way to his ugly yellowed teeth, taking great pleasure in stopping me from moving forward—taking away any hope I was foolish enough to have.

Suddenly, Hailey walks in.

"Jill, its noon, ready for lunch?" She frightened me again.

"What, noon already?" I gasped. "Gee, guess time flies when you're having fun," I said in a cynical way.

"Sorry for making you jump again," Hailey chuckled once more.

"I'm famished. Want to go to Dingo's for lunch? I'll call and order ahead. What would you like? Oh wait," she paused for a brief second and then continued, "your usual!" Hailey rolled her eyes, mocking my predictability.

I'm a woman that doesn't like change. I had enough change going to ten different schools. I came to rely on my customary life. It was straightforward and I was content as things were. Hailey knew I had a slight case of OCD when it came to organization, but she didn't know that it stemmed from my childhood—packing up the very few things I could call *mine* in cardboard boxes just to move to *another* place we'd call home. Everything was always so scattered, disorganizcd, and I felt with every move, I lost any sense of control I had.

Hailey ended her call with the restaurant and looked at me. She didn't say anything, but by the squint in her left eye, she knew something wasn't right. She tried to hide it from me with no luck.

Sliding our badges at the time clock, Hailey glanced at me as if she had something important to say. Ignoring the glance for the time being, I opened the heavy brown door that separated our confinement for freedom and headed for the imperial blue metallic hard top sports car that I fell in love with the moment I saw it. Four hundred and twenty-six horses under the hood with a six speed transmission was more than enough power for the both of us. Twenty-one inch chrome wheels only added to the magnificence this car had to offer.

As we buckled our seat belts, I felt a bit of tension between the two of us. Maybe I was just reading too much into Hailey's body language. Instead of getting into a deep conversation, I decided to keep it light on our five minute drive to the restaurant.

Being regular customers, the small town waitress knew us well and seated us in record time. Hailey and I expressed our gratitude of quick service and awaited our lunch. We received our drinks and Hailey started out the chat.

"So, my friend," she paused and smiled. "There's something

I've wanted to tell you for a while. I know that I can trust you."

Her bright cheery face immediately went somber. Her eyes darted down to her drink while she fidgeted with her fork. I envisioned there should be a dark cloud above our table ready to spew out hail stones. I immediately felt guilty for not trusting in her with my dilemma. But how could I? I never even told my husband and I knew I couldn't tell Hailey now. I wanted to apologize and try to explain it was complicated.

"I'm," I tried to spit out an apology until she put her hand up for silence.

"Sshh," Hailey began. "Just listen. I want to confide in you something that I have trouble with to this day. However, I was young and naïve and felt it was the right decision."

I chimed in before she began again and asked, "Hailey, why are you saying all this?" I wasn't trying to sound rude because she is a dear friend.

"Well, it's like this; you're a very good friend. I've noticed you've been struggling with some sort of battle and I believe it's within yourself. I want you to know that *everyone* has those secrets that nobody wants to whisper, including me. We always talk about the positives in our lives, never the bad. It's like there's a road block between us since neither of us knows each other's previous history. I feel like now is the time. So, I want to tell you what happened to me."

As Hailey ended her sentence the waitress, Mary, brought

our lunch. We thanked her and then prayed a blessing over our food and the hands that prepared it. Then we turned our conversation back to where we left off.

Speaking low, almost a whisper, Hailey leaned in closer fearing another soul might hear in the tiny diner. I felt a little nervous as my stomach became tangled in a rope full of knots.

"I will try to summarize a long story. So, here goes. When I was eighteen I went to the prom with my then boyfriend. I was still a virgin and unbeknownst to me, Tom decided that he was tired of waiting for me. Throughout the dance he seemed extremely antsy. I sensed that something was up, but shrugged it off as him being bored. As the dance drew to a close, we were supposed to go to a party. So, afterwards we went and we were hanging out talking with friends. I told Tom that I had to use the restroom and I went to find the upstairs bathroom. I didn't realize he was following me. I had been drinking so I wasn't aware of my surroundings like I normally would've been."

Hailey stopped for a moment, rubbed her eyebrow and prepared herself to go on.

"Next, he pushed me into one of the bedrooms and ripped off my clothes. All I remember was I was lying there naked on top of the bed and he took full advantage of me. When Tom was finished he looked at me and said, 'Two years is too long to make a man wait'."

Hailey paused for a brief moment to regain her shaky voice and continued. "I was crying profusely and embarrassed that I had been made a fool of. I felt dirty and used like a cheap rug. I gathered myself up and had a friend take me to my house. I didn't say a word the entire ride home."

"Oh my goodness," I gasped. "I am so sorry." I wanted to say more but couldn't find the right words.

Hailey's mouth turned up with appreciation and then quickly went back down and went on. "Five weeks later I found out that I was pregnant. Tom never pulled out or used a condom. I feared there was a chance and I was right. I never told a soul what he did to me that night but I knew I had to now. For that reason, I confided in my mom. She was heartbroken of course and angry as hell at Tom for doing such a thing. We talked about my options and we both determined it was best to have an abortion. So, I did. It was the worst and best choice I ever made."

Hailey's shoulders were limp from shame. Her eyes were filled with tears by this point. The table began to bounce up and down knowing her leg shaking under the table like she does when she is nervous.

I slowly placed my hand upon hers and said, "You're right. We all have skeletons. We all have choices to make and that was yours. I'm grateful that you were comfortable enough to confide in me."

My mind was swirling with thoughts and opinions.

21

Everything seemed jumbled like the dozens of boxes placed at random after every move to a new house when I was younger. I tried to smile so that Hailey wouldn't have the impression that I was judging her, even though I think a part of me was. I didn't want to judge her. And the good Lord knew I had plenty of sins.

When we returned to work my emotions were getting the best of me. My stomach was still tangled in a web of despair. I became ill and extremely clammy. My director seen my condition and asked what was wrong.

"I'm not sure, I just became really queasy," I told her knowing it was only half true. I knew exactly what was wrong but I wasn't about to tell my boss.

"Go home Jillian. Get some rest. You look green!" exclaimed my boss.

"Gee, thanks," I said sarcastically. "I'll see you tomorrow then," I added.

I didn't tell Hailey I was going home. My emotions were in overdrive while my stomach was threatening to turn inside out. I got in my black SUV and sped off. As I reached Route Thirty, my reminder chime prompted me of my need for gasoline.

I pulled in to gas station. It was quarter until one on a Monday afternoon and the lot was full. Evidently half of the rural town needed fuel. The sun shined down scorching through my windshield. Knowing I had a wait, I turned on my air conditioner and put my vehicle in park.

"Your mom is a killer! How does that make you feel?" my dad boasted the surprise information.

I was heartbroken. Even at my young age of eleven, I understood what an abortion was.

I sat down on our dingy brown couch, which was once a tan color. We were in our new place that we moved to four months before in the neighboring town of our last. Again, this meant another new school. The air followed us from house to house, filled with cigarette smoke and the scent of beer. A cold draft made its way through the generic trailer window. It sent a shiver through my spine and into my fingertips. The feeling seeped into my chest and ice began to freeze around my heart. The panicked reaction made me unable to breath. Was it true? Mom couldn't have had an abortion. No! Mom couldn't do that! I know her, she couldn't have!

I looked at Mom for reassurance. Pleading with her displaying my grief stricken eyes, "Please, Mom, tell me it's not true."

"I'm so sorry, Jillian. You were *not* supposed to find out. I'm sorry honey. Please don't hate me. I love you too much. My mom made me do it a long time ago. I can explain."

Mom looked desperate for forgiveness. I had to forgive her.

She was my mom. My mom was the victim. Right?

"Of course, Mom, I forgive you." Was it really my place to forgive her? I was just a child and yet I knew she needed it.

My dad snickered as he cracked open another can of beer. As he walked from the kitchen to the living room he had already drank a half case of beer throughout the day. His mood was elated with himself as he turned and looked at me, resting himself against the oak colored paneling. He knew he hurt me deeply. My mom wasn't a saint, she committed wrongdoings too. I wasn't ready to accept that yet.

Dad staggered over to his stereo and reached out to open the glass that housed his pride and joy. The stand was made of oak wood and a bit wobbly from him falling on it earlier in the year. Dad began flipping through his numerous albums and found his selection. He pulled the old twelve inch record out of its protected sleeve and twirled the vinyl with his long bony fingers. Placing it in its appropriate place and putting the needle on the second song, he turned on his record player. He gave one glance back and smirked.

"Time for bed," he demanded over the ninety decibels streaming through his speakers.

The intro echoed through the paper-thin walls of my shared bedroom with my sister, bare of any decoration, except a picture of my Grams. My heart felt crushed into tiny pieces of sand as the artist began to sing about how bad love can truly be.

Just as the lyrics sang through my memory, I was interrupted by the sound of yelling with a radiating blare of a horn. This had been the second time in one day! I have to get home, immediately to my safe haven. Evidently, my spacing out wasn't the safest thing for me since obviously it has been a nuisance to those around me.

Chapter 2

Hello, God…

I pulled in to our medium sized yet ideal home. At the beginning of summer, my husband re-coated our cedar log home with the same red cedar stain as before. When we originally picked out the color, I swayed more towards the darker woods. My husband was a lover of the lighter options so we compromised with the red cedar. I really liked the way the wood glistened in the sunlight. As I walked onto our rather large front porch, I noticed my day lilies to the right of me had started to bloom. The pale pink lily reminded me of how beautiful nature can truly be. With a bit of strength that flower gave me, I headed inside.

I walked into the living room and to my right I see the answering machine light blinking. "I don't care right now," I said aloud. I knew if it were my kids they would call my cell phone as would my husband with any emergency. Throwing my keys on the table next to the telephone, I made my way to the kitchen. I opened the double doors to our stainless steel refrigerator and grabbed a water from the bottom shelf. It was only little after one o'clock in the afternoon and the kids wouldn't be home from their friends house for another two and a half hours. I headed to the basement of our home to the craft room my husband, Nick, constructed for me. He was an electrician by trade but carpentry was a passion for him. Nick enjoyed his love of fabricating miscellaneous projects and I had no problem asking him to create things for me. Being the easy going, relentless to please kind of guy, he happily obliged to most of my requests.

I pulled open the door to my fully stocked, well organized escape, I began to look around. The ten foot by twelve foot room was large enough but for some reason everything looked bland and felt stale. My mural-painted wall seemed comatose without color or joy. It was as though it had lost its life. I had my sister in law, Emma, paint a mural straight ahead as you walked in to the room. She completed the painting years back when she first married my brother in-law, Fred. I once saw a breath taking photograph of a picture-perfect scene that I HAD to have. The sky was a rich blue and the earth was a vivid green, filled with grass while a still pond sat to the left of an old dirt road. By the pond was an old weeping willow with a tire swing attached to a low but sturdy limb. I knew I wanted to incorporate my two, at the time young children. I photographed them at a distance from their backs to signify their silhouettes. Once Emma added my then five and almost two year old children running to the swing, the mural came alive. I fell in love with the painting she mastered for me and my love only grew deeper as the days passed and my children grew older. It symbolized God's love and faithfulness He has for each of us.

Having our daughter three months shy of my twenty-fifth birthday was the best thing that ever happened to me besides my husband. I was old enough to appreciate all the wondrous things she taught me as a new parent. Della Grace was an exceptional baby and toddler growing up. The only issue we had with her was that she didn't sleep much which was definitely a challenge for me. But, I remember taking each day and finding something special about it. It made life so much more worthwhile instead of getting lost in the monotony of the day-to-day tasks.

When Della turned a year old I recalled singing happy birthday to her. Her sweet smile melted my heart into a puddle of butter. When we began to sing I remember how I started to choke up and tears streamed down my face.

I had such a bittersweet sentiment that our daughter had turned a year old. At that time I thought our lives were complete with Della in tow. My husband and daughter consumed my life. I was certain that God had surely blessed my beaten path with a life filled with more love and happiness than the wealthiest person on Earth. I understood that I had to cherish the little things because without those, life wouldn't have much meaning. Life couldn't be more perfect when you had a family to love.

We learned our lessons with Della, teaching and learning as we went along. The wonderful qualities and values we've passed on to her, we wanted to do with our son, Kevin. I was four years older when I delivered Kevin. An easy pregnancy and labor, he was a delightful baby. He picked up on small achievements faster than Della had because he wanted to be just like his big sister. Kevin even started walking at nine months old because he was determined to keep up with her, delighted that he could now chase her around. Busy was an understatement when it came to our daily living.

Finally coming out of my trance, I was at my work station. I pulled out my old blue padded Queen Anne chair to sit down and find myself. The chair was quite old and worn showing the wear and tear to which it's been subjected to over the years. It never bothered me and re-upholstering it was a task I put off for the last five years. It was one of the only things I had left from her. I envisioned her relaxing in the arms of her beloved chair like a mother holds her child. In a sense, she was holding me while my body rested in the arms of an angel's chair. Della Saunders, my beloved grandma, was one woman I'll never forget.

My emotions were in complete disarray from the day's sizable revelations. I left the drama behind me at the age of seventeen, venturing out on my own. When I met Nick two long years later, my days of dealing with theatrics were over. I've not had to deal with it for so long, I find myself forgetting how to do just that—*deal*. The littlest of things will cause panic — even if it isn't evident on the outside, I sense it.

I closed my eyes, then, folded my hands and started talking to God as if He was sitting beside me and we were chatting like old friends.

"Lord, I found out something about Hailey that I honestly disagree with. As her friend, I'm not sure how to handle this. Please, please give me strength and understanding. Help me not to judge Hailey. She's a wonderful woman, Lord. Guide me. Amen."

Ending my prayer, I opened my eyes and unfolded my hands. My heart not quite as heavy, I looked around again and things seemed to brighten. The mural on my wall came alive as though it was merely frozen in time. The brokenness inside me mended. "Thank you God, just took a little bit of faith."

Soon after, my cell phone rang.

"Hello?" I answered.

"Hey, it's me. I have to work late tonight. Can you have dinner ready around six-thirty?" asked my husband, Nick.

"Sure, hun, no problem. Do you have any special requests?" I inquired.

"Um, how about grilling up some steaks and baked potatoes. Oh, and maybe some rice or something," Nick responded.

"Okay, that sounds really good. I'll start that in a bit. I love you."

"Love you too, babe," he said. Honestly, I have always secretly hated when he called me babe. My father had called my mom that after his drunken rampages when his rage had seized and he wanted to kiss up with one thing on his mind.

We hung up and three seconds later my phone rang again. "Boy, am I popular today," I thought. Chuckling to myself, I glanced down to see the caller ID. It was my very best, most trusted friend since the summer before fifth- grade. Gretchen and I met at the fence separating my cousin's house from her own. Oh, how I needed to chat.

When I answered the phone Gretchen said, "Hey woman! I tried calling your house and left a message. I had a feeling something was wrong. Talk to me. You working?"

Sensing one another's feelings was a routine for us. Gretchen knew ALL of my past. She never once judged me for who my parents were. She was wise beyond her years. Gretchen, coming from an upscale family, was thought by others to be snobby and full of greediness. However with her, in this rare instance, she was blessed with the heart of a saint. She always appreciated what was given to her and has worked hard all of her life when she didn't have to. Knowing that not everyone is dealt the same hand as hers, she respected people no matter what the circumstances. In the last thirty-one years that we have known one another, I have never witnessed Gretchen display any sort of malice to anyone she knew or met.

Her appearance was impeccable. She stood five foot seven inches with poker straight blond hair down to the middle of her back. Gretchen's eyes were like crystal blue diamond's glistening off the sand. Her skin was golden brown that she maintained throughout the entire year. Gretchen Turner was a pin-up filled with grace and compassion.

"No, I'm not at work. I am home in my craft room actually. I'm so glad you called. I just got off the phone with Nick so your timing is perfect," I began.

"Everything okay with Nick?" she asked.

"Oh yeah, Nick is fine. We're all fine here at home; however, I learned something today at lunch with Hailey. She told me something that honestly bothers me. I'm not sure how to deal with the situation. I'm hurt, Gretchen. But, I know I need to get over it and not dwell on a choice made years ago. And, considering it wasn't my choice nor did it affect me, I'm trying hard not to pass judgment."

"Oh okay, Jill, sounds like a pretty in-depth situation. Should I know more or would you rather keep things private?" Gretchen asked. She was the type to never want to overstep her boundaries.

"I honestly think this should be kept between Hailey and me. This is her personal business and I don't want to tell anyone. I'm not one to break confidentiality," I countered.

"Oh this must be something, something not good to say the least. Okay, well what can I do to help YOU, Jillian?" asked Gretchen.

"That's just it Gretch, I'm not sure. When I got home I prayed. Things seemed to be a tad better. I think this is something that will take time for my memory to fade. Something I have to not dwell on. I guess I just need to move past it like she did."

"Okay girl, you know what you got to do. I'm here for you whenever you need me. You know that. I'll be in touch in a day or so just to check on ya. Call me before if you want," Gretchen replied.

"You know I will," I responded.

"Oh and Jill...remember when it comes to Hailey, friendship is helping someone through the hard times to get them to the good times," Gretchen ended.

"I will. Thanks Gretchen."

With that we ended our call. She always gives me food for thought. She certainly is right. I need to think of how Hailey trusted me with her secret. I have to remember mistakes are made, we learn, and move on. I can love someone, but that doesn't mean I think their actions were right. Hailey has her reasons for what happened. Unfortunately, I don't know of any justification had I been in that situation. Then I am reminded of my mom's and the struggle inside my head begins again. I tell myself over and over, "love the person, hate the sin." But what about my sins? I've done plenty wrong throughout my life. How can I judge? The battle never ends.

Still in my comfortable blue chair I glanced down at my calendar. It was middle of July already. Suddenly, Mr. Hopkins flew into my thoughts. His funeral would be held Friday. One day for his viewing and service. His family said it was going to be quick and easy. That put a little stab in my heart. I know the bastard he had to of been to his family. Nevertheless, the man was still their father and he changed two years before his wife died. I suppose with all the hatred he created, the timing of him changing was simply too late. Still, I wanted to be there for his service. I grew to love the man with the wicked history. When he and I chatted I could always see the hope in his eyes that his children would one day forgive him. Sadly, that day never came and now it never will.

My father once told me I was too forgiving. I feel differently of course. When I held a grudge when I was younger, I wasn't at ease. I felt like the devil had me in his grasp. When I let go of the grudge I felt a sense of peace. I can't be truly happy if I can't forgive those who hurt me. By me forgiving them, I feel like I can move on and not dwell in my past. I'm not carrying around the pain and hurt that once filled my heart. I was miserable. I want to be happy. I made that oath to myself a long time ago and I am still upholding that vow. Until recently, when all hell broke loose internally.

I made a mental note to myself to let the Director of Nursing know that I will be taking a personal day for Friday. There shouldn't be any problems and they can always page me if something would arise. The state health department was due to come in to do their annual survey of our facility so there is always a chance to get called in at any given time.

I made my way up the oak stairway to our kitchen. I needed to pull out the steaks for dinner. Turning my head to glance at the clock, I knew I still had plenty of time. The kids would be home in another hour and half and Nick wouldn't be home for another three hours. I'm not sure what to do with myself considering I'm rarely home alone and don't have to rush to get things started for dinner or run the kids to either baseball or dance. Deciding to at least thaw the meat, I went to our freezer and pulled out the meat for dinner and placed the package in the sink for the time being.

Exhausted from the emotions of today's events I decided to prop my feet up on our black leather sofa. It was comfortable but I always felt chilled so I permanently kept a throw on my side of the couch. I pulled out the built in recliner and turned on the massager. Oh, was this nice. I drifted off to sleep instantly.

"Don't we have to go to the gas station and get some kerosene tonight, Mom?" I asked.

"I think we'll be okay for the evening. It's only supposed to be down in the twenty's tonight. We should have enough kerosene to last us until morning."

With that, Mom smiled trying to be confident in her statement. I knew in my heart we would run out. This happened all the time. Mom and Dad didn't have the five dollars to get fuel to heat our uninsulated, tin can of a trailer. Yet amazingly they had money for cigarettes and a case of beer. I was baffled by their inability to manage their money. Dad made sure there was money for beer and cigarettes and if they didn't have the cash, he made Mom borrow the money from family or friends.

"Okay Mom, if you think so. I'm going to bed. Goodnight, love you," I told her as I was walking the four steps from the living room to my bedroom.

"I love you too, Jillian. Sweet dreams."

Dad had passed out earlier since he started drinking at noon that day. Evidently, he was having a bad day and needed to relax. Whatever. I was just thankful that he didn't start any fights.

Six o'clock in the morning and I hear my alarm buzzing to wake me for school. Oh, not another day of hell. School was horrible. I was terrible at making friends and my fellow classmates always picked on me. I felt feeble and my self-esteem was nonexistent. The lack of instability, lack of sleep, lack of love, and lack of life was evidently written all over my face for my classmates to see. "Hit me when I am down," I felt as they took any opportunity to bring me down with their snide remarks. Being bullied daily was not my idea of the great time you're supposed to have while being a kid and enjoying your school years. So, I retracted from others in school and became quiet and shy. Even the teachers hardly noticed me.

As I pulled down the same blue, stained, and tattered comforter I knew right away that we ran out of kerosene. Wow, is it cold in here. Taking a deep breath in, when I exhaled I could see the warm moisture escape my lungs that reminded me of smoke from a cigarette. This is ludicrous! Throwing on another sweatshirt from my broken dresser drawer I headed to the kitchen and turned on the oven. Hopefully I could get the trailer warmed up before Chris, Chloe, and Andy had to wake up for school. Pulling down the white oven door, in the back of my mind, I knew my mom had let me down - again. Some things never change, no matter how much you will them.

I heard a door slam and I jumped up and out of my dream. The dream, it was so authentic. Wait a second, it was exact. I never dreamt of my past before. How odd I thought, puzzled by my dream of what was once my reality, I shook my head, as if doing so would jiggle the thoughts right out onto the carpet and free me. I felt incredibly cold as though my bones were smothered in ice cream. My body shivered and Della saw me.

"Mom, it's like eighty degrees in here. How can you be cold?" she asked.

I never went in depth of my childhood with my kids. I was afraid to expose them to the truth of my private inferno at a young age. "Once they get older," I always told myself. Since Della turned fifteen this past May I suppose I can start telling her, but I haven't gotten around to it just yet. Kevin is only eleven, and being a typical boy, I don't believe he is interested in what "Mom" is all about. However, Della has asked questions here and there, but fortunately for myself, I have always been able to dodge the bullet.

"Oh, I just had a bad dream, honey. I'm okay though," I answered quickly.

"Okay, Mom. So, what's for dinner?" Della asked.

"Steaks on the grill but Daddy won't be home until six thirty so I'll start dinner in a little bit. Right now though I want a hug and kiss from my two best kids," I tried to sound cheerful.

Kevin groaned but gave in while Della was glad to offer me some love. I held on to them extra tight with my hug and looked at them with more love and joy than I had in a while. It was like looking at them with a new set of eyes. Knowing what Hailey had done brought on a perspective for me with my children that I sometimes forget. I cherish them one hundred times more than I had before. Which I didn't even think was possible since I have adored my children since they were conceived. Della had noticed my new found feelings as we sat down on the couch. Feeling the coldness of the leather below me I shivered again. Della grabbed my hand. They were like ice cubes. My hands were always cold but usually not this cold. She noticed that as well and asked, "Mama, are you sure you are okay today? You seem like something is wrong. Your hands are freezing, and you keep shivering as though you were in a freezer all day. And you looked at Kevin and me weird. What's up?"

Della reads people all too well. She looks like my mother in-law, Kathleen, and my sister in-law, Isabella, a great deal. Della was blessed with medium thick dark chestnut hair that shimmers as her long locks flow in the cool summer breeze. Her dark brown, almost black, eyes are filled with mystery. Della's oval face has a perfect complexion with her golden tan she acquired from our boating expeditions already this summer. She gets her athletic build from me though and does very well with water sports, volleyball and softball. Della stands at five foot five inches. I know she will pass me up at five foot six inches within the year. God granted me a gorgeous daughter with a wonderful heart. On the other hand, she is an extremely intuitive young lady that scares me sometimes. I feel like she knows my past — without me ever saying a word.

Kevin understood his older sister just as well as his hand signals for baseball, and he could sense she wanted a little girl time with me. "I'm going out to shoot some hoops." I nodded in approval and out the door he ran.

Never letting go of my hand, Della said again, "Mom, what's going on?"

"Well, sweetheart, I just had a bad day. One of the residents at work passed away today and it just makes me sad he is gone."

Again, I was dodging the true cause. My past will find a way to trouble me, no matter how much I think I forgave my kin and worked to bury the ache. Too smart for her own good, Della insisted on more explanation.

"Mom, you're trembling for a reason. People have died many times before and you have never been this shaken up. What's the difference? What's with this guy that died? And what is up with the dream you had that you are so cold?" Della asked with more assertiveness.

Am I an open book today or what? First, Gretchen and now Della. What is giving me away so easily? I used to be good at hiding my worries and the events that happened. I suppose being forty years old and the twenty years it has been with Nick I lost some of my tendencies to protect myself.

"Alright Della, I guess you're getting older and are capable of understanding situations better than I would like you to be," I started as she grabbed both of my hands and held them to her chest. Her heart was beating quickly as she knew she was about to learn something that I didn't share with anyone. She nodded for me to continue.

The conversation with Mr. Hopkins loomed over me. I suppose it's time to come clean. First and foremost I should start with Nick. Then again, I knew that Della deserved some answers.

"Oh man, where to start? Well, Mr. Hopkins passed away today. I grew a special bond with him throughout his seven year stay. His room was right next to my office so I would see him every day and we would chat. You see, honey, he was an alcoholic for many years. He caused an abundance of pain to his family. He changed many years later but the change came too late. His children hate him and his wife died a while ago. He had no one left yet always had hope that one day his children would forgive him for their tainted past. Unfortunately, that dream never came true," I paused to ponder how I should continue. Instead Della helped me along.

"Mom, it seems like there is a huge connection between you and this Mr. Hopkins. I don't want you to get mad, but I have a feeling that Mr. Hopkins reminds you a lot of your dad. I always wondered why we never see him or our great grandmother. I know they live in Ohio but it's honestly not that far away. I can't even remember the last time we saw them, if ever. So it kind of makes sense that if he is like Mr. Hopkins was then you don't want us around him."

I felt my heart skip three beats and my breath was caught in my wind pipe. How could this be? I don't recall my daughter being *this* perceptive. She is only fifteen years old. This day just doesn't like me. My mind is working triple time filled with an extreme amount of anxiousness that I can't seem to process it all properly.

"Um, okay. Wow. I had no idea you would be so observant. I don't remember teaching you that." I teach my children to be observant, but hope that when it comes to my own transgressions they miss the details that threaten to spoil my perfect image. I was flabbergasted. I didn't know what to think or say. My defenses quickly came back and forced in to high gear. I felt panic strike.

"Well, Mom, you always said I reminded you of a girl you used to know."

I looked down to find myself wringing my hands in my lap and caught a glimpse of the dingy couch—the one my mother deemed a 'treasure find' for only ten bucks. I sniffed the air and in place of Warm Vanilla Sugar, a whiff of beer smacked me like a bitter winter morning, assaulting all five senses. The crash of a lamp echoing over and over, the radio blaring, and Della's voice was somewhere in the mix, "Mom, Mom." Flashes of the thin carpet, stained with a drop of my blood, danced around like the makings of my own haunted kaleidoscope. It was all here. Or was I back there? Della's voice, louder this time, "Mom!" She doesn't belong there— or here, whichever was the case. Her innocence shouldn't be subjected to the depravity of my childhood. I need to put her with the kids. Where's Andy, Chloe, and Chris?

Wait, where am I? My eyes moved from left to right not stopping. My vision was blurred and my heart was pounding out of my chest. I pulled my hands to my core and stood up. This is too much for me in one day. Pacing the cherry hard wood floors I started to scratch my arms. My nervousness was exploding out of my skin. The fright of the old memories rekindled and I was pushed back in time. They just kept coming. The shotgun was at her head. The dark metal a stark contrast to her bleach-blond hair sticks, the image forever etched in my mind. Her body trembles with fear until the weight of her ninety-five pound frame nearly buckles. He wasn't going to let her get away. His free hand latched onto her arm, just above her elbow, and he pulled her up and she crashed into his chest. His pedophilic-looking mustache was pressed against her ear, making sure she heard every word. I'm on the stairs, peering through the banister rails and although I'm far enough away, I heard him threaten her life—and mine. The bastard—my own father— wanted me dead. I've never saw pain in my mother's eyes like I did at that moment. It wasn't fear for herself this time—it was for me, her first born. I hear him threatening to pull the trigger. Tears streaming down my face. "No, Dad, No! " I shrieked.

"Calm down Mom, it's only me, Della. Hello? Mom?"

I was still scratching my arms and pacing while my breathing started to be labored. My chest muscles began to tighten. I heard the heel of my shoes clattering on the wood. The adrenaline coursing through my veins was like someone shot me up with an eight-ball of hot lava. Unable to put out my personal inferno, I was plagued with yet another scene. I watched as my mom was being thrown against the refrigerator and her limp body slid to the floor. My father shakes his fist at her asking if she wants more. As my hands started to spasm seeing his face and smelling his beer breath, I reached out to punch him except I punched air instead of the invisible demon. My mind was in a whirlwind of scattered visions wishing them to disappear.

43

I felt something wet below my fingertips. I saw red liquid oozing out from the outer shell of my body. Oxygen seemed to be scarce in my lungs as I started to hyperventilate. My legs were weak; they started to shake and my footing slipped beneath me. It was slow motion as my body crumbled like an accordion, hitting my head on our square cherry wood coffee table, sending a throbbing sensation throughout my body.

"Mom! Mom! I'm calling 911! MOMMY!" screamed Della. I could barely hear her though. She seemed so far away. I could hardly hear anything except for the jumble of thoughts in my mind. Where am I? Who am I? Help me. I can't breathe, I thought. Just then, darkness clouded over me.

As I started to regain consciousness I could feel something in my nose. Cold air was filling my nostrils, helping my brain supply the oxygen I was lacking. The sound of constant beeping and then quiet conversation filled my ears. Something warm was on my right hand. I started to flutter my eyelids open. They were so heavy. My surroundings were nothing but white which scared me to the center of my chest. Am I dead?

I have never been afraid of dying since my faith is strong with my relationship with our Lord. My only worry was that I wouldn't be able to say goodbye to my family.

Anxiously, I open my eyes again and I slightly turned my head. Oh thank God, I saw a familiar face. A tear fell when I saw Nick. He instantly came closer to me. Crying and laughing all at once, his plump moist lips met mine. With the urgency in his kiss I knew something had happened. I just didn't know what. Looking in to Nick's light brown eyes I wanted to ask him what happened but he already knew my slew of questions so, he began.

"Sshh, it's okay now, honey. You're in the hospital. The doctors think you had a severe anxiety attack. When you started to hyperventilate you fell and hit your head on the coffee table at home. You got a gash on your head and needed four stitches. Other than that you are fine and will be released soon."

I nodded to let Nick know I understood what he said. As I brought my right hand up to touch Nick's face I seen my right arm was wrapped in gauze. Blood was peeking through the white cotton. The puzzle was slowly being built, making me wonder what else had happened. I looked at my left arm and found the same sight. Confused as to why I was bleeding on my arms, I surveyed Nick's face again.

My voice was groggy, but I was able to ask him why my arms were bleeding.

"It's okay Jillian, we'll talk once we're home. I promise I'll tell you every detail," said Nick.

"Okay," was the only thing I could muster up through my

voice box.

An hour and a half passed before I was eventually released from the hospital. The doctors wanted to check the lab results and echocardiogram that they ran on me while I was unconscious. The physician on duty wanted to make sure I didn't have a heart attack. All the results were within normal limits and I was cleared for discharge. The discharge nurse reviewed my paperwork which indicated I was treated for a head contusion and an anxiety attack. The prescription she handed me was for a new antidepressant that was on the market. I'm not a fan of medicating, but the worry in Nick's face tells me I gave everyone a scare. Maybe meds will help me *handle* my stress triggers a bit better next time. God, please don't let there be a next time.

As Nick wheeled me down the hall in the wheelchair the nurse insisted I use, my memory started to clear from the fog as we made our way to the elevators. My husband looked afraid and confused; he glanced down at me and kissed my forehead. As he stopped to push the elevator button to go down he knelt beside me.

"Jillian, you scared me to death. I'm so thankful you're okay though. Whatever caused you so much anxiety, well, you can talk to me about it. I'm here for you babe. Always and forever."

He smiled and kissed me softly on my lips as the elevator door opened. The ride down was short and quiet. The dim lighting of the elevator made the three other passengers look ghost-like. The

46

white doctors coat I seen to my left was filled with a slender American doctor that I recognized. He was the psychiatrist that saw and treated patients at the nursing home. He tried to dig for information from me once as if he knew I was hiding something. Quick as a fox, I was able to dodge his questions. With my recollection I became a bit embarrassed, so I put my head down and pretended to read my discharge papers. I saw how he looked at me thinking he may know me from somewhere. Hopefully he won't recall from where and continue on to his rounds. And the question popped into my head, "Am I really all about appearance?" Before I could answer myself, the elevator opened on the second floor and the doctor got off the small confinement that shuffled people from level to level.

Reaching the ground floor, Nick left me in the front lobby of the hospital sitting next to a small pink table with magazines. He had to pull his truck up to the main entrance so that we could go home. The stale hospital air was almost unbearable making the few minutes it took Nick to bring the truck around feel like an eternity. Within a few minutes, I saw him walking back in to the hospital doors and I stood up. I felt better with more energy. Wrapping my arms around him I didn't want to let go. The smell of his masculine cologne overpowered the hospital aroma.

"Let's go home," Nick said lovingly.

It was nine-thirty at night when we pulled into our driveway. I instantly thought of Della and Kevin and wondered if they had eaten dinner. I let out a small gasp and Nick chuckled. He also looked at the time and knowing me the way he does, he knew exactly what I was thinking.

"Don't worry Jill, the kids were well taken care of and yes, they ate dinner. My mom kept an eye on them. Dad dropped her off after Della called them."

"Oh thank goodness!" I exclaimed.

Nick and I walked hand in hand to our front door. Kathleen saw the headlights from the truck pull in and opened the door to greet us. Nick walked in behind me and Kathleen quickly pulled me close to her for an unexpected yet welcomed hug. Kathleen and Everett were wonderful in-laws. They welcomed me into their hearts and home from the very beginning. However, they were not the type to show their love or emotions on their sleeves. With that in mind, our hug was truly cherished.

As we pulled away from one another I saw the concern in her eyes. She was overly worried about me seeing the lines in her face deepen. She never asked me about my childhood and knew that it was a raw subject for me to talk about. She hadn't pressured me but I know she has always wondered what I was hiding. Looking at Kathleen I saw my two precious children standing behind her with tears in their eyes. Waiting for their cue to embrace me I stepped to the side of Kathleen and knelt down. They both ran to me and wrapped their arms around me with such force we all almost toppled down to the floor.

The emotion of the day's events was so intense I couldn't help but to cry as I held my children in my arms. Della and Kevin sobbed in my arms like two feeble babies longing for comfort and security. I held them as tight as I could to show them that everything would be fine and Mommy is okay.

After about ten minutes of soothing the kids I motioned to the couch so we could all be a bit more comfortable. Kevin was on my left side while Della was on my right. Kathleen sat next to Kevin and Nick next to Della. I was nervous and unsure where to begin. Just then, the thought of apologizing popped in to my thought process.

So I began, "First of all, I want to say I am very sorry for the scare I caused everyone today. I had a very long day at work and then once home Della and I started talking about things that I'm very uncomfortable discussing. She's more observant than I wanted to admit which made me quite uneasy. My nerves went through the roof and I started to panic. I'm sorry everyone."

Waiting for the line of fire to begin I braced myself. How could they not ask all of the how's and why's and explain how afraid they were. I waited for Della to start but instead Nick stood up. With his biceps showing their definition he slid his hands in his pockets and I saw his slight wink to the kids. With that prompt the kids hugged me again and told me how happy they were that I was okay and to be back home. They headed to bed and gave us all a kiss goodnight. Then, I saw headlights through our living room window, knowing that it had to be Everett to pick up Kathleen. She quietly grabbed her coat and purse, kissed my forehead and headed out the door. This was all definitely pre-planned.

The only sound I heard besides silence was the crackling of the sweet smell of cherry wood burning in our fireplace on the opposite side of our living room. It wasn't typical for us to have a fire burning in the summer time so I found it odd. Nick knew it was something I enjoyed since it relaxed me so much in the winter. Maybe he just wanted me to relax. I don't know. Nick sat back down beside me after the kids went to their rooms and his mom left. Still nervous and unsure of what was to come, I felt uncomfortable and vulnerable.

Being a man of little words, Nick chose his words carefully, not wanting to upset me even more. He began with his soft, deep, soothing voice, "Jillian, I love you more than life itself. I want you to know that I am here for you. I always have been. For reasons only you know, you have left me out of your past. You have pretended it never happened in some ways. So, when you're ready, let me know and I'll be here to listen."

With his words I felt remorse yet comfort all at the same time. I know he didn't want to overwhelm me and according to the physician I need to be stress free for a while except, I knew that I couldn't achieve that until this was resolved. So I had a little meltdown today. Everyone breaks at a certain point. Regrettably mine was today. What I am baffled at is why now? I handled a lot more stress when I was younger and never broke down like I did today. And it happened in front of Della. That hurts the most. I never wanted something like this to happen in front of my kids. I am a strong independent woman. Someone wise beyond her years yet knew how to relax and enjoy the moment.

Leaning over to Nick, we hugged and I thanked him for his patience. Looking into those brown eyes captivated me every time. We kissed slowly and the hunger for each other began to ignite. We retired to our room and after we both reached our ecstasy, both of us lie in each other's arms and fell asleep peacefully.

Chapter 3

It's Not Your Fault, It's Mine

I woke to Della bringing me breakfast in bed. She had made my favorite morning foods, french toast smothered in syrup with powdered sugar and fresh sausage patties from our local butcher shop. I wanted to go to work, but according to the doctor orders I wasn't allowed. Instead, I was to stay home and rest. Apparently during my unconsciousness Nick called my boss and let them know I wouldn't be in for the rest of the week. So, I suppose I will try to enjoy my vacation from work. Hopefully the state health department will hold off their visit until next week. At least I won't have to confront the situation with Hailey. I also plan on preparing myself for Friday since I know it will be difficult with Mr. Hopkins funeral service. As I was thinking about the reason all these thoughts started I heard a knock on my bedroom door.

"Good morning Mama. I hope I didn't wake you. I made you some breakfast. Hope you like it," Della said with a smile.

She must have woken early since it was only seven in the morning. She was like her dad in that aspect. She was so chipper and ready to go in the mornings. I, on the other hand, was a night owl and hated mornings. I'm thankful she gets that from her father.

"Well, good morning to you too, sweetheart. I see you're up with the chickens this morning. Breakfast smells fabulous." The aroma of sugary syrup wafted up as the dish was placed in front of me. "Thank you very much, that's incredibly sweet!" I kissed her cheek and Kevin appeared with my morning must have. Coffee!

"Oh my little man, thank you! It's just what I needed!" I exclaimed cheerfully.

"I figured Della couldn't carry everything so I told her I would help," Kevin said.

Kevin was a night owl like me. He loved staying up with me when he was younger. Just hanging with Mom and having our special time together. He reminds me of my youngest brother Andy in a lot of ways. Andy always stayed up late with our mom when he was young. Andy would sneak down the steps when the coast was clear and say, "Mom, I got the kids to bed. What do you want to do tonight?"

Looking back I see Kevin is an image of him. Kevin even resembles Andy a great deal except Kevin has light brown, almost blond hair. Andy's hair was very blond, nearly white as a child. Kevin has grown to be a lean, tall young man at eleven. He stays active with his friends and recently started to notice girls so his hair must be styled at all times. He eats healthy, dresses respectable and loves giving compliments. Kevin is a charmer of sorts with his left dimple peeking out as he gives his boyish mischievous grin. His brown eyes compliment his long eye lashes while his teeth are perfectly straight showing off his killer smile. Kevin loves sports and is the quarterback for the junior football team at school. In the spring he enjoys playing short stop for the school fast pitch baseball team.

"Now what would I do without my two favorite kids? You two treat me too good. Thank you both," voicing my gratitude.

I always make sure to thank my family even for the little things. Having a childhood like mine, I wasn't shown that. Instead they only expected more from me. Having the life I had before taught me a great deal of life lessons early. I have always tried to be thankful and learn from my parents' mistakes - taking the negative and turning them positive when it came to me and my family. I believe I had succeeded for the most part until recently when the ache in my heart started to overcome me.

"Well Mama, you better eat up before it gets cold. Kevin and I will be dusting for you in the living room. So just yell if you need something," Della said. She then leaned down and whispered, "I'm sorry I made you so upset yesterday, Mama."

I felt a lump in my throat as a lonely tear crept slowly out from my right eye. My baby girl thought this was her fault. How could I not realize that? She was not responsible for my crazy emotions. She has to know that, right?

As Della and Kevin turned to leave my spacious bedroom I grabbed Della's hand for her to stop. By this time I was weeping and in agony for hurting my daughter. Della was too sensitive of a soul to have to be in anguish like this. I'm so mad at myself for what I have done. Maybe I should have seen a counselor all those years ago when my mom wanted me to. How dare I bring my demons into my family's life? This is my battle and I must triumph over this.

As she turned back I saw how upset she was with tears streaming down her delicate bronzed cheeks. I quickly set my breakfast to the side and jumped out of bed and took my girl in my arms and hugged her like a mother should when their child was in despair. This was my fault and I needed to rectify this fiasco.

"Della, listen to Mama. You did NOT cause what happened. I have been having a battle in my own head for quite a while now. I never wanted to burden anyone with it so I kept things to myself. I didn't even tell Dad. Please, baby, please understand you had nothing, and I mean *nothing*, to do with last night. Della, please, know that it was *not* your fault," I pleaded with my daughter hoping she understood it was me who was to blame.

Looking at her square in her bloodshot, water filled eyes I asked, "Do you understand?"

Through her tears Della nodded her head yes and said, "Mama, I was just so scared. I didn't know what was happening. You couldn't breathe and started scratching your arms. I was so frightened I panicked. I kept thinking if I wouldn't have speculated about Pap then this would have never happened. See Mom, it is my fault. I made you get upset for no reason."

By this time Della was re-living the moment and I had to stop her. She would have a panic attack next feeling guilty for something that was out of her control. Saying a quick prayer to myself for strength and words of wisdom I pulled Della to the bed so she can sit and I can try to calm her.

"Listen to me Della," I began trying to quickly ponder how to reply. "Yes, I had a hard past. But so did so many others in this world. I overcame my obstacles and made right in my life when I met your dad. Once we married my theory was that chapter of my life had been written down and closed forever. I chose to ignore it and pretend to myself and my family that no bad things ever happened. I never wanted you or your brother or even Daddy to know the truth. I thought at the time that it didn't matter and it wouldn't hurt anyone. Instead, twenty years later, it started to eat at my soul. I don't know why things started bothering me but they are. Instead of turning to Daddy to try and figure out a solution I never told him. Then, something happened at work with a friend that shocked me and I didn't expect it. We all have rotten days and yesterday was one of mine. I can't apologize enough for scaring you and having you go through everything like you did. It hurts me to know that I caused you fear. I never, ever wanted to do that, *ever*!"

With my words I saw Della become less tense and seem to relax a bit. I wanted her to know that the peacefulness that she felt inside two days ago will return. The mountain that I had to scale was for me and not her.

Looking into Della's eyes and holding her slender long fingers in my own I said, "Listen, make me a deal. If you promise to not take any blame upon yourself I will start to tell you everything that happened when I was young. Deal?"

The girlish look peeked through her gorgeous dark eyes with a spark of interest. "I promise, Mom."

As we parted ways for her to dust the living room and I to eat, Della swiftly turned her head back, smiled and said, "I love you, Mama."

I winked and blew her a kiss as I sat back down on the bed. I felt like such a failure. I get so upset with myself when I mess up. I keep telling myself I'm not perfect. Nobody is perfect! So why do I obsess about trying to be? The word 'image' came to mind. I ignored the word just as I had tossed it out during elevator ride at the hospital.

Pulling my tray of breakfast close I took my first bite of now cold food. Taking a sip of coffee I heard my cell phone ring. Contemplating on answering with a mind full of thoughts and a grumbling stomach I grabbed my phone to see who was calling. Gretchen. I should have guessed. I haven't talked to her since the chat we had in my craft room. I know Nick must've called her while I was in the hospital with my meltdown.

"Well hello there my dear friend," I began.

"Hi. Okay so I know it has been less than twenty four hours, but how are you? Nick called me on his way to the hospital and filled me in on what Della told him."

"I'm fine. I promise. Just more angry at myself than anything. I can't believe I broke like that in front of my daughter. Never in a million years did I ever want that to happen. I feel like a failure for last night." I was heartbroken and Gretchen could sense that through the miles between us.

"I know dear, and I'm truly sorry. I wish I was there to take Della's place last night. Unfortunately, that's just not the case. You *have* to start talking girl. And not just to me. You built up this barrier and literally erased your past from your life. You pretend life before Nick just doesn't exist. But Jill, you have to come clean. This has been eating at you for months." Gretchen paused for a moment and then added, "Nick deserves to hear it all from you, Jill."

I stopped Gretchen before she could continue her lecture.

"I know Gretch, you're right. I can't hide where I came from any longer. And yes, Nick does deserve the truth. I heard a hint of hesitation in your voice when you said that. I need to be honest with him. I have hid from this extensively. I fought this too long with only you. Nick deserves my honesty."

A sigh of relief came out of Gretchen. "Thank you, Jillian. I agree fully with your decision to tell Nick. However, I was afraid you might need a shoulder to lean on so I booked a flight for this afternoon. I will see you this evening."

That was undeniably a surprise and a gigantic weight lifted off my shoulders when I heard that. "Oh Gretchen! I certainly could use some support. Thank you." My chest was beating fast from the excitement of seeing my best friend. I knew the reason for her short visit wasn't going to be all that pleasant but I am thankful that I'll have her there when I need her most. I always find refuge with Gretchen and I am ever so grateful to have her in my life.

"What time should I pick you up at the airport?"

"No need to go out of your way, Jill, I'm going to get a rental. No biggie. See you soon girl."

After our conversation I forgot my hunger and threw on my favorite pair of cargo shorts and a relaxed burnt orange t-shirt. The rest of the morning I was in high spirits given the circumstances. The kids did a fantastic job dusting and making our home tidy. In truth we are all neat freaks. When the kids were small our house was always destroyed. The chaos was out of control so when I went back to work after Della and Kevin got older I realized that I'm not the only one that should know how to clean. So, Nick and I made a plan and held our ground. Della was always eager to please us so when we asked her to help out we had no complaints from her. Kevin on the other hand was a bit of a fighter. He thought cleaning was a "woman's job," thanks to his grandpa Everett. Evidently, Kevin saw how Everett expected certain things from Kathleen a little too much. I swear that man thinks he is from the early nineteen hundreds. But after a few groundings and a long talk from Nick, Kevin realized that he had a part in our family as well and needed to help out.

Once we developed a routine it became second nature as a family instead of me being the only one beating my head against the wall trying to keep a clean house. We divided chores up and made things fair to each of us. Our system has been working ever since, which I am ever so grateful for. I thanked Della and Kevin for being such wonderful kids and told them I would be downstairs if they needed me.

As I made my way down our basement steps, I felt a feeling of relief. I know the next couple days will be extremely difficult for me but hopefully, just maybe, I can finally put my past to rest and let go of the hurt and anger I thought was long gone.

As I opened the passage to my escape, I immediately saw the mural Emma had painted for me. It was a lovely piece of art that I cherished as much as I treasured Emma. She and I became instant friends when she and Fred first started dating years before. We mirror one another in numerous ways especially with how quirky we can both be. Each of us love to have fun and are artistic in our own way. Emma, the artist, loves creating life on canvas. I, on the other hand, find my creative side writing poetry. We respect one another and accept each other as we each are. Just as Gretchen accepts me; no fakeness, no jealousy, no guilt, we are who we are without pretending or putting on a show.

Emma and I had a very in-depth conversation once about

how many people show off their monetary purchases claiming it was for self-expression.

I believe self-expression has been taken out of context in recent years. People seem to think it's about the clothes or jewelry they wear, how many tattoos are permanently imprinted into their skin or the piercings all over their faces. To me, self-expression is something personal that occurs when no one is looking. It's the thoughts that linger in your mind, the choices you make to decide which path you will take, the words you speak aloud, how you treat others, and how you live your life. People's appearance shines through without all the glitter and body art. We as individuals take steps every day to prove to the world exactly who we are as a person. And that makes self-expression all that it should be.

I don't think that there is anything wrong with any of those accessories some choose to have, like expensive clothing, electronics, vehicles, tattoos, or make-up but I do think people use those to the extreme. Putting items on display only to try to show others who they are. It has changed our world and fooled people into believing it makes our self-esteem better and feel good about ourselves. To me, none of that matters because I am a woman of faith. I believe Jesus Christ is my Savior and He makes me feel like I am good enough the way I am. That doesn't mean there isn't room for improvement; it just means I know I don't need the traits of society to make me feel better about myself.

As I remembered our conversation I thought to myself, "but

that was material things. What about who we are as a person? The things we hide deep within our hearts and refuse to let escape...like my childhood."

Pushing away my newest question to myself, I finished recalling my response to Emma. My point was that if we eliminate all the glitter and stars that supposedly makes us feel better, we may dig deep into our soul to find that the way we think, act, and treat others and ourselves is enough self-expression to show others what we are all about as individuals and be able to hear our message to one another.

Regaining my senses back to the present, I focused my eyes and I found myself staring at the willow on my wall. I smiled because it reminded me of the weeping willow Nick planted for me ten years ago. It was my thirtieth birthday gift he surprised me with. Somehow he managed to find a great looking young weeping willow that was exactly like the mural on my wall. It's matured now and perfect in every way. The willow stood tall in our backyard by our pond he dug out for me a year after my willow took root. It's a short walk from the back of our house that sits on our four acres. Remembering how much comfort my special tree has given me over the last decade I decided to take a stroll outside.

It was a beautiful seventy-five degree sun-filled day in our small town of Pennsylvania. I heard the birds singing throughout our many trees as a small gray squirrel nibbled on an acorn to my right near our property line. I should have grabbed my camera to capture the wondrous sight God granted me. Instead, I took the brief walk under the willow. I felt safe here from the beast inside me that I have concealed from my family, mostly my husband, for the past twenty years. The meaning behind the weeping willow was sacred. Something that only I knew about, as many other things that I kept hidden from the world.

I ducked under the low branches that dangled in the breeze of our valley. I decided to keep the landscaping around my tree as the earth is. Grass and dirt with no flowers so that I can sit under the tree without the worry of stepping on vegetation or any other design I might have chosen.

As I sat down on the ground I felt the cool grass under my legs and fingertips. The grass was soft to touch as the blades ran through my fingers. The earth was so soothing to me in every aspect. Leaning against the jagged bark I felt myself relax for the first time in days. I have missed this old tree these past few days. It seems like life becomes a contest full of the hustle and bustle of business. However, I feel like the one who finishes first actually finishes last. If we don't take a moment to realize what we have, then we have nothing in the end. Just a blur of memories and a heart filled with regret.

I closed my eyes and let my conscience take me away. Thoughts whirled around like the air in the breeze. My gram instantly came to mind. Della Saunders was a woman of strength.

63

The one I consider my guardian watching over me from Heaven. She passed away when I was thirteen and I thought my world stopped forever. My heart ached for weeks knowing she wasn't there to protect me any longer. Her home was my safe haven until cancer decided to attack her body once more and eventually took her away from me. I was heartbroken when she finally took her last breath. We lived with her during her last bout of cancer and took care of her. Gram had a brain tumor when my mom, Carol, was a teenager. She managed to beat the tumor but little over two decades later cancer came back with a vengeance and attacked her throat. It was as if the cancer had something to prove; *"it"* was in control. At the age of sixty-one, cancer won and took my only hope away.

I started to feel the familiar ache in my chest that I always experience when I think of my gram. I know she wasn't perfect; however, she was perfect to me - almost. We even named our daughter after her.

I had this great woman in my life who taught me so many of my morals and values that I still uphold. One explanation came to mind as I thought of how differently I remembered Gram than my mom. Mom loved her mom, which is undeniable. But, I believe Mom thought of her in an authoritarian way because Gram was her mother. Parents treat children differently than their grandchildren, I am certain of that. When I was young, it was a different growth period in Gram's life and she had changed in many areas. Mom viewed her as the disciplinarian. I never saw that side of Gram.

I still have a hard time with the fact that she told my mom to have the abortion, a decision that robbed me of an older brother or sister. Every time I think about it I get extremely upset. Still, my mind proceeds with the memory. Gram never talked to me personally about it since I was only thirteen when she passed. However, as I got older I was curious as to what happened and why Gram would tell my mom to do such an awful thing. As the facts came to light in my late teens I found out the story behind it all…

My mom was eighteen years old and was dating a guy named Chad. She became pregnant and soon after he was caught cheating with my mom's cousin Tracy who Chad married later on. My mom was devastated of course and wasn't sure what to do. Talking to her mom about it was extremely uncomfortable for her. However, Mom knew she had to tell Gram the unfortunate situation. Given my Gram's background with men, having a daughter of her own out of wedlock to a married man, she didn't want her daughter having a child without marriage vows either. Gram felt that being shunned in the family wasn't the route she wanted her daughter to take. So, instead of having a child without a father, her solution was to have my mom get an abortion. Mom, being young and incredibly naïve to the world around her followed the direction she was lead. I know that having a child unwed would be frowned upon, but if other members found out about the abortion, wouldn't they see that as a bigger sin?

I certainly don't agree with abortion. Unless, circumstances arise that the child or mother are terminally ill and life will be lost no matter what action is taken. When it's a choice of personal reasons, I am highly against taking a life away without ever having a chance. Adoption is always an option. God grants us the blessing of a child and I feel that we should cherish that child no matter how he or she came about. The baby is still a life from God from the time of conception. In the end, it's something that is dealt with between the person and God himself. Forgiveness and redemption are extremely important for any Christian who falls short of His glory daily, including myself.

As time passed and I grew older and a little wiser I had a personal growth after beginning to read my Bible. In the book of Matthew, Jesus clearly states the standard you use in judging is the standard by which you will be judged. We are to love our neighbors as we love ourselves. The fact of the matter is their hearts are the one that becomes heavy. Deciphering all of the warnings He tells us, I came to the conclusion that we need to be extremely cautious on how we judge others. As a whole, many people believe that each sin is on a tier of bad to worst. With further interpretation of our good book, in the eyes of the Lord, every sin is considered the same as the next. In the end, it's still a sin against God's commands. Since then I have tried very hard not to criticize others for their actions but love them that much more. With what had happened though, I still find it difficult to accept.

I became conscious that I started battling in my head, positive I would lose, trying to defend my grandmother for a poor choice she made; I decided I needed to change gears. "She was trying to protect Mom," I said aloud trying to force any negative thoughts about Gram away with the breeze.

Pulling myself back together and wiping away the dampness from my face, I stood up under the luscious green of my willow and took a deep breath. The air suddenly became thick with moisture and I figured a thunderstorm was on the horizon. Dusting off my shorts I wanted to check on Della and Kevin.

Walking up towards the house I spotted Kevin shooting some hoops. I decided to quietly come up behind him and stole the basketball off of him. As I dribbled around him I threw up a hook shot. Score!

"Wow, good shot, Mom!"

"Thanks Kev. Didn't think your old Mom had it in her I bet!"

Laughing he shook his head no and we decided to play a game of Horse. A quarter through our game Della came out and said she wanted to play the winner. The clouds started to part ways so the rain never did come. I was glad because spending time with my family like this was just what I needed. The rest of the morning we had a wonderful time together laughing and playing basketball.

Chapter 4

The Dark Angel

That afternoon was smooth and relaxing. I was eager for Gretchen to visit. I knew her schedule was jammed throughout the summer months. About twelve years ago she decided to start her own photography business. Although it was a slow start, business started to pick up within the first year as her name went around by word of mouth. She had an eye for spectacular scenes and was lucky enough to capture such a view and have it published in her local paper. That's how the idea started for a career change. She then decided to take some photography classes and she has been pleased with her choice since then.

The phone rang as Della and I was cleaning up our lunch dishes. "I'll get it, Mom."

Watching her walk to her bedroom while her voice was low, I knew it was a friend for her. I was certain she was assembling some sort of afternoon outing.

As she got off the phone she came over to me and gave her sweet innocent "I want something" look.

"Yes my dear, what is it?"

"Well, Shelly called and wanted to know if Kevin and I

68

could go over and swim for a while. Shelly's little brother Steve will be there so Kev will have someone to hang out with. Please, please!" she begged.

"And how are you getting there?" I inquired thinking she wanted me to take them.

"Shelly's mom is off work today so she can pick us up if that is okay with you. Shelly said they have to pick up some milk and bread so they will be out anyways."

"Alright that's fine but I want you guys home for dinner. Remember Gretchen is coming tonight." I don't mind them going but I want them here this evening. Gretchen always loved spending time with the kids since she and Jake never had any of their own.

A squeal with delight came out of her lungs that hurt my ears followed by a hug and of course, "Thanks Mom, you're the best!"

Children are able to express their emotions like adults wish they could. Della was no exception to that rule.

"You're welcome but make sure Kevin wants to go. If not he can stay here."

"Okay, KEVIN…" she yelled out for him.

Two minutes later Della ran out to the kitchen where I was finishing up and confirmed that Kevin wanted to go as well and promised to be respectable and mind their manners. Those are my two main requirements when my children are out in public. I think I have stressed that to them since birth and they know if their manners weren't on cue, they would be grounded, taking away privileges.

Della said that Shelly and her mom would be here in about fifteen minutes so I wanted to finish cleaning up in the kitchen. Then, all of a sudden, I remembered I didn't have my phone on me. As I fumbled around my bedroom forgetting once again where I put my phone, I heard it beep. Eventually, I found it under my pillow so I checked my cell. Seventeen missed calls, holy smokes! As I scrolled through the calls I saw my grandmother or father called, my sister and both brothers. My father still lives with his mom in Ohio. He is sixty-three-years-old; you would think he could be on his own by now however, he has been with her for decades. With that said, they share the same phone. With all these calls something must have surely happened; I just dreaded to know what.

Since my sister Chloe and I are the closest I wanted to call her back first, knowing she would fill me in. She and I became extremely tight when she moved back to Pennsylvania, right before she had her son Ethan. Chloe has always been a free spirit and when she was younger I tried to guide her. At the time she didn't want anything to do with what was right and did the exact opposite of my advice. We fought constantly and honestly couldn't be in the same room together for more than an hour. As time passed and she began to mature with her son, we grew a very special bond. I began to trust her. She was more than my sister; she was one of my closest friends. As I was about to hit my speed dial for her, I heard the doorbell chime. I guess Shelly was earlier than expected.

Della yelled out she would get the door. I heard a noise as if she had fallen down the stairs so I rushed to make sure she was okay.

"Are you okay, honey?" I asked my clumsy daughter.

"Yeah, Mom, I'm fine" she chuckled. "I was just running down the steps too fast and my footing slipped on a couple steps. I'm good!"

Again we heard the doorbell. Still laughing Della ran to the door and I followed. As she opened the door expecting to see Shelly her eyes filled with concern when she saw the expression on Chloe's face. My sister, oh not good; not that I wasn't happy to see her but given all my missed calls I knew this was going to be something big.

"Hey, Aunt Chloe," Della gave her a hug.

"Hi, sweetheart, how are you?" Chloe began.

"I'm good, but you seem extremely upset. Are you okay Aunt Chloe?" Della questioned. Her natural instincts were always at their peak. Della obtained a gift where she was able to sense when a troubled heart was bound by chains of uncertainty and distraught. Always sensitive to others, not wanting to over step any boundaries considering her age, Della made sure to word her questions delicately.

"Well honey, I just really need to talk to your mom first. I'm sure she will fill you in. Please don't worry that pretty face of yours. Uncle John, Ethan, and I all are okay."

Chloe let herself in as I watched her face for any sort of clue

71

as to what was going on. Chloe was always a bit of a drama queen, so I was trying to get a grasp as to what had her so upset.

She beckoned me to join her in my bedroom for some privacy. I nodded and followed, although before she started to shut the door I wanted to make sure the kids got picked up and I quickly explained they were leaving soon. Noticing Chloe's face was puffy and her eyes bloodshot I could tell she had been crying. I wanted to comfort her but I also needed to make sure my children were ready and give them a time to be home. Chloe understood and I went to find Della and Kevin.

Once I got the kids out the door I called for Chloe to join me in the living room. We hugged since it felt like forever that we last saw one another, even though it was only about a week's time.

Hearing the leather crunch underneath us as we sat on the couch, Chloe sighed and started crying. I leaned over and held her like a mother should and stroked her hair.

"It's okay, let it out and just start when you're ready," I began. I felt my stomach knot up thinking someone must have died. It was probably our grandmother. She was in her mid-eighties and hasn't been in the best of health these last thirty years. I chuckled inside thinking of how she has managed to still keep kicking after all the prescription drugs she has taken over the years. How an eighty-seven pound petite old lady can take sixty pain killers and sixty pills for her anxiety in six days and still be alive is beyond belief.

Nevertheless, she did and blamed my father, her own son, for stealing her medicine and freaked out when her doctor told her she couldn't get another prescription. One hundred and twenty pills in less than a week was insane. How she lived is madness.

I suddenly remembered that I forgot about why my sister was so upset and needed to redirect my attention to her. My opinion had me prepared to hear that Gram had passed away. Working in a nursing home, I witnessed multiple occasions when the angel of death knocked three times. I assumed this was the second knock.

"So, what's going on Chloe? I had seventeen missed calls while I was outside with the kids. Even our brother Chris called me and you know I *never* talk to him."

Sniffling and grabbing a tissue out of her designer handbag she began. "Well Gram called me a little bit ago. Dad did it. He finally succeeded. Damn him Sis, he shot himself."

My jaw felt like it dropped to the floor with her news. Certainly not what I expected to hear from her because it took my breath away knowing it was Dad instead of Gram. I never thought him to live a long life and make peace with himself and his faults but I certainly didn't think that his mom would outlive him. I was surprised however, that I wasn't as saddened as I probably should have been.

"Um, wow, okay. What happened?" I questioned. I was disheartened although I didn't feel the urge to cry. I know he is, or now, *was* my father - however he was just that; a father and not a dad.

"According to Gram he had been drinking all last night and into the morning. He found a twenty dollar bill on the city street while walking to the drug store for Gram. You know how Dad is, he gets money and he has to spend it on beer and cigarettes. Well, he went and bought a bunch of beer and a fifth of vodka. He didn't even get Gram's laxatives. When he got back to the apartment she said they got into it because he didn't get her stuff. So he went in the bedroom and turned on his stereo. Well, about two in the morning he started fighting with her again and she called me saying she was going to kick him out tomorrow. You know Gram, he drinks and fights with her and she threatens to kick him out. She wanted to call me to make sure us kids wouldn't get mad at her. Oh, Jill you know how they are."

"Unfortunately, yes I do. So, they were fighting and she called you at two in the morning? I wouldn't have been a happy camper." They have always called late. Both are night owls, which is where I get my bad habit.

"Yeah, I was mad because she got me and John up. But I answered because you know if I didn't they would just keep calling. I talked to her for a little bit and then to Dad. I told him just to leave her alone and go back in the bedroom and go to sleep. He slurred a "yeah" and I got back on with Gram. I told her he promised to go to bed so we hung up the phone and I went back to bed. Next thing I know she is calling me again late this morning. She said that Dad went into the bedroom as promised and kept drinking. He must have passed out for a little bit because Gram said she checked on him around four this morning. Gram had fallen asleep after that and woke up at ten o'clock this morning to a loud bang. Gram went to check on him thinking it was something outside. When she opened the bedroom door she saw blood and said she called the cops. I don't know Jill what actually happened. I just can't believe he had enough guts to pull the trigger. He's gone though. Gone. Forever."

I saw a tear run down Chloe's slender cheek. I knew the only thing I could do was try to comfort her. I'm not sure why I don't feel as upset as Chloe. Until recently, I thought I made my peace with him years ago. I forgave him for all the garbage that happened. Maybe it's because I know that I really have no loss. My love for him is minuscule in comparison to anyone else and other than him being my sperm donor he really has nothing to do with neither me nor my children.

My sister, on the other hand, has always held a soft spot in her heart for him. She realizes who he truly is, yet has always overlooked his failures and has loved him unconditionally. Me and that unconditional thing never really saw eye to eye. Regardless of my feelings, she has always told me she feels bad for him. Why, I'm not quite sure. Maybe it was because Dad always adored Chloe. I think she reminded him of Mom to a great extent. They divorced when I was fourteen and he never stopped loving her, never. They both re-married afterwards yet when he talked about Mom I heard the twinge in his voice that said he still missed and loved her. He knew he is the one that ruined that relationship.

Anyhow, Chloe was his little girl, his "Little Miss Marilyn Monroe". I remember when she was three years old she climbed up on his lap, grabbed his face with her tiny little hands and said, "Dad, you're drunk". That happened to be the same night he busted my mouth open. When Chloe did that, he laughed hysterically and thought that was the best thing since alcohol was invented. She always did no wrong in his eyes.

For so many years I was jealous of her for that. I knew that because I stood up to him, he was sure to bring me down anyway he could. Ironically, he told me I was his rock. I could never grasp how I could be his stone of logic and reason when he continuously tried to bring me down. Growing up wasn't a treat but instead, it felt like a trick. For me to want to go back to a time that was supposed to be fun and easy without the worry of a job or family was never something I wished for like so many others I knew.

All the hatred I used to feel came rushing in like a lion in the safari hunting its prey. The contact he had with my kids was always very limited and monitored when they were younger. Eventually, as my children got older, I completely ceased all contact after my grandmother called me one evening while we were at Della's cheer practice. She asked why I told all of my family that I thought she killed her husband. She threatened me that she would sue me over the matter and my last words to her were that I would see her in court. Court never happened and our communication was stopped after that.

I have worked very hard at keeping my secrets and I wasn't going to let him or her ruin it for me. Now that he is gone maybe I can rest a bit easier. I know once Gretchen is here it will all come out though. The weight of what I have to do later feels even heavier on my shoulders.

Chloe came back from the bathroom. I hadn't even noticed she walked out of the living room being so wrapped up in my own mind-set.

"Oh Jillian, I am so sorry! How are you? Nick called me Monday evening. I was going to go to the hospital but Nick said to wait and give you a day or two. And your arms, oh my Jill, are you okay?"

"Yes, I'm alright, just had a little melt down. A lot of stress and it got the best of me. Sadly, it happened in front of Della which still bothers me immensely. But other than that, I am fine. The scratches on my arms will heal. I am relaxing this week and not working as you know. Now, let's get back to Dad. I guess it's a good thing that you and I bought that life insurance policy on him years ago. It's not much but at least it should cover the funeral costs. Are they going to autopsy him? And where in the world did he get a gun? If Gram knew he had one she would have freaked."

"She did know he had a gun. Gram gave him the money for the gun to buy it off of a local store clerk. According to Gram the police didn't really see a need for an autopsy. The forensics said the way the gun was laying and where the bullet entry was, matched up to suicide. They knew he was a drunk so I don't think they will push the issue." Chloe paused as if she wasn't sure she had the courage to ask her next question. "Jillian, do you think she could have done it? You know the story about Pap better than I do. What exactly happened with that situation?"

"Oh my Chloe, that is a long story. How about if I just give you the basics because Gretchen will be arriving in a few hours," I said.

"Oh cool, Gretchen is coming up! I haven't seen her in forever. How has she been?"

"She is doing good. After my little episode we had a talk and I decided that I needed to start to tell Nick and even the kids about our childhood. You know I have hid it for so long and it's something that I literally hate to discuss. She is coming up for support. Hopefully, we can talk about where to start with Nick and figure out a guideline."

Chloe's face was in shock of what I just said. She knew that our childhood was under lock and key for what she thought would be all eternity. After a shy smile and nod she said matter-of-factly, "I'm proud of you big sis. You're doing the right thing. Now tell me the short version of the story about our pap."

Rolling my eyes I began the brief synopsis. Nothing was ever proven, but I always had a shadow of doubt on how our grandfather died. Back in the early seventies Pap allegedly shot and killed himself. He suffered from rheumatoid arthritis for years. There were rumors that he also might have had some sort of bone cancer or disease that debilitated him further but I have never seen any medical reports. As time passed, it got worse and he ultimately was unable to perform daily tasks for himself. Even trying to hold a cup of coffee to his mouth or raise a cigarette was useless. He was forced to stop working and when that happened, he gave up. According to Dad, he confirmed that his dad had told him multiple times that he wanted to die because he didn't feel like a man. Pap's dignity and manhood was shattered by his disability.

Evidently, Pap had an idea one day. He started to have his son work with him every day to help with his range of motion so that he could hold a cup in his hands again. At least- that is the story he convinced Dad with. At the time, they owned a thirty-eight special semi-automatic pistol and that is what they practiced with. It was Pap's pride and joy. He loved the gun for his own reasons.

After a couple months passed by and all the pain Pap had to endure, he was finally able to hold that cup of coffee. Dad was excited about the progress he had helped his dad accomplish. Unfortunately, his happiness came to a cease when the cops and his uncle showed up at the Catholic school he attended. Dad was fourteen and in ninth grade when this all transpired.

To no surprise, when Dad heard that his father shot himself and died, he lashed out. He was angry and distraught that his own father was gone forever. How could he do that? He departed his son, sending his soul to the torments of Hell according to his Catholic upbringing.

The police whisked Dad away to the station and questioned him as if he pulled the trigger. The cops went as far as calculating the time it took to walk from school to Dad's home and back to school. After their interrogation and testing him for GSR, they realized Dad didn't have enough time to leave school, kill his dad, and then return back to school. The cops decided he had nothing to do with the shooting and moved on in their investigation. The real suspect was at home - his mom. As the story was told to me, she was asked by police what happened. She gave her alibi and even provided a store receipt and a bank deposit slip showing her whereabouts. Since she was allegedly innocent and her husband's death ruled suicide she felt she had to place blame on someone. That someone was Chris Cochran, a fourteen-year-old child. Her own child. She held him responsible, saying that if he wouldn't have helped his father, this would have never happened.

I'm not sure why she put that on her only son. The single reason I could make sense of was due to her guilt. I asked my father once about everything that happened. I suggested that through a rumor, it was thought that she did it. At first, he was reluctant and said there was no way. However, as he was telling the story, halfway through he started thinking of the time of events.

Sorting out everything we believe that Gram had to know what Pap had planned. So as directed, she went out to run some errands. He had the gun beside him, loaded and cocked. Pap put the gun to his gut and pulled the trigger. I'm not sure if he wanted to go higher, but as it unfolded, he had a chance shot that ricocheted throughout his organs and hit a rib that went into his lung. He didn't die instantly. Instead, he lay in bed, bleeding internally until he took his last breath. My instincts tell me that Gram got home and found Pap still alive. I can't imagine the conversation that took place that day. I'm not sure I would want to.

One thing I do know is it scarred our father forever. He blamed himself all his life. Gram beat it into his head for decades that it was his fault. I can't envision how it felt to reside a life with a guilt-filled heart. The repercussion was the childhood we had to endure because of it.

What I thought happened is purely speculation and he still took fault. I am sure that she will take that day and its truth to her grave. She had completely dictated his life and made him incredibly dependent on her. It's probably best that he died first.

"Okay, so you seriously think she didn't do it? All these years and you never told me. Why?" Chloe asked as I finished the tale.

"Well, honestly, I never said anything because it was part of the life I left behind. He was such a weak person all his life. I figured you knew prior to that and there wasn't much more to tell. I didn't envision Pap's suicide would ever be brought up again. I certainly didn't think that you would consider Gram killed Dad. I honestly don't think she literally killed Dad, however I think it was a very slow and long process that put him over the edge," I said as a matter-of-fact.

"So Gram made him weak and Dad was dependent on her all his life. How pathetic," she blurted out.

"Yes, I agree. He chose to drink to flee from his reality. It was like he was having a dreadful dream and instead of waking up to peace, the nightmare was his realism. I never understood how the weak survived. I'm still trying to figure that one out." I have always wondered about that so I thought I would share my question.

"This was very enlightening, Jill. Thanks for letting me in on our family history. For now though, I suppose I should be going. We have to figure out what day we want to have Dad's funeral. I will be in touch, Sis. I love you." Chloe grabbed her purse and headed for the door and I followed.

"I love you too, Chloe. Call me and we can decide on the day. Can you contact the insurance company and keep me updated?"

"Sure will, Jill. I'll call ya. Bye." Chloe left and I was left with astonishment that Dad *died*.

Chapter 5

Angel of Inspiration

Nick got home from work before the kids, which gave me time to sit and tell him the news Chloe delivered earlier. Asking what happened, I filled him in with all the details.

"Well babe, I suppose it's up to us to take care of things. What do we have to do?" Nick asked.

Frankly, I was stunned he said "we" and even more so when he implied taking care of the funeral arrangements. Nick was never a fan of my father. He could sense the tension I had whenever I spoke to him on the phone and visiting him was never an option. Nick made little comments in the past about my father and being thankful he wasn't in the picture. I never indulged on his comments for fear of Nick asking questions.

"That's a good question. I haven't had to deal with taking care of funeral arrangements so I thought I would ask your mom how she handled things when Grandma passed away." I figured it was my best bet.

"When do you plan on telling Della and Kevin?" Nick then questioned.

I could tell Nick was curious as to how I was going to explain it to the kids. The one man, my own father, was someone I dreaded to be around. The only plus out of this was that he could no longer talk and reveal the truth I've hidden for so long. Now, it's me who was going to tell my story, with my voice, my way, my time.

"Well," I began, "I was thinking of telling them after dinner. Gretchen will be here as well and I am going to try to prepare myself for the questions that I am sure will follow."

"I wish I could help you with that." Nick looked forlorn with his response. I could tell he was saddened by not knowing the whole story. I felt the guilt rise within me wishing I could turn the hands of time back. If only I had the confidence twenty years ago.

"You have no idea how much I want to start over. I would confide in you all that I was, all that I had to endure. I was so afraid, I just couldn't."

Nick wrapped his arms around me, knowing I was hurting; for the both of us.

Gretchen arrived right before dinner was ready. I cooked enough food, expecting her company. The kids helped me with some last minute tasks like getting Gretchen's sleeping arrangements ready. We have an upstairs loft that was our office space. We added a spacious king sized bed and matching dark chestnut dresser for these instances. Nick built a partition so that any company that we may have can obtain privacy in the event that one of us needed to use the computer. In most cases, there weren't any issues since I keep my laptop and extra printer in my bedroom. When Nick was re-designing our home, I had him put a nook in one corner of our bedroom just for that reason. At first, he fought me on the idea, saying that it was just a waste of space. I told him it will pay off in the end. It has proven to be a positive choice when we've had company.

During dinner, we all chatted lightly, enjoying the sight of my best friend. I couldn't have be more elated seeing her across the table from myself. When Gretchen entered our home, it instantly lit up, filling the area with energy. Small talk continued through desert, telling funny stories about one another. Della and Kevin volunteered to clean up the dishes while Gretchen and I went out on our back porch to talk. The kids knew why her visit was so important and respected my wishes to give us some space.

"So, Jill, how are you?" Gretchen started getting to the root of why she came to visit.

"I'm a lot better now that you're here. I can always seek refuge under your wings. Thanks Gretchen for coming up."

"Oh now, don't swell my head! You are doing the difficult part. I am simply here to pick you up if you would stumble."

Gretchen, ever so humble, took my hand and looked straight in to my eyes. "Okay girl, when do you plan on talking to Nick? Tonight, tomorrow?"

"I knew you wouldn't waste any time! I was thinking of showing you my secret scrapbook. I have it hidden downstairs. After that, we can decide on where to start with Nick."

Gretchen looked a bit puzzled. I always told her my latest and greatest ideas of what I was scrap booking. However, this project I kept all to myself. It was something I was very protective of, in fact, so guarded I kept it in the safe I have tucked away in the black filing cabinet of my sanctuary.

"I'll explain," I reassured her.

I also knew that I had to tell Gretchen and the kids about my father's passing. I was just procrastinating and I was well aware of my actions. The words were on the tip of my tongue and before I knew it, "So my father died today." I blurted out the news as if it was some random thought.

I heard a gasp escape Gretchen's ideal frame. It wasn't that big of a deal, was it? I'm fully aware he is my father, and I know the commandment that we should honor thy father and mother that rings through my ears. I thought I moved on from all these feelings that conjured up over the past couple months. My father is gone, it shouldn't matter anymore. Right?

"I talked to you earlier this morning, when did all this happen?" Gretchen questioned.

"After I got off the phone with you, I went outside and had some quiet time under my willow. Then, the kids and I played a little basketball. After lunch, Della and I were cleaning up and I realized I hadn't checked my phone in a while. So, when I went for it I saw I had seventeen missed calls, all from my family. Next thing I knew Chloe was at my door. The kids went to a friend's house and that is when Chloe told me the news," I stated trying to summarize the events.

"You've had quite a day, Jill. How are you handling all the stress? Your doctor said to limit all the aggravation. It doesn't seem like you are doing as the good man prescribed." Gretchen was showing her protective instincts over me. I appreciated her concern but I knew the time was right. I felt it in my heart to proceed with my plans.

"I know you are concerned Gretchen, but have no fear! Jillian is here!" I stated laughingly as I made a superman stance.

She began laughing as well, as she knows I like to bring humor to any delicate situation.

"You don't like to listen to reason, do you Jillian Davenport?!" Gretchen exclaimed.

"Now as long as you have known me, you ought to realize I am not a woman of reason. When I want something, I go after it with full force. Besides, I know it's time. I feel it in my heart and I am ready to share my past with my husband and children. They deserve the truth." I was very adamant with my words. Actually, I felt a bit gratified as I declared my independence, stripping away the ties that my family has had bound me to for so long.

"Well now, I see there is no way to sway your thinking, so that leaves me with one option. I'm here for ya!" Gretchen said smiling.

I can't believe God blessed me with such a loving, compassionate soul as Gretchen. I reminded her on a regular basis how much our friendship meant to me. She was my sister, although not by blood, but by spirit. Gretchen was a friend to me through thick and thin, regardless of the circumstances. I cherish her more than any words could express and I made sure she knew that after she confirmed what I already knew. She's there for me; whenever, wherever, and however. Gretchen Turner was my angel of inspiration.

I explained to Gretchen why Chloe stopped by today and the story she had told to me. I included Chloe's questions about our grandfather and if I thought Gram could do that to Dad. Gretchen wasn't astonished that he died, but was intrigued by my sister's doubts and uncertainty.

Looking at my watch, I realized forty-five minutes had passed and I needed to talk to Della and Kevin about my dad's passing. Gretchen knew what I was thinking and stood up. Leaving our cushioned lawn furniture, Gretchen and I headed inside.

This was it, this is where it starts. I had a thought run through my mind like I was attending my first Alcohol Anonymous meeting. "Hello, my name is Jillian Davenport, and I am a survivor of domestic abuse." I chuckled at the thought while Gretchen looked at me strangely, probably wondering what was going through my sometimes foolish mind.

"You don't want to know," I said still laughing.

Walking into our kitchen and around the island that housed our stove and dishwasher, I saw the kids had finished up the dishes. Pleased with their help, I went to see where they were. Glancing in the living room, the television was on and Nick, Della, and Kevin were all there lounging on the couch. I decided now was the time to initiate the news I had to share. Gretchen followed behind. I motioned for her to sit in the most comfortable chair that Nick took pride in calling it 'his'. I was surprised he wasn't sitting in it, but knowing me, I would have kicked him out of it when Gretchen and I returned from the deck. He probably knew that, so he chose to avoid his male ego being slightly bruised and retired to the couch with the kids.

I asked Nick if he would turn off the television and figuring what I was about to announce he obliged. Standing in the middle of the room, I could feel my heart begin to race. At first, my words seemed jumbled in my head as I looked for the place to start. Swiftly, my words found their voice.

"I need to talk to you all about my dad," I began. I saw Kevin squirm and Nick told him to behave because this was important.

"Aunt Chloe came by today as you all know. After Della and

89

Kevin left she had told me that Dad had passed away today." I heard a slight gasp escape Della's tiny body.

      "I know you guys didn't really get a chance to know him. But I assure you there were plenty of reasons why I kept you shielded from a man filled with immoral tendencies. He was a drunk, an alcoholic honestly. As a child I hated him for it. As a woman I learned from it. In the end, beer won the war, taking his soul and purpose of life. He drank daily to forget his memories. Always living in his past yearning for his future to bring back his time of yesterdays to try and change it. He was a man I had little respect or love for. He gave me life so for that I am grateful. Because of him and my mom, I knew what I didn't want out of life and I made sure that I broke the cycle that seemed to be predestined. They made me strong in that sense. I was an independent child, an old soul as so many people have told me over the years. I kept you all away so that none of you had to endure the pain I once did. For that I am not sorry. What I am sorry for, is that you will never know the man I know he could have been."

      As I ended my speech, I saw tears running down Della's face. She was such a sensitive soul as am I. The difference between her and I is that I hide it from the world where she shows it on her sleeve. Nick was consoling Della, holding her in his arms. Sensing what she was feeling, I knew that Della had questions regarding the man she never knew that brought her mom so much agony. She would slowly come to terms with the death of her phantom of a grandfather. That, I recognized, would not happen until I fully explained the mastermind that helped form my personality.

I glanced over to Gretchen's direction. She was crying as well. It seemed odd to me since she didn't cry when I told her initially. I looked at Kevin and found him noticeably calm. Walking over to him I wanted to be sure he wasn't suppressing any feelings.

"You okay, Grover?" I asked him. Grover was a nickname I always used since he was two years old. He loved Grover and the "montners" from the TV program. As long as I live, he will always be my Grover.

"I'm fine mom. To be honest, I didn't really know Pap, so I can't miss what I never had."

I was astounded by his adult-like response. Never have I heard such maturity come from my little man. Impressed and depressed at once, is that possible?

I gave Kevin a hug and kissed his forehead. I was so proud of him. I then headed over to Gretchen. How ironic I thought, considering I was going to comfort her instead of the other way around. I knew I was ready to tackle my endeavor and nothing was stopping me.

Looking down at Gretchen, I felt my heart sink as my fear of messing up overpowered by thoughts trying to ponder the reason why she was crying. What if I said it all wrong? What if I was too brutal with my speech? A thousand what if's came to mind and I started to panic. Gretchen sensing my nervousness stood up and put her arms around me. I had the comfort of her embrace and felt a little more at ease.

And then I heard in a light whisper, "I have never been as proud of someone as I am of you right now."

Chapter 6

Expressions of Poetry

I reassured Della that we will have a long chat about the situation that transpired. Once I felt comfortable that she was calm, Gretchen and I headed downstairs to the basement. Holding on to the banister down the steps, I felt a bit nervous showing my most treasured work. In it contained all the poems that I wrote. I also included the year I wrote them as well as giving explanation to the meaning of each poem. The entire book is a brief summary of my life. I felt absurd for the butterflies that were soaring around my abdomen, I then realized exactly who I was sharing my endeavor with; Gretchen. And for right now, it was only Gretchen.

Flipping on the light switch as we entered the room, I felt my confidence rise. I fumbled under my desk for the undisclosed black box that helped contain my concealed character. I slipped the top off and produced the little silver key that protected the magic to my inner most feelings. Holding it up high, I felt a bit of triumph. Being candid with my best friend was not difficult. My family was a different story.

With key in hand, I stepped over to my black metal filing cabinet. I hated having a piece of furniture such as this, since that is all that I see at work. It reminded me of all the restless souls, stuck in a nursing facility that was not their 'real' home. Pushing the thought out of my head, I opened the bottom drawer and revealed the fire proof safe that contained the legend of Jillian. I chuckled inside thinking of the impractical contemplation. Turning the key, I found the brown leather collection sealed with my heart, my soul, my sincerity. I imagined it glowing with pride as I turned to hand my creativity to Gretchen.

Her blue eyes danced with anticipation and a nod to show her appreciation for sharing. And the launch of a new era has begun for the Davenport family. I felt exhilarated knowing my past was soon to be unchained. Nothing holding me back now, Gretchen and I dived in to reading. I gave an introduction on the first page, telling why I was doing this and what I wanted my children to know should anything happen to me before I was able to.

I decided to start my poetry out with one of the very first poems I ever wrote about my Gram Saunders who passed away. She meant everything to me and I declared that in many of my poems. The second was dark. I wrote it at the age of nineteen and it was about how I felt when I was in second grade. I was terrified I would come home from school to find my mother dead by the hands of my father. I sat on the floor as Gretchen, in my Queen Anne chair, started to read out loud. Clearing her throat, she began.

"The Ticking Clock

94

Safe Under the Willow

Flashes of light flicker

As the clock ticks

Soft sobbing of a woman

Drowns out the whimpering of her child

As she glances at the clock

She fears the ticking time bomb

Ready to explode

She hears the slamming of the door

Like an exploding shotgun

A moment later

A command for fear of her life

Stepping forward ready for the blow

With a deep breath she takes the beating

For an endless hour

Crawling from Death's door

She gathers her child

Vanishing from Satan's presence."

I saw goose bumps on Gretchen's arms as she finished. "I forgot how powerful that was, and you writing it at nineteen…" her voice trailed off.

"Yeah, I was pretty young. Analyzing it now, I see how I could have improved it. But, knowledge comes with age." I always knew my writing wasn't perfect; nevertheless, I made the attempt and wrote with my emotion instead of my brains.

95

"You always were too critical of yourself. Take pride in yourself girl. You deserve it."

"Honestly, I take pride in my job and being a mother and wife. However, when it comes to my creativity and writing, I suppose I just need some reassurance saying either, 'yeah' it's great or, 'no' it sucks!" I giggled and Gretchen joined in.

"Well my friend, you know I have always loved your work, but knowing how you are, you will just say I am being biased!" We laughed even harder at her outlook knowing full well she was precisely right.

After we finally had our fill of laughter, we went back to our task. As Gretchen read and I answered a question here or there, she came to the final page. Her look became very serious which kind of frightened me for an instant.

"You know Jillian, by you beginning this process of opening up to your family; it's going to change everything. Are you ready for that?" Gretchen seemed concerned that I was rushing in. I knew I was ready and I told her just that.

"I have never been so sure of anything in my life. The time is right and there comes a point in your existence that you must take the reins and hold on tight. It's like taming a wild stallion; you have to be ready for when it rears up taking claim on its independence, its pride. But being diligent and patient, gaining the horse's trust proves to show your love in return. I know my family will give me the respect and love I deserve without pitying me. You know as well as I do, I *don't* want pity." I was exceptionally steadfast with my words.

Raising her hands in the air, Gretchen declared, "Okay, you win! I just wanted no shadow of doubt that you are prepared for all the questions that I have no doubt, you will be asked. I know how difficult this has been for you all these years. To jump in like this, I am worried you may accepting more of a challenge than you can handle." She paused and placed her hand upon mine. "I'm just trying to protect you, Jill."

"I sincerely appreciate your genuine concern. And without you here I am not sure I would feel as secure. What I am confident about though, is that I'm primed. I promise." Smiling at Gretchen I then added, "Now, I intend to figure out a game plan as to where to start. Any ideas?"

I didn't want to fly by the seat of my pants with this like I did telling the kids about my dad. It just so happened, that the words came to me as they did. Lord knows, I usually manage to put my foot in my mouth most of the time. I have plenty of friends who can attest to that!

"I think you should start from the beginning and recall the stories you remember and go year by year. Make sure they are significant stories so that Nick and Della can make sense of what you're saying. I'm not sure Kevin will be too interested in all this, but you can offer, nevertheless. Let's establish a list of what you recollect and then we can arrange all the short narratives in chronological order."

"It sounds perfect!" I exclaimed happily. Gretchen was like me when it comes to organization however; my mind was full of stories in no order. Usually, I just had random snippets play through my head like a movie. I knew it was best to write everything down and create a timeline.

The next morning was certainly hard getting up at seven in the morning. Gretchen and I didn't get to sleep until well after one in the morning. Rolling over as I heard the knock on the door I let out a small grown.

"It's too early! You can't make me get up!" I was fully aware I was whining. I didn't care. I never enjoyed waking up with the chickens.

I heard chuckling outside the door. From the feminine tones it sounded like Della and Gretchen. Then I heard Nick's voice, "Get up you lazy bum!" He was joking but everyone knows, I am *not* a morning person so, getting irritated I threw my pillow as Gretchen opened the door. Oh no, I hit her. Well, at least it was just a pillow!

"What did I ever do to you to get hit with a pillow like that?!" I think Gretchen was a bit stunned from my behavior but knew nothing was meant by it.

Starting to find the humor of the situation, We both started laughing.

Feeling extremely hungry, I asked Gretchen if she wanted to help me with breakfast. She agreed while Nick volunteered to make the coffee. I was happy that Nick took a vacation day so he was off work. He knew that today was of importance to me, so last night in bed he told he would be home all day.

Making small talk as the bacon fried, grease filling our arteries with just the smell, Nick turned to a more detailed conversation. "Babe, when do you want to start?"

I knew exactly what he meant and a wave of rapid heartbeats filled my upper cavity. Nick surprised me at times, being he was a man of little words for the most part. On occasion, he surprised me with being so blunt.

"First off my dear husband, I love you very much as you know. But *please* don't call me babe. I don't want to sound rude or mean; however you must know that 'babe' was my father's pet name for my mom when he was drunk. It sends a little bit of rage throughout my body every time I hear it. It's quite irritating to be honest. I'm very sorry Nick, but please, can you find a new name?"

I know I hurt his feelings. I saw the guilt plastered on his face and I felt horrible for putting it there. That has always been one thing that bothered me over the years and I finally had to bring it to light. I wasn't trying to hurt Nick, but I had to tell him.

"Oh…" Nick's voice trailed off. He was so forlorn in his look. Stepping across the room, I reached out for him. Taking his hands in my own, I looked at him and tried to brave a smile. "Please honey, don't be upset. It's not your fault. You never knew. I love you more than ever so let's just learn from each other and make the best of it. This is going to be very hard on all of us. I'm ready to make peace within myself and in order to do that you and the kids are included. Are you with me?"

He leaned in for a kiss. I knew his answer was yes. He stunned me again, when our kiss was long and sensual. He was never one to show his affections in front of company. However, I felt his passion burning within him. He loves me, which I know for sure and I am indebted for his faithfulness. I heard the kids giggle and Gretchen guided them into the living room so that Nick and I could have a bit of privacy. After a few intense moments, I pulled away from Nick and called out to the kids and Gretchen. "It's safe now; you guys can come back in." I had to giggle because I felt like a school girl with watchful eyes around Nick and me.

Gretchen came in first and gave me a girlish grin. She tended to the bacon and Nick and I departed our embrace. Slapping my behind I knew what he was thinking, so I had to strip his idea away. I shook my head no with a stern look and started cooking the eggs.

Gretchen and I shared smiles while at the stove, as she gave me a little nudge. "No," was all I said quietly.

Then I heard Nick clear his voice and asked if anyone wanted coffee. Gretchen and I said yes in unison as we finished preparing breakfast.

After we enjoyed our breakfast and dishes were done, I asked for my family to join me in the living room. Kevin let out a groan and Della punched him square in the arm.

"Ouch! Mom, Della hit me!" Kevin had shouted as if I were two rooms away.

"Please, no fighting you two," I asked in my stern mother voice. Glancing at the two of them, Della was smiling as she knew she won the dual between her and her brother. Kevin had a pouted face with his lower lip fully extended to show his displeasure however, I knew his revenge wouldn't take long. Oh, the joys of motherhood.

I grabbed the notebook off the brown granite countertop in the kitchen that I put there earlier this morning before Gretchen and I went to bed. As we all sat down to get comfortable, I knew exactly where I wanted to start since Gretchen and I created the timeline the night before. Nick and the kids took their positions on the couch and Gretchen in the recliner as the night before. I grabbed a chair from the kitchen and took center stage. Taking a deep breath, for once feeling comfortable in my own skin, I began.

"Kev, I know you're probably not too interested in your

mom's past, but some day you may want or need to know this. I believe it's important for you to hear. I would appreciate it if you would humor me for a while." I saw his eyes start to roll but then decided against it, fearing his father's punishment for being disrespectful.

"Yes Mama," was all he said.

"Thank you. I will try to only include the necessary parts and then you can go off and play. Now, I think it's best if I start from the beginning."

I saw Della and Nick sit up and scoot up to the edge of the couch as their interest peaked. I felt terrible that I never had the courage to tell Nick from the start. The fear of rejection was too great when I met him. Not wanting to scare him away with my insecurities, I pretended to be someone I'm not. Not that I ever put on a show of fakeness. I just never told him the story of who I am and why. But I knew this was a fresh start and my chance to make things right.

"I was born while my mother and father were separated. He was living in Ohio, working in a factory. My mom was living with her mom in Pennsylvania. She had never been away from home before and missed her family terribly. She left my father and filed for divorce. As the months passed, he had convinced her to re-join him in Ohio. Loving him deeply, she accepted the invitation back while I was still a baby. Deep down, Mom knew that when she did that he would make her pay for leaving in the first place. Blinded by love and false promises, she made the trip. I was eight months old before he ever saw me, his only daughter at the time. It was always a fear of his and his mother that my mom might have chosen not to grant me life given her past history. They always said they were scared to death thinking that I would have been taken away from them without their knowing.

While living in Ohio, my father continued to work. He had a good buddy that worked with him as well named Don. Don opened the door to awful temptations. Granted, it was each a choice on their parts. My father told me the story one night when I asked him about how things were when I was a baby. He admitted that both he and Mom used cocaine. Evidently, it was the thing to do which Don only added fuel to the fire by coaxing it along. One night Dad had taken a hit of acid. The trip was bad and he wanted to come off the high. He took the medicine him and Mom kept at the trailer in case I would have ever gotten a hold of the cocaine. I admit I was angry when I heard him tell me that. How could they do drugs with an eight month old child in their home? The truth is, it's over and I never did get into the paraphernalia by the grace of God. And that I am certainly appreciative for."

I finished the first of multiple segments. I was sure that questions would arise from what I had divulged. Taking another deep inhale I cleared my throat and asked if everyone was following so far. As they all shook their head yes I seen Della raise her hand as though she were in a classroom.

"Mama, why did Pap and Great Gram think you might not have been born?" Della asked shyly. I knew this would be tough. I wanted to take a firm hand on making sure this didn't get too detailed, especially for Kevin's sake. I decided that the best plan of action was to wait on answering the question.

"Della, I hope you can understand when I ask that you and I talk about that in private. I don't want to get too in depth with certain topics and that's one of them." I knew it was too late since the question had already been aired. However, still wanting to preserve Kevin's innocence I chose to wait.

Della shook her head understanding that Kevin was still too young to explain such a complex matter. I decided to go on with my story.

"My first memories are when we lived with dad's side of family. His mom and grandmother shared a home with us in a neighboring county of Gram Saunders. I was four years old and I remember that summer quite well. My brother Chris was born and just a toddler. Mom had just found out she was pregnant with Chloe at the time. We had a large garden in the back yard filled with fresh vegetables. I used to go out and help Dad in the garden except, that my helping him was sneaking sips of his beer when he wasn't looking. Before I knew it, I was drunk and staggering. Of course, Dad thought it was cute that his daughter took after him and liked the taste of beer.

I believe it was after kindergarten when my dad's grandmother, Bubba, had passed away because we moved. My grandmother claimed she sold her soul to the devil and married a man to please her mother's dying wishes. With the new marriage came a new house. Not far from the one before nevertheless, I had to change schools. First grade was a horrible experience for me. I distinctly remember hating it. The kids were mean and treated me like garbage. Making fun of me and picking on me any chance they saw an opportunity. I even remember the teacher belittling me in front of the whole class. I was mortified. I never did tell my parents though. Instead, I kept all my secrets to myself. Feeling like a nobody without any self-esteem at six years old, I hid in my shell. I was shy. In fact, I was extremely shy. Making friends was never my forte and I knew I was different from my classmates. I understood that things at home weren't right but I wasn't sure how it was supposed to be. From that point on, me and school never got along. It was more of a nuisance than a learning facility."

My voice splintered a bit recalling the memories. Glancing up over to Gretchen I seen tears streaming down her face. Always a sensitive soul, I wanted to comfort her. Instead, she stood up and headed to the kitchen. I paused and said, "Okay, let's take a break for a moment guys."

Kevin jumped up quick and ran to his room. Della and Nick continued to sit on the couch. She put her arms around her daddy fully understanding the amenities and love that she has been granted. I made my way to the kitchen to find Gretchen. I wanted to reach out to her and let her know that it's okay. I learned from all this and it was going to be alright.

I saw her walk out of the bathroom with the box of tissues in hand. She started laughing and said, "Sorry, I'm such a wreck, Jill. I'm supposed to be being strong for you. It looks like it's the other way around." I saw a smile peek out from her distress.

Taking a hold of her arms, I told her, "I'm getting all my strength through you. You inspire me to do what's right. You are my voice of reason. Trust me when I tell you, I couldn't do this without you here."

We embraced one another for a loving hug. As we parted, I felt my throat was dry and needed a drink. "Does anyone need a drink?" I called out.

"Yes please," I heard in echoes. I refilled the adults' cups with coffee and poured orange juice for the kids. Everyone wandered back to the kitchen for their refreshments.

While sipping my morning cup of delight, I sort of felt like I was procrastinating. Inside I just wanted to get everything out like I was on some sort of deadline.

I sat down at our kitchen table and started to lightly skim the top of my coffee cup with my index finger. My childhood was being revisited, playing like a movie. Except, only *I* could watch the film, as the little girl I once was, walk through the scenes.

Unbeknownst to me, my eyes closed and my tone started out soft as I recalled the emotion I felt as a child. The scene was all too real as if I were walking along side that sad, broken little girl. I wanted to reach out and hold her hand. To let her know she would make it. But I couldn't.

"During my first grade school year we moved to the projects. The community consisted of five rows of houses which we resided in the fourth row. It was a yellow house with four bedrooms. I remember the layout of the house well. When you walk in the front door you were in the living room. To the left were the steps to the upstairs bedrooms and bathroom. Straight ahead of the living room was the kitchen. What's more intriguing is that I even remember our furniture and where it was all positioned. This house reminds me of the scariest of times. We lived there until the summer after third grade. During the two and a half years stay, my father was at his worst. Rob and Chuck, the two neighbor guys, always taunted him to drink more than his fair share. But Dad always had the choice. And he made his choice daily."

I stopped, opening my eyes to the present. I was actually talking out loud when I thought it was only the movie playing in my mind. As I looked up, I saw Della, Nick and Gretchen staring at me intensely. Getting a bit embarrassed for not being conscious of my vocalization, my eyes shifted down to my coffee as my index finger was still circling my mug.

Trying to regain my reminiscences of where I left off, I slowly took a mouthful of coffee. I felt the warmth of the smooth liquid slide down my throat. Now, I was ready to go on.

"This period of time was by far the worst of my memories. Dad drank every day. He didn't work except for twice during those years. Once he was the paperboy for the community that we lived in. The other was when he was painting for a guy on the side. So technically, neither one of them were real jobs by today's standards. He spent most of his time drinking and listening to his vinyl records.

"The late Eighties proved to be the best and worst decade within the history of my life. Gram Saunders always called me her, "Nineteen eighty lady." She made me feel so special when she called me that. I was born that year and that was the upside to the decade. Mom had Chris, Chloe and Andy so that was good too. Other than that, most of my early childhood memories are poignant."

My words ceased as the movie snippets streamed like a Youtube video. Most of it was quite jumbled as different scenes flooded my very soul. I felt the loneliness all over again. I knew I couldn't talk to anyone about my father hitting my mom, fearing that Children and Youth services would strip us off our mom. For so many years I felt like Mom was the victim. Later on, I realized she played the part of being the sufferer quite well.

Snapping out of my trance, I put those snippets into reality. Just talking about all this made everything finally seem real. It actually did happen and it wasn't just my mind playing games on me. I have hid from everything for so long that I sometimes thought it was all just a figment of my imagination.

I explained to my husband, daughter and even Gretchen that I was a lost soul that constantly expected the worst. I hated to go to school in second grade because of my fear of coming home to see my mother dead. Yes, I did expect the worst. Only because Dad proved to me time after another that he can and will make our lives a living hell. And after all the beatings and cruel words, I would hear them making love at the end of the night. Hearing her beg him for more made me livid. I felt betrayed as if she chose him over her own children. Like, I said before, I am a night owl. I always had trouble sleeping - I couldn't protect anyone if I was sleeping.

Chapter 7

Whispers From Kin

During the summer of nineteen ninety, something amazing happened. Every summer I would visit a cousin of mine. It was a like a mini vacation that I desperately needed. Having the relief of knowing I didn't have to keep up my guard for seven days was a true blessing. Sparky was twelve years older than I and married right out of high school. She had two daughters and honestly was wonder woman. I was in awe at how well she ran her home. I drew confidence knowing that one day; I too, can have that.

This particular summer she had just moved to a small town about forty-five minutes from where I was living. I remember being extremely excited that summer to see her. I was feeling quite frail and knowing Sparky, I knew she could give me the drive I so desperately needed. The funny part was that I never said anything about what happened at home. I simply kept the secrets to myself. I gained everything I needed just by watching her. Being around her I found the fundamentals that lacked with my parents.

"There is a girl about your age that lives next door. I will take you over by the fence to meet her in a little bit." Sparky's words have been embedded in my brain since the moment she said them.

"And that day," I said smiling looking at Gretchen, "is the day that I met my best friend."

"I remember the day well," Gretchen said as she touched my hand cordially.

Throughout the morning I caught several glimpses of Kevin trying to listen intently from afar. I knew he was interested yet, afraid to say so. I wanted to talk to him about it one on one. He was the type that liked individual conversation. I suppose it was due to him being comfortable asking questions without being made fun of by his sister.

Just then, Kevin appeared from the living room. His face showed mixed emotion and I wasn't quite sure what to expect. Just when I thought I knew my son, he asked a question that shocked my inner core.

"Mom," he began.

"Yes Kev?"

"With all this bad stuff that happened, why didn't you just give up? I mean, things seemed horrible for you, Mom. I don't understand how God let that all happen. And then you had us. What if Daddy was like Pap?"

My words faltered and I was afraid my expression was filled with shock. I wasn't sure where to begin with that.

"Uumm," my eyes darted from Nick to Gretchen for answers. Nothing but open mouths and surprise in their eyes.

"Kev, what do you mean when you asked why didn't I just

give up?"

Scratching his head, his thought process wasn't able to be put into words. Taking a few deep sighs and tapping his lip, Kevin found what he was looking to ask.

"Okay, so I know you couldn't move out so how could you have the hope to keep thinking one day it will be good?"

Gretchen pointed to her heart and I knew then where to begin.

"Well honey, yeah there was a lot of bad stuff. I understood years later that God was teaching me how to have strength. It was the hope that He gave me during those hard times that kept me pushing forward. I knew one thing though," I said trying to smile to comfort him. "I knew in my heart that things weren't right. So, when I grew up I didn't want to settle for someone like Pap. When I met Daddy my entire world changed. I felt God telling me that Daddy was a good guy and would *never* act like Pap. And I wanted you and Della because I felt something was missing. I needed you guys. To teach me what it would be like to have love and happiness. Daddy, Della and you *are* the reason I kept going."

Kevin immediately threw his arms around my neck and started crying. "I love you, Mommy." He had no embarrassment or shame, only a heart bursting of tenderness.

I felt the sting of fresh tears roll down my cheeks. The lump in my throat restrained my words. The affection and adoration for my family I felt surged throughout my veins. My little man, my eleven year old son, made all my earlier sorrows evaporate with four little words. This - this exact moment, is why I continued.

Della and I started to prepare lunch. The hour hand on the clock seemed to pass by in seconds. The morning was nearly over. This has proven to be an extremely emotional day already. Nevertheless, I was thankful that everything was finally coming out.

We kept the conversation light as we had lunch. Nick was chatting to Gretchen about her photography. I think she finally convinced him to get a family portrait done. Twenty years married and never had a photo session all together. That is one thing that has always bothered me about Nick. I have asked him on many occasions about it. Usually he's working so the timing never worked out. I honestly understand he has to make a living for his family but every once in a while, I wish he would humor me when it came to trivial things such as pictures.

Anyway, Gretchen said we could set a session up in early November since her schedule wasn't so chaotic. I was incredibly happy that Nick was in agreement... now if only he keeps his word. He usually does so I'm not going to worry about that right now. There are certainly other things that needed to be dealt with before November.

Once we cleaned up our mess, I pulled Gretchen to the side to make sure I was following along with what we discussed the night before.

"So, Gretch would you want to sit out on the deck for a minute?"

"I'd love to," she responded.

The outside warmth was a breath of fresh air. The clean country air was refreshing to my soul. I smelled the lilac bush's lavender scent dance around my nose. It's such a calming aroma which is why I planted it where we enjoy relaxing.

Gretchen and I sat down on the cushioned chairs. Her gorgeous white smile brought such comfort, knowing I was doing something right.

"I want you to know how I'm incredibly proud of you." Gretchen hesitated for a brief instant and continued. "We've all had things we've had to shoulder, and God knows yours has had the weight of ten people for all the burdens you've carried over the years. To think, I thought I knew all there was but you've proven today that there are so many stories you kept to yourself. I'm touched that you included me, Jill."

"Gretchen, you are my dearest and most treasured friend. I couldn't imagine you not being here right now."

We exchanged smiles and then I knew I wanted to ask her something important.

"So, do you think that I am saying too much with Della there? I don't want to take away her childhood or her innocence."

Waiting for a minute, with her brows furrowed, I could tell she was in thought. Knowing her, she was weighing the pros and cons.

"Well, thinking about it all and knowing Della is fifteen, let's weigh everything out. She is getting older and if I remember correctly, at her age kids need to hear the truth. Reality will start once she is out of high school and she only has three more years. The new found knowledge will probably help her when it comes to making choices, particularly when it comes to her dating. She will look for signs that she might not have realized before. As far as taking away her innocence I certainly don't believe that is the case. You are helping your daughter in a way not all mothers can. So, to answer your question, I believe you are doing the right thing."

I felt relieved. Gretchen was right, I was helping Della. I realized being over protective wasn't always a good thing. Kids need to learn and I certainly would rather them gain knowledge from me than from friends or bad relationships.

"You always have an excellent way of rationalizing everything out." I wanted to add that she would have made a wonderful mother; however, that is one bridge I will not cross.

We had many discussions about the topic however, it always ended up that they just weren't ready. I guess time ran out and they never were inclined to do so. By the time we turned thirty-seven,

Gretchen put that dream I had for them to rest. She told me that it's just not in the cards. I was heartbroken. I knew that she had so much to offer a child. Her talents and brilliance would never get passed along to her offspring which I felt was a misfortune. It wasn't my life so I couldn't make it happen. I just really wish they would have reconsidered.

The door opened as Nick appeared and asked if he could have a turn. He always liked turning things into jokes if he could. Being funny was his way of dealing with unpleasant moods or conversations.

"Sure Dad, take the stage!" Della chimed in standing behind him, trying to be humorous imitating her father.

"Thanks babe…I mean honey." I knew he felt guilty as his eyes darted to the pine beneath his feet.

"It's okay Nick, I understand." I tried to console his wounded self-esteem still; this is something that will eat at him.

Rebounding his ego, his long stride headed in my direction. I was a bit nervous wondering what he planned on doing. Usually with the way he was looking at me, he would try to make references that he wanted to make love. *Not now* I thought giggling inside.

Instead, he pulled me close and declared with all of his affection, "I love you, Jillian Davenport." He then held me close so I felt the constant thud of his heart against my cheek.

Once we released our embrace, my cheeks were flushed with

embarrassment. I wasn't used to Nick showing such affection with friends around. I felt like a school girl getting caught making out in a car. Sad part was, all we did was hug. Yeah, I guess I am getting old!

We all agreed that the sun-filled day was certainly not a thing to waste as Kevin wandered outside looking for the bodies that once were in the kitchen. The sky was a rich blue just like my mural with a few cotton-like clouds that painted a surreal display of God's handiwork. The fresh summer air was filled with fragrances of our landscaping.

Catching a glimpse of my prized willow, Gretchen read my mind and wanted to take a walk. Nick, Della, Kevin and I followed. Knowing that more of my story was about to be unveiled, I took a deep breath. My words came out easy once I started. It was the moment right before that my nervousness increased as the saga came to mind. I felt like I was re-living a part of me that died a long time ago. It hurt to drudge up all the pain I once had. Seeing exactly how lonely I once was made me remember how blessed I am today. The little girl that was afraid to talk, scared to make friends, and ultimately made a loner was no more. I must admit, once the memory was said out loud I felt freed. As if, once it was voiced it was over. I can move on.

Walking the familiar path to the sacred ground felt peaceful. My demons seemed to be afraid of the willow tree. It was as if they knew that the war between us was soon over. The horror of my loved ones discovering the truth has been set free. Now, it was a matter of finding the peace within me that I undoubtedly believed was there for the last twenty years.

Thinking we should have brought a blanket, we all sat down around the weeping willow. Viewing my beloved tree, I placed myself on the prickly texture of the grass. The deciduous weeping willow was *me* in a sense. Remembering back to a time when I was miserable, I had always wept internally without any notice from others. The delicate branches hanging downward like tears descending on my cheeks demonstrated that. The body made of solid wood just like my teenage heart after years of abuse. I grew up all too fast, identical to my refuge. The trunks distinctive bulges of soft, watery wood uses its bark for protection against nature explaining why I built a wall against those who tried to weaken me. It's quite sensitive with late frost just as I'm susceptible to being hurt easily. The root system is remarkable for its toughness and tenacity for life which is similar to my drive for true happiness and being complete. Yes, if I must compare myself to something, it would undeniably be this tree…

As I collected my next group of stories, I wanted to make sure that Nick and my children fully understood the revolving cycle domestic violence entailed.

"Dad was a true alcoholic. He drank every day when I was growing up. It wasn't just a beer or two; I mean he drank an entire case of beer by the end of the night. I will always believe he drank to escape his depression and own nightmares hidden within himself. That doesn't excuse his actions and curses he acted out as I was growing up. I hated him for what he did and for a long time I secretly resented my mom for living with him for fourteen years."

I took a deep breath as the jitters I had earlier dissipated.

"The minutes passed on the clock with no hour truly turning to a new day. It was a cruel cycle that never faltered. A different scenario with various reasons and by the end of the night one thing was for certain - abuse. By noon or a little after, Dad would have already had his coffee and cracked open his first can. By dinner he was feeling pretty good. Depending on his mood, depended on how dinner went. He usually cooked since he felt that he was the better cook. I must admit, he was right when it came to cooking. Mom's talent was baking. Anyhow, throughout and after dinner we usually walked on eggshells knowing that the slightest comment would set him off. It never took much, something as simple as song lyrics would cause the ticking time bomb to explode. Usually he blamed Mom or even me for his outbursts. He was certainly never at fault for his own actions. After the damage was done, Dad would always apologize and promise Mom it would never happen again. There were times he even tried to claim nothing happened or Mom made it out to be worse than it really was. Well, let me assure you that it *certainly did happen* and I remember *exactly* how bad things got."

I began shaking my head thinking of my mom's words I overheard her telling to a friend. "I want to fix Chris." I chuckled a bit. "Yeah, she was delusional at that time in her life! To her defense, she had other reasons too as to why she stayed. He would threaten her that she couldn't take us kids. He told her he would kill her first. The reasoning's were many and varied but ultimately she stayed."

Della spoke up then. "Mom, what do you mean by she thought she could fix him? He was his own person and made his own choices. She could never change him, if that's what she meant."

My daughter who is fifteen years old understood more than my Mom did as a young adult. What Della didn't realize was how love could sway one's thinking. And due to her young age and inexperience, sometimes, learning the hard way is the only way to actually learn. I figured I'd better enforce her logic now though.

"You're exactly right Della, she couldn't 'fix' him," I said using my fingers to signify quotation marks. "Unfortunately, a lot of women think they can fix or change a person. In truth, only God can change the heart of a person and it's up to the person to allow Him."

"Your Mom's right," Nick confirmed. "When you start dating remember that."

"I will Dad," Della said with a sheepish grin being a bit uncomfortable talking about boys to her dad.

"Don't worry girl, me and you can chat later about all that boy stuff!" Gretchen nudged Della with a wink.

I gave Gretchen a stern look and cleared my throat as a reminder that she is *only* fifteen! She was my daughter and I guess my instincts wanted to protect Della even though I knew in my heart Gretchen would never go too far.

"Mom, can we get back to your story?" Kevin bit his lip, as it was evident that he was uncomfortable the question shot out with such urgency.

"Sure Grover," bringing him in close for a much needed hug. I kissed his forehead while weaving his light brown mane through my fingers. He remained on my lap as I unveiled more of my history.

"As you all know, both of my parents were only children; or so we thought at the time. My mom found out about a half sister and brother from her father but that was when you kids were very young. Anyhow, there were no aunts or uncles that we could turn to. My mom had a few great aunts and one great uncle. We were pretty close with her great Uncle Ray. He lived right down the road from my gram's house. Uncle Ray knew what was happening but didn't know what to do to help. The other three aunts lived close by as well however chose to turn their heads in shame. Mom was, after all, a fatherless child and shunned most of the time. Her marrying a man like Chris Cochran proved to them that she was beneath them."

As I tried to think of how to word the next bit of information,

I shifted my weight. Family gatherings were painfully strained causing my shoulders and neck to tense up almost immediately. I decided to start with that.

"Family cook-outs were always uncomfortable. They looked at us four kids with misfortune and indignity. I felt like it was my fault that I was born into all this. It was like they all deemed us unfortunate and not worthy and we would just follow the cycle of what we were produced from."

I sighed heavy remembering the failure I felt just being around them. Frankly, I detested them for judging who they thought I was going to be as an adult.

"The common whispers and instant silence as we walked past merely proved their conversation topic. Their fakeness was thick like the smog in California. Their pollutants reached each of us in some way. All four of us kids used to talk about it and how they made us feel. I was speechless when my sister, Chloe, asked why they thought they were better than us. She was only six at the time. I couldn't answer her with the truth because she wouldn't have understood. So I shrugged my shoulders trying to protect her young mind."

"Looking back now, I can see how my siblings and I simply survived. As the years passed, we had to choose to unlearn the truths as we saw them when we were younger. Some of us did, but not all of us."

I ache for my siblings even to this day. We all aren't as close as I'd wished. Unfortunately, there's times when we are forced to make a very difficult decision to protect our spouses and children, and I made mine.

"Our extended family certainly doesn't know where we are in our lives. A few of them passed on and the two remaining haven't tried to keep in contact. So it is what it is."

Della raised her hand as if she were in school. Trying not to laugh I said, "Yes honey?"

"So, that's why we only talk to Sparky and her daughters?"

"Yup, they are the only family members that never looked at me negatively because of my parents or made me feel like I was worthless. There's a few other cousins who I hold close in my heart but we don't really keep in contact except through social media," I confirmed.

Kevin questioned, "Hey, why do we call Sarah, Sparky?"

Oh yes, the reasoning has always been one of my fondest. When I was three years old, Sparky had gotten me a stuffed dog for Christmas. On its red shirt, it read, "Sparky". For whatever reason, I loved the name and started calling Sarah that. It just stuck over the years."

Smiles came across my children's faces.

Della then added, "It all makes sense now, Mom. I know why Daddy's family has always been such a huge part of our lives and most of yours were always a mystery."

"There's a reason for my concealment Della. I was only trying to protect you and Kevin. Daddy too. I never wanted you kids to be subjected to such negativity. You kids have a bright future and I pray that you become the best you can be. You don't need anyone trying to falter your aspirations. Dream, hope, love, and have faith regardless of what others say."

My words were passionate when I spoke to my children. These are the life lessons I've needed to teach them. I had to learn the hard way and there's no reason why my children should have to do the same.

I recognize that in the end, the reflection of Della and Kevin will be who I am today. That makes me strive even more to pass along my knowledge to help them grow as individuals.

"So, all of your family just pretended that they didn't see anything? How can someone do that?" Nick seemed puzzled that abuse took place and no one seemed to care enough to do anything about it.

"Yes, I believe they pretended except for my great uncle. Oh and an aunt. She was a social worker and spotted the signs very early. She would give her speech like she would to someone at her office. 'You just need to leave.' But it wasn't that simple to just leave. And for my uncle, you have to realize that when they were growing up, in the nineteen thirties, forties and fifties certain subjects were kept very quiet. They honestly were never taught how to help. I learned that later in life, of course. It wasn't their fault that my mom chose Chris and stayed with him. What their mistake was, how most of them acted toward us because of my mom's choice."

Nick, being his protective self, appeared irritated that they didn't help and only tore us down more.

Sensing he was about to say something he would regret, I looked at him and said, "We can talk about this later if you want, okay?"

"Alright," Nick relented and let it rest.

Kevin wanted to re-adjust his positioning so he got up and laid on the sweet smelling grass. Resting belly down with his arms bent while his hands propped up to his chin, Della decided to follow his lead. Nick and Gretchen remained sitting with their legs crossed. I rearranged myself to prop myself against the willow facing my audience.

It felt odd to have such attention brought upon myself. My forte was distracting the interest. I shoved the peculiarity aside and went on.

"Living with an alcoholic wasn't easy. Friends were never invited to our house for fear of my dad making a spectacle of him and us. Not only that, but it was a sure thing that people would know the kind of life I was living. I wanted to hide that part of me. I was embarrassed and terrified of what others might think or say.

"Me or the kids joining any extra-curricular activities was an easy answer; no. We had to have the finances for that first and foremost and secondly, we had to have transportation which was a rarity. Chloe was the only one who was in cheerleading for a year. I remember Mom complaining about the cost which told me anything that I might have been interested in wouldn't be possible. Besides, I would rather see my siblings in sports or other activities before myself.

"My grades were horrible. Concentrating on school work wasn't my top priority and it showed. Somehow, I managed to slide by. I'm not sure if it was due to me being so quiet or teachers knew and felt bad.

"So, as you can see living with an abusive alcoholic had a high price to pay. Opportunities weren't an option for me. Even as young as I was, I knew that I could either let it define me, let it destroy the person inside, or it could strengthen me. I chose strength, learning what I could even if I had to suffer during the process."

Nick reached over and pushed my hair behind my ear. "I'm happy that you chose strength, Jill. I couldn't imagine living my life without you."

I was touched by his sincerity. I was also troubled that he pitied me for my past. Pity does nothing but wish for a different life or circumstances. I was always thankful for my history. It taught me important lessons in life that I would have had to learn later in life. I felt one step ahead of the game to have all that knowledge before I actually started my own life. It's not about wishing something else for me. God provides for every need we have. Even when our days look meek or scary, when we as mortals, feel like we've been given the short end of the stick, we must trust the Lord knowing He will provide regardless of the need. So, for me to wish for better parents, more money, a bigger house, a different childhood is like telling God He screwed up. No- He didn't. Those are earthly things. Possessions and people are temporary. They have no lasting qualities. However, once you accept Jesus as your savior, you will have everlasting life and that makes all the trials and hardships you may experience here on Earth worth it as He teaches us what it means to be a child of God.

I knew in my heart the truth had to come out sometime. The only problem now was I felt like this wasn't the only step towards healing. Hopefully, the pieces will fall together and I can figure out why this all happened in the first place. Resurfacing old baggage from twenty years ago with no reason just doesn't make sense. God has a plan, of that I am sure of. Waiting for the answer tended to be the difficult part.

Gretchen perked up after my long pause as I thought of Nick feeling sorry me. Something was up because I caught a wink between Gretchen and Nick.

"Hey I have an idea!" Gretchen exclaimed excitedly to Della and Kevin. "How about I take you kids to get some ice cream?"

"Yeah!" they both shouted eagerly.

"I figure the kids need a break and so do you, Jill. You and

Nick stay here and relax for a bit while I take the kids. You want anything brought back?" Gretchen inquired.

"No thanks, Gretchen. We can all go if you'd like." I didn't want my best friend to feel obligated to take my kids out for ice cream.

"Don't be silly. I think you and your husband need some time together alone." Gretchen flashed her mischievous smile in Nick's direction.

Then it clicked.

"You dirty little scoundrel! Do you and Nick have some sort of secret code or something?"

By then, Della and Kevin had run up to the house and were on the porch waiting for Gretchen. As she turned, she gave another playful grin, whipped her blonde hair around her shoulder and said, "I'll never tell!"

After they left, I turned to my husband of twenty years. He came to sit next to me against the willow tree.

"You're the best thing that ever happened to me, Jillian."

"I have to disagree, Nick. You showed me what life was supposed to be like. I can never repay you for the happiness you've brought me." I meant every word.

I quickly got lost in his gaze. Time stood still as he held me in his muscular arms. His lips were plump and moist that dared me to reach for them. Yearning to feel his touch against my skin, Nick caressed my neck with his mouth. Inching as close as we could get to one another needing to feel his burning body, our desire ignited. The moment became intensified and our infatuation confirmed it as we kissed deeper with more passion. My breathing became labored with anticipation. I moaned softly releasing all of my concerns.

"You captivate me, Jill," Nick admitted.

His hands went back to operating and began to wander south. Nick started to work his magic as I got carried away in the bliss he was creating.

Chapter 8

Foolish Love

Gretchen returned with the kids a little while later. Nick and I had walked back to the house and were cuddling on the couch. I was beginning to get worried since they were gone for two hours. They must have milked the cows and waited for the milk to freeze so they could make their own ice cream.

"So, did you have to make your own ice cream or what?!" I knew they had to go somewhere other than the local ice-cream hut. Knowing my best friend she wanted to treat the kids with more than just creamy frozen deliciousness.

"Della and Kevin were showing me around town. More than I expected for this one stoplight village. And you don't have horse and buggies anymore! I'm impressed," Gretchen jokingly said.

She has lived in the city for far too long. The hustle and bustle type of lifestyle wasn't for me. Though, it fit Gretchen's personality well.

I couldn't help but laugh and hope that my quick wit would kick in.

"At least, I know how to ride a horse!"

Yeah…witty wasn't happening today.

Everyone laughed at how ridiculous that sounded. After making fun of myself, I looked at my watch. Six o'clock in the evening. Time was escaping us all too quickly. If I could just bottle up time and use it for special occasions such as this. All the stop lights and grocery store lines are just a waste when I could use it for times such as this.

Daylight was still upon us thankfully, so I asked Nick if he could grill some chicken. The kids disappeared quickly. I'm sure Gretchen bought something for them.

"You will be joining us for dinner right?" I wasn't sure when Gretchen had to leave. I never thought to ask, not that it mattered.

"I have a flight out first thing in the morning. So, I will be leaving around four in the morning to head to Pittsburgh."

"Oh shoot, I hope you don't expect me to wake up with you!" I couldn't help but torture her after she won earlier.

"No, my dear friend, I know you don't wake up until noon!"

Well, wasn't she just a regular comedian now a days.

Pouting and crossing my arms, I hung my head as if I were hurt. Truth be told, I would absolutely love sleeping till noon. I guess I'll have to wait until I retire at the age of ninety to sleep in.

"Fine, see if I brew *you* coffee in the morning! I'll just make *me* a cup. There!" I was being facetious and loved teasing Gretchen.

Nick decided he needed to put his analysis into the conversation and only confirmed my love of sleeping.

"That's it; see if you get anything special for the next

month!" He knew I could never keep my word but it was amusing to threaten him.

Nick grabbed his chest as if I put a knife in it. Next thing I knew, Della walked in to the kitchen and said matter-of-factly, "You guys are gross!"

"Sorry sweetie, but Daddy started it," I tried to plead. It was always Daddy's fault even when it wasn't.

"Oh Mother, you know I'm too old to fall for that," Della stated extremely sassy as her head shook like a bobble head.

"Well aren't you acting like Miss Thing! Watch it, missy." I gave her the all mighty mothers eye for a warning. Teasing is one thing but attitude is another.

We enjoyed our dinner, thanks to Nick's awesome grilling capability. Conversation was kept light with talk of the next school year and everything we've done over the summer thus far. Once everything was cleaned up, my cell phone rang. It was Chloe so I decided to take the call privately.

After our short conversation, I returned to the living room where everyone had gathered. My expression was raw with emotion. Nick picked up on it and asked, "Is everything okay, honey?"

"Yeah, I'm fine." Everyone should know that when a woman

says she's 'fine', she's honestly not. Most of the time, men don't realize that, including my husband.

"Nick, do you mind if we girls have a little time together, alone?" I didn't want to be ignorant towards Nick or Kevin. Truth is, I wanted to have a little girl time with Gretchen and Della since I was trying to stick to my outline. While my courage was still at its peak, I had to tackle one topic with Della before her friends at school did. The conversation at the willow tree sparked the realism of necessity for this talk.

Chuckling Nick said, "You don't have to ask for permission, my dear. Go ahead!"

I told the girls it was probably best to go downstairs so they followed suit. Seeing the excitement on Della's face made me smile. Rarely did I let the kids hang out in my craft room. I always felt like I had to keep it private. After all, it did house my secrets.

I grabbed a couple folding chairs so that everyone would be comfortable. Placing a cushion on each seat, I told them, "There you go girls."

Then, I thought of my etiquette and asked, "Gretchen, would you rather have my comfy blue chair?"

"No, this is perfect. Thanks though."

Thinking back to our chat at the willow, I wanted to discuss the whole birds and the bee's thing with Della. I've been dreading this conversation for some time now. Every time I thought I would bring it up, I chickened out at the last minute because I knew I had to bring up my past. Della may have acted naïve when it came to sex yet I knew she was in public school and kids talk.

Unsure how to begin or even explain the reason for bringing Della down, my words faltered for air. My lungs seemed to collapse just as the thought of Ryan came to mind. One man, an entire lifetime ago, had a way with my heart. Over the years, I was able to forget about him except on that rare occasion when I'd hear his name or visit an old town where we created so many memories. I would get a soft spot for the blue eyed, temperamental guy that stole my affection for two years. Just the thought of him and my heart started to flutter thinking of all the greatness that we could have been.

I pulled myself to reality, I reminded myself that the romance was no fairytale and the Lord had other plans for us; separately. Thank goodness for unanswered prayers.

Exposing my most treasured book of poetry to Della was certainly going to be difficult. Delicately pulling it out of its living quarters, I flipped to the poem I wanted her to read.

"This will start to explain to you the woman I was before your father. Time has passed and wounds have scarred over but the memories are still alive. Remember that when you read this poem, it was not for your dad but another man that I loved deeply over twenty two years ago. He showed me life beyond my parents. He taught me lessons that only a man can do. Love can be incredibly glorious and then sometimes love will also be a burden so heavy that you must let it go."

My daughter, with her dark captivating eyes, drank in every word that I spoke with magnitude. She had been yearning for this for so long that I didn't realize how significant her craving was of our new found openness.

Gripping the hardback with her long delicate fingers, I saw her eyes dart down to my creativeness. This poem echoed silently as I remember when I took the pen to paper and brought the past back to life.

My nerves were getting the best of me as my leg kept bouncing up and down. Gretchen put her hand on my knee to stop all the shaking. Her expression was comforting however, I couldn't help but be nervous about the questions that was about to stem from this.

Della looked up from the page with wet cheeks. "You really loved him, Mom."

"Yeah baby, I did. *Did* is the key word though. Ryan was my first true love. Your daddy is my second and means the world to me which I am thankful for."

"What was Ryan's last name?" Della queried.

I was puzzled because I wasn't sure why it mattered but, I answered her nevertheless. "Ryan Dodson is his name. Why do you ask?"

"I'm not sure Mom. I guess I just wanted to know who

captivated your heart so much that you wrote a poem about him."

Raising my right eyebrow for the shear truth of her statement, I swallowed hard. I remembered his eyes of blue ice cut through the armor that I desperately tried to sustain for protection.

"Well honey, you're right. Ryan certainly engrossed me for two years. I fell fast and hard for him without a doubt. And his smile gave me comfort when I needed it the most. I gave him every part of my being except one crucial fragment – communication. I never had the courage to speak up for myself and tell him what I was feeling. Nor did I open up and show him the person I was and explain why. Instead, I clammed up and tried hard not to cause tension. I was afraid to start a fight so I just kept quiet. Essentially, I enjoyed the ride for what it was worth."

"Why didn't you speak up?" Della asked curiously.

"Growing up with the men that my mom had in our life, we always had to watch what we said so not to upset them. It always caused a fight or an argument. Sometimes I would say something and it ended up that I was inappropriate with my behavior. Thus, with my own relationship I thought that if I didn't speak up then everything would be okay. The boldness I had with my father wasn't there with my own adult relationship. I was wrong."

"So you tried to learn from your childhood and make things better when you grew up. But, you ended up wrong anyways. Geez, life isn't fair, Mom."

Gretchen and I couldn't help but to chuckle from Della's fine observation. So, Gretchen had a few words of truth she wanted to share. "Yeah Della, that's exactly right. Remember, that life is full of lessons. We may try something different however, that doesn't always mean it's right. We just have to try harder next time to make the decision that works best for you. Life is like a rose. Its beauty can captivate you yet its thorns will prick you. Watch when getting pricked but learn from them when you do. And enjoy the beauty as much as you can." Gretchen's intellect poured out of her soul as she stated her analogy with grace.

Lightly stroking her shiny dark hair, I caressed her cheek thinking of all the heartache she still has to encounter. It broke my heart knowing I couldn't stop it.

"Don't forget to see the beauty in the midst of the downpour," I gently added.

"Your mom is right, honey. Listen to what she has to teach you. We all have different avenues to take throughout life. Knowing which one to choose is never easy. Follow your heart but don't forget to let your intelligence have some input. Let them both work together. And most importantly, ask God first before you act."

Gretchen so full of wisdom was a natural when it came to offering advice. The paths she chose to take over the years have proved her expertise and explain why I have trusted in her for so long. She's more than my best friend, she's my soul sister.

"I promise," Della vowed to Gretchen looking extremely

determined not to select the erroneous lane that leads to hardships.

"We all make mistakes, Della. So don't get too upset when things don't go your way. Nobody is flawless so don't expect perfection all throughout your journey." I felt like I had to throw that out there knowing my daughter. She has always expected to be the best at everything she tries. I fear that once reality hits it could whirl her into depression and anxiety. Lord knows, it's nothing to mess around with.

She shook her head in acknowledgment yet, I still wasn't confident she truly understood. I suppose it's a topic we'll have to revisit often throughout her teenage years, as it is with most teenage girls.

"Mom," Della began and then paused as if she were afraid to ask. She found her courage then inquired, "What happened with you and Ryan? I mean, what made you guys break up?"

Blowing a big puff of air out of my frame, the movie played in my head like it happened a week ago. The night everything happened stemmed from so much. It wasn't an easy break up for me. I convinced myself I fell out of love with him. There were several details I wasn't willing to reveal to her however; I knew I had to give Della the key elements of our relationship. I'd give her some, but certainly not all.

"Everything in my heart told me I wanted, no needed, to be with him. The fire between us burned like a forest in flames. I was infatuated with Ryan from the moment I met him. It was a warm summer evening at the restaurant I used to waitress at, a local hotel, during my senior year of high school. Within six months, things got rocky. I found out he had cheated on me and I was so hurt that he did that so, I left him from the advice of a so-called friend. The break didn't last all that long and soon I was back to living with him. We had many little fights after that because my trust in him was nil."

"So you left him and went back? Geez Mom, that's stupid. My friends told me once a cheater, always a cheater." Della's words stung like a bee. I couldn't answer why I went back; I just knew that at the time, I couldn't let him go, at least not yet.

"I assure you that's not always the case, Della. Someone can cheat and realize how wrong it was and never do it again."

Shaking her head, Della's lip turned up as she was about to battle me on the topic. Gretchen quickly saw a fight brewing and stepped in before things went too far.

Placing her hand on Della's shoulder, Gretchen reassured her that people are capable of change. "Yes, Della, many times when someone cheats they do it more than once. However, just because you cheat on one person doesn't mean you will cheat on another. People grow up and mature. They realize cheating is wrong so they devote themselves to one person. Like your mom always says, 'Things aren't always black and white, gray creeps in and changes things' And she's right, you know?"

"Yeah, you're right, Gretch," slumping her shoulders,

knowing she lost the debate.

I mouthed "thank you" to Gretchen since I knew she saved an argument. Nodding with a smile, "So, where were we?"

"Well, let's see. Ryan got a job working for an airline company as a mechanic. As it turned out, it required him to relocate from Pennsylvania to Virginia. I was going to college for massage therapy at the time and I knew that my schooling choice was not what I wanted. So, being young and dumb, I quit school and followed Ryan south. My heart told me it was the right thing to do since my feelings for him were incredibly bold and intense.

"I soon got a job working at the mall. I loved it there and proved myself as a serious worker so I was quickly promoted to supervisor in the shoe department. I was proud of myself for my accomplishment and so was Ryan. I thought that things between us could finally get better with the new scenery and no family or old friends to get between us.

"Then something happened. New Year's Eve of the new millennium changed me. I was home at our apartment alone watching Dick Clark count down to the year two thousand. I started to cry as my worst fear, at the time, unfolded. "Seven, six, five...I didn't love Ryan anymore...four, three, two, one. And that was the dawn of a new era for me."

Cold chills ran up Della and Gretchen as I watched them both shiver from my description. A small gasp escaped from Della as she covered her mouth.

"Oh Mama, so just like that, you fell out of love?"

"I'm afraid so, sweetie. Sometimes love just vanishes. We may not want it to but, you can't control your heart. I do want you to understand that there's so much more to love. I suppose saying it vanishes isn't a good way to describe it. With Ryan, it was feelings I pushed aside for a while. I was falling out of love with him for a while. I just wouldn't admit it to myself. New Year's eve I finally allowed myself to accept it. So it felt like it just vanished but in reality it was slipping away months before that." A tear had escaped as I quickly tried to wipe it away. I didn't want Della to think I still loved Ryan because I didn't. I may miss him and the fun we shared from time to time but, that hardly counts as love.

"Well, what about you and Daddy then? What if that happens to you two?" Della had shakiness to her voice as I was aware of her concern for her father and me.

"Things between Ryan and I were sketchy to begin with. And there were a lot of factors involved that helped turn my heart against him. Now, for Daddy and me, we are at our strongest. Daddy and I love each other very much. We make sure we make time for us, which is a great component that couples tend to forget once they have children. As much as we love you and Kevin, we also have to take time for just the two of us."

"I couldn't agree more with your mom, Della. I remember when you used to get very upset that they went out without you.

Now you should see it was for the good of all of you." Gretchen was ever so gentle with her words as her voice was soft and delicate as a petal on a lily.

Della stood up from her chair, seeming to try and digest the story I had just told. Evidently, gravity wasn't helping the tales down, as her shoulders straightened and her stance reminded me of a Marine.

"Okay, so let me get this straight. We fall in love and just hope for the best? That's what you wanted me to learn? I thought you said we control our own destiny? What if I don't want to fall in love? Is it worth all of it?"

Her questions fired like an automatic weapon at the enemy. There is a tremendous amount of ground to cover with my fifteen year old daughter.

"Slow down, gunner!" Gretchen on cue to what I was thinking stole the words that entered my mind. I swear this woman has a sixth sense of reading my mind!

Amused by Gretchen, I couldn't contain my laughter. Della's girlish grin was fully exposed as she realized the line of fire that flew out without a second thought.

"Sorry Mama, I guess I just don't understand the whole love thing and why we put ourselves through it. With everything that you said tonight, it just makes me wonder why we let ourselves be so foolish to let emotions take control."

"You would think that it *is* foolish. Then again, as you get older and your interest in boys ignites, as well as your hormones, your questions will be answered without any response on my part. I do, however, want to tell you that as I have said in the past, we have control over our destiny to a point. God controls all but He gave us the power of free will. We have choices to make that govern what we do and how far we can succeed in life. That doesn't mean that there won't be bumps or sometimes boulders to climb over. Love can be one of those mountains. My advice to you is to make sure you don't let love get in the way of your goals and dreams. If he is supportive of that ambition you have then that is wonderful and continue with the relationship but, if he tries to hold you back...let him go. In return, you must be supportive of him and his hopes too. If you are both equally yoked, then go for it."

I pulled Della close, I wanted her to know that life wasn't always going to be easy. I told her I would always be there for her and support her decisions regardless of the outcomes. As close as I thought I was to my daughter, tonight has proven just how distant I've kept myself from my family. I was hurting more than just myself by keeping secrets. I haven't been fair to the ones I love the most which showed me how selfish I have been. God was starting to open me up to unconditional love and what it actually meant.

Wanting to beat myself up further, I decided to stop focusing on my screw up and go onward with our conversation. The hard part was about to unravel. It was the almighty parents' worst fear for their daughter…*sex*. Inhaling too much air into my lungs, my palms sweaty while my nervous shaking leg banged against the cabinet to my right, begging my heart to stop racing, I exhaled and made the attempt to speak.

"Honey, I wanted to tell you about Ryan for a reason. As I said, he was my first true love. That doesn't mean he was the first man I had sex with. I know you are at the age where girls are starting to experiment and do what the in crowd is doing. I don't want you to be like everyone else, I want you to be a leader and direct your own way."

When I paused, Della took the opportunity with her quick assumption to ask, "Were you one of those girls, Mom?"

A quick, "No," flew out. "I was eighteen before I chose to have sex. And if I were smart, I would have waited until I met Ryan. I was dating a guy that I knew was below my standards. Someone I settled on because I wanted a boyfriend. He was the reason that I got into a fight on the bus because his crazy ex-girlfriend paid this big dude-looking chic to beat me up."

Della's eyes lit up like the ball in New York on New Year's Eve countdown. "Mom!" she exclaimed in a high pitched tone. "You were in a fight?! No way!"

Concealing my eyes in my sleeve from shear embarrassment, I nodded shyly.

Looking back up, I felt my cheeks flushed, knowing full well my face looked like a pickled beet that had been soaking in its tart vinegar for a week.

"Oh, now hush. It isn't that big of a deal," trying to brush it off as a mere exchange of words instead of fists.

"You get into a fight and say it's no big deal?! Mom, that is huge!"

"Well, it wasn't by choice. The girl was paid to beat me up. She took her man hands and shoved my head into the window of the bus. I had to defend myself!"

"Did you win, Mama?"

"No, but it wasn't a total loss. I got her a couple good times with a few punches to the jaw. It felt invigorating at the time, to release some of my anger. The swings were full of fury as the tiger was released from its cage. I didn't want to stop; on the other hand, I had to block the punches that were headed for my face. Her hit was hard, but so was mine."

Gretchen was shaking her head which made me wonder what exactly she was thinking. Probably how much of a fool I was for staying with the guy after the fight.

"Yes, Mrs. Turner?"

"Oh, just how you act like the fight was merely an argument over who got the last bowl of ice cream instead of the whole pint!" By this point, Gretchen was in a full belly laugh that went from her the tip of her nose to the bottom of her toes.

Now, extremely embarrassed, I shook my head and figured I

might as well join in the laughter.

The incident happened my junior year of high school and before I ever had sex with him. The girl was paid to jump me on the school bus however; she enhanced her punch with a pair of brass knuckles for an added bonus. Once it was all said and done, I ended up with a black eye and in school suspension. I stayed with Heath, for an unknown reason. I knew in my heart I didn't love him, yet he was there…just there. Things at home were still a downward spiral of messy situations which lead me to move out prematurely. But that is another story. I wanted to finally talk to Della about sex and I was determined to do so now.

"When I turned eighteen I promised Heath I would give him one of the only precious parts of me that can never be returned-my virginity."

As soon as I said the words, it was then Della's face turning into that jar of beets.

"I know this is extremely uncomfortable for you sweetie. Trust me, it's been a topic I've been dreading."

"I still remember the talk I had with my mom," Gretchen stated.

"Oh?" I was intrigued because this was new trivia I didn't know about Gretchen.

"Yeah, it was pretty brief. 'Guys want one thing. Be careful who you choose.'"

I waited for Gretchen to continue. The silence was deafening, so I spoke up. "That's it?" I was truly astonished.

"That's it," Gretchen stated matter-of-factly, as I heard the snap of her hands down onto her lap.

Rubbing my chin, I said, "Interesting." The statement was bland like no salt added to french fries.

"Well, that makes me feel ten times more confident as to why I needed to open up." Winking with an upside down frown at Della, I knew I was doing the right thing.

"Okay sweetie, I'm sure you know what sex is. I know you are fifteen and kids talk. However, I want you to know the truth and not just what others think is the case. So, what do you know?"

Shifting slightly in her chair, I saw how uncomfortable Della was. Twiddling her thumbs then twirling her hair as we waited for her answer.

Then, a horrifying thought entered my mind, had she had sex already? My breath caught in my throat as I felt my heart sink to the cement floor. I had to ask.

My voice was soft and hopeful that her answer would be no. "Have you had sex yet?" My voice was low and calm even though my heart was racing and felt my emotions sky rocket.

I saw a smile come across her face and I started to breath heavier. Usually, when I see that smile, she is trying to hide something. No, please God, no.

"Mom, I have to say it's funny to see you squirm in your

seat." Della started laughing knowing that she pulled one over on me. "No, Mom, I have *not* had sex."

Whew! That is a relief off my shoulders. "Della Grace! How dare you scare me like that?" I felt like I was half scolding her and half myself for believing she would have sex and not tell me. She's always been pretty open about stuff that happens at friends' houses and school. However, we have not chatted about sex or anything of that sort so I honestly wasn't sure.

Gretchen and Della both bumped fists while laughing hysterically. I, on the other hand, found no humor in her little trick.

"You two are going to get it! Now, let's focus girls or you two girls will be sleeping down here!"

Clearing their throats and directing their attention back to the conversation, both girls sat up straight with their eyes focused on me.

"Okay," Gretchen began, "we're ready."

"So, as I was saying, Heath was my first. It wasn't exactly what I expected. No dimly lit room with rose petals blanketing the bed. No soft music with candles burning like our bodies. Instead it was an old house with a mattress on the floor. Not exactly romantic like most guys say it will be. Remember, guys will promise you the moon if they think they will get in your pants." I was being very blunt and honest. Maybe even a bit too descriptive for my fifteen year old. Fact is, I can't change it. I want to warn her of guys never ending false guarantees if they think they have a chance.

"The deed was done in a matter of minutes and I felt no different inside. The only thing I felt was discomfort and pain from having an area that has never seen the light of day be ravaged by a foreign object."

"I did hear that your first time is painful but they said after that it's great. Is that true, Mom?"

Twisting my lips up, pondering her question I admitted that the first few times were extremely uncomfortable. I also made sure Della understood that protection was of most importance when protecting herself against pregnancy and STD's. Stressing the fact that sex is for two mature adults, not young teens, who love one another. It can be beautiful, almost magical when it's with the right person on the other hand, when it's with a random person that's exactly what you get; randomness with no satisfaction emotionally. And I couldn't tell her enough that when she thought she was ready to please talk to me first because I will be there to answer any questions.

I caught Gretchen's lips open slightly when she caught her breath as if she wanted to say something but stopped. I knew she had something on her mind but thought better of it. But, me being the curious creature that I am, I had to know.

"What was it that you wanted to say Gretch?"

"Oh, well, honestly it was a question that I always wanted to ask you but never did."

"No hold backs tonight girl. What's your question?"

"Well, if you knew you didn't love Heath, then why did you sleep with him? Was it because you promised him?" Gretchen asked.

I was a bit afraid to answer that. The real reason had nothing to do with the promise I made Heath. It was a stupid reason and I didn't want Della to take it the wrong way. I don't want her making the same mistake I had all those years ago.

"Let me try to explain this while making sense. Honestly, it is the most asinine reason for doing something I have ever done. Peer pressure was outrageous in high school. All the girls by then had already had sex. I felt like a minority because I was a virgin. Things were said like I was a lesbian or no man wanted me. Truth was, I always said I was waiting until I was eighteen to have sex so that I can make adult decisions without being judge by my family. Essentially, I did it to get it over with. It seemed more of a burden than it did a pleasure. Unfortunately, I realized later that it was the wrong choice. I should have never given up that part of me for someone who didn't deserve it. He was a twenty year old man that was just there. He had a simple high school education, no ambition to make something of himself, and little fundamentals that I found appealing."

I was looking up to the right for a description of who Heath was. Sadly, I can't say a lot of good about him. My judgment was poor when it involved men. After Heath but before Ryan I had a little fun if that's what you want to call it. Once I met Nick, I knew the men before were simply fillers. They were men to share my bed, with no meaning. I looked for meaning, I wanted meaning. In the end, I was just another notch in their belt. Only one, I believe, thought about having something more than just sex.

Della interrupted my recollection by saying, "I won't do that Mama. I know you want me to be careful who I choose and do it for the right reasons. I get it," she stated, giving the scouts honor her brother learned in boy scouts.

"Remember baby, when you think you are ready for sex, ask yourself, are you ready to be a mom or have a disease that isn't curable. Are you ready to deal with all that goes with sex including the emotions that will forever bind you and the man you choose forever. If you think those are chances worth taking before you're an adult and get married then talk about it. Whether it's to me or Gretchen or any of your aunts or another woman you feel comfortable with just make sure it's someone of value and trustworthiness. I know in today's society and world, things are different and faster than twenty years ago. I only ask that you not let society or your peers help you make your decisions."

"I promise."

Feeling confident in her vow I caressed her cheek with the tips of my fingers with a smile filled with love and adoration for the beautiful daughter God had granted me. This amazing child has given me more than I deserved, more than any mother could hope for. What's more is Della gave me a glimpse of the childhood I could have had with different parents. She is proof that I made some good choices in life. She is one of three reasons why I have to tell my story, my hardships, my lessons, and my pain. Because of them, Nick, Della, and Kevin, I am here today with a heart filled of tenderness and devotion instead of sorrow and resentment.

Chapter 9

To Be Different

Eight o'clock in the evening and I was utterly mentally exhausted. The girls and I had ventured back upstairs to find Nick sprawled out on his overstuffed lazy boy, half asleep while Kevin was watching his favorite movie on the big screen. Kevin knew the actors lines by heart and always pretended to swing his bat at the imaginary ball. I'm not sure if he was trying to correct his swing or imagining he hit a grand slam as the crowd roars with cheers for the game winning runs that he batted in.

I picked up Kevin's feet and sat them on top of my lap as I plopped myself down on the cool leather. Nick had perked up realizing our return.

"Hey girls, you have a nice talk?" Nicks voice heightened in tone as he asked.

Della, still extremely introverted with her father, nodded with her quiet girl grin hoping that neither Gretchen nor I would mention the topic.

We all said a simultaneous, "Yes," as a heavy sigh left our bodies. The memories were exhausting, reliving the moment as the words left my mouth. I could feel my jaw clench as it tightened when I became angry and my teeth grind wearing down my enamel

like my father did to my spirit. The emotions were from one extreme
to the next because I would then notice my eyes squint and burn as I
tried to hold in the water that was about to escape. Next, I would
notice the fear that riveted my very essence of life. My breath
catching as I inhaled or my hands shaking like a washing machine
off balance on spin cycle. The reverberation thumped, echoing in my
ears like the wind blowing angrily through our valley.

I didn't think I could utter another word until Nick brought
up about my favorite birthday gift that generated another movie reel.

We were living at my grandmother's old company house the
coal mine used to own. While we lived there, however, my great
aunt owned the property after she finagled her grip on the deed from
my great grandparents. Ultimately, my grandmother had life-time
rights to the place. Then, it was supposed to get passed on to her
offspring, my mom. My aunt disagreed having her own unknown
reasons, so she obtained the deed unfairly.

Gram had passed away earlier that January and my mom was
comfortable staying in her mom's home feeling the closeness of her
that still lingered. Mom knew that in time, her aunt, who supposedly
loved her, would eventually evict her. Mom fell a couple months
behind on our one hundred dollar a month rent because of *him*, the
inebriated worthless piece of, well never mind. However, until that
time came, we remained where we were.

It was a humid day that July as the sun beamed its rays upon the old shingles of our home. They barely held their placement from the old rusted nails. I had turned fourteen that Wednesday with no party planned since the drunk of a man that I called Dad made it impossible. The small amount of money that my gram had left for my mom went mostly to my father which then went to the local beer distributor. I admit I was furious with the jackass that he made of himself. I couldn't wait until Mom finally left him for good. Except, I wasn't sure that was ever going to happen now that her mom had died.

This day was no different than any other. Dad fought with Mom, I got in the middle of it as usual but by the end of the day, I received the most special birthday present I could ever ask for.

He was yelling at Mom, claiming some sort of nonsense when I wiggled my way in the middle. I was fourteen now and old enough, or so I thought, to protect my mom. Not that my age ever stopped me before. Half laughing he tried to push his weight into me in hopes that I would either back off or fall. I felt his entire six feet stature barrel over top of me, taunting me to test him. My adrenaline was pumping like a freight train late on its run. He couldn't budge me. It was quite an exhilarating feeling as my patience grew thin of his commands. When I wouldn't stand down, he relented and backed off both of us. Next thing I knew, something clicked inside my mom's head. She called our great aunt, the social worker who owned our home, and asked her to pick us up because she was finished with Chris.

155

I couldn't understand why Mom just didn't kick him out by herself. This was *our* home and I didn't feel that we should have to leave. This old dwelling was one of the only things that I felt connected to. Since we moved exceedingly often, when Mom whispered in my ear, "we are going home", I knew she meant Gram's. The delight I had to hide radiated my morale knowing it was going to happen. Except now, Gram wasn't here. She couldn't protect me, no more winks, no more smiles, no more dinners at the table with her in the chair to the left of me. She even convinced me to try liver and spinach once. I just about puked, nevertheless; I tried them both with Gram by my side.

The memories, still vivid in my memory, I felt like they were being stripped away from me. Leave? Why us? Why not- *him*?

My great aunt came with her husband and son so that there wasn't any trouble from my father. He was half passed out anyways so honestly, my brother Andy could've beaten the tar out of him without much difficulty.

The night we left, was the last night my father and mother shared a home. I never felt my heart lift so high above the clouds full of joy when I realized it was over. The abuse would stop after fourteen years of my life. I could be happy and free to be a kid.

Unbeknownst to me, that cloud of darkness loomed ahead, I just couldn't see it quite yet.

Mom officially filed for divorce and a smile crept across my face. Contentment was pouring throughout my veins. Who would have thought a child wanted to see their parents' divorce? But I did. In fact, I prayed for it for years.

"You were pleased that your parents divorced?" quizzed Nick.

"Yes," as the gratifying smile lurked across my face while my eyes danced with pleasure. "Sad, I know Nick, but honestly it was for the best." Trying not to show my utter pleasure from the event was rather difficult. To explain to someone who grew up with the typical role model parents was challenging. And, unless you actually experienced the realness of it, comprehending the ordeal isn't all that easy.

Just then, Kevin turns his attention from the television to my direction. "Mom," he began, "why are you telling us all this?"

It completely astounds me how parents think their children don't listen and not pay attention to their surroundings. Many times, we think our children are busy watching a movie or interested in something else like a video game. When in truth, kids drink in all sorts of information, taking it all in and analyzing the new found knowledge in their growing brains as to what it means.

I, at times being one of those parents, was shuffling my words. It wasn't the fact that I didn't know why, it was that my son, who I thought would be the least interested, has asked me the most intricate questions to respond to. His inquiries were prolific in thought that opened your soul to the passionate desire of truth.

157

Kevin has proven that age can have no significance when compared to perception.

Angling my head slightly to the left when I am amazed, my heart was reaming with pride for my son. I decided to offer the choice between the long, drawn out version or the short to the point reason.

Kevin, eyes me with a crafty grin, put his pointer finger up to his lower lip and began tapping. It was adorable knowing that he was mimicking his father as he debates within himself.

"Can I say a middle version?" Kevin concludes.

Being the type to never be outdone, a middle version came as no surprise. Kevin is constantly trying to pave his own way, a born leader.

"Sure Grover, we can do a middle version," I said as I ruffled his brown ash colored hair that reminded me of wet sand from my favorite beach in North Carolina. Emerald Isle has always been a cherished advantage when visiting my mom and step dad.

I began painting a canvas before them that was full of swoops and turns, revolving around to the center where a lonely young girl stood underneath her only safe haven; the old willow. That same judicious child was placed hidden in its branches, hiding from the hurt that shadowed over her very existence. Feeling like she will never be that perfect girl, exiled from society because she was different. I may have been wise beyond my years but my endless skepticism of others made them think I was unapproachable. At least, that's what I speculate. Trusting others was an unmistakable no since I couldn't rely on my own parents to protect me. So not trusting others seemed logical. I was too young to be taken seriously, yet old enough to realize the hypocrisy that surrounded me. The cave that was embedded around me was dark and cold with no light or warmth. The only comfort I found was the protection of the willow and its glory that shined in my heart. He protected me…He instilled His holy spirit.

Next, I divulged to my loved ones about Mr. Hopkins and the brief chats we would share. I explained that he reminded me of my own father. And how I grew a love for a man that reformed his ways. Unfortunately, it was the eleventh-hour for his children's' acceptance and forgiveness because subsequently they denied his plea. I went on saying that during our last talk, I realized that I needed to make changes in my own life. I had to end concealing the silver screen that was persistent at reeling those images and eating at me inside, unknown to the people around me. I acknowledged this is my time to make things honorable and morally righteous. This was a moment of self-healing; to be able to admit that I came from the wrong side of the tracks. Proving to all those who knew me, that I was someone, I deserved respect, and I am no different inside as the next person. To put it bluntly, I was exhausted from pretending.

I then went on and apologized for my crazy anxiety attack that scared my family to its core. "You have no idea how upset I am with myself for crumbling in front of you Della. It wasn't intentional, I assure you that. Knowing what I had to do and the events of the day, I broke. Because of that, I will forever be burdened by. I have to learn to accept that *everyone* has a breaking point. Regrettably, I found mine that day. I know there is a lesson to be learned from it, but that doesn't mean I like it."

I felt the pain of that day when I collapsed inside. My heart ached for the horrifying scene my daughter had to endure. Lord only knows the terror that overpowered her on Monday which rips my heart out knowing I was the reason. Yet, here we are two days later pouring out my inner most secrets and I'm stronger than ever while Della is learning and growing as a beautiful young woman. I suppose it's the initial pressure knowing that the weight I've carried for so long was about to be released and my family's judgment could disintegrate my perfect world that I worked so hard to create. Truth is, the fear of them casting me off was a foolish distress. They are my family that accepts me, that loves me, that doesn't condemn me for who or where I came from. That was huge because so many others have in my past. God reminded me as I felt Him tell me, "Unconditional love, my child."

"But, the Lord knows what He is doing so, I won't question it."

I concluded portraying my painting by letting them know that because of the girl I was, because of whom I was from, molded me to why I kept quiet for so long. Mr. Hopkins helped me grasp the fact that second chances are necessary. Mistakes are made routinely, judgments are made regardless, but maturing, maturing is evolution. My favorite old man, showed me that in order to find inner peace, truth and acceptance must be obtained. Thank God for him, because he taught me a valuable lesson without even recognizing it as it happened.

Chapter 10

Seeds of a Dandelion

We all decided to turn in for the night after I finished my thought of dear Mr. Hopkins. After tucking the kids in, I nearly ran in to Gretchen as our shoulders collided. I felt the sharp pierce of pain radiate down to the tips of my finger. I certainly didn't mean to bump her as hard as I did. I was biting my lower lip with one thing on my mind…tomorrow.

"Oh Gretchen, I'm sorry hun! Are you okay?"

"Yeah, I think, but you might have dislocated my shoulder if you would have hit any harder. Geez girl, you lifting weights?"

Slightly chuckling I responded with an affirmative no.

"You need ice?" I questioned as I softly touched her shoulder.

"Nah, I'll be fine." Pausing for a moment Gretchen's sixth sense sparked. "You have something on your mind, Jill?"

Desperately trying to shield my eyes to conceal my lie, I sharply darted my gaze to the floor and denied her suspicion.

Wanting to drop the subject like the hot handle of a skillet full of scorching grease, I bid her good night and scurried to my bedroom after apologizing again for running into her.

Closing the door behind me, I saw Nick snuggled comfortably under the paisley blue Egyptian cotton comforter. The aroma of sweet honeysuckle filled the air thanks to picking it earlier that day to replenish the vase of wilting blossoms.

Nick being the light sleeper he is, stirred as he heard the door close. I knew he couldn't have been in a deep sleep so, I was thankful I seen his eyes flutter open. His smile comforted me and tonight was no exception. It soothed me knowing what I had to tell him next. I felt the lump of grief rise in my throat. My expression must have changed as I noticed Nick sit up in bed with a puzzled look on his face.

"Something wrong, Jillian?"

I wasn't sure how to break the ice for what I had to do tomorrow. The conversation I had with Chloe earlier today was kept quiet until now. Without any further hesitation, I blurted out, "I need your truck tomorrow."

Nick's brow slanted inward with curiosity, as his posture became more defined instead of slumped. Nick knew I never liked driving his truck since he always reprimanded me for driving too fast especially, on our back roads. Like it was my fault he drove like an eighty year old man!

"Okay, but why do you need my truck?"

"I got a call from Chloe today. She was panicked and unsure of what to do, so she called me to ask who could clean up the mess that was left by our father. Before I realized what I said, I told her I

163

would go and take care of it."

"Are you crazy?" Nick's voice boomed as his shock was blatant. Sensing his guard was on high alert my own self-defense went into code red.

"What Nick?" My tone was sharp and curt preparing for a battle.

"You didn't answer me, *why* do you need my truck?" His questioning set my temper to blazing instead of a minuscule flame.

"I have to dispose of the mattress. So, my plan is to bring it back here and burn it." I felt the vibration of my voice deepen as my head began to pound from my increased blood pressure. I was absolutely certain my face was a deep cherry color from the extra blood flow.

Nick's eyes began to glare at me as he clearly showed his disapproval of my intentions, while his jaw clenched so tight I thought he would fracture his teeth.

"After everything you have told me about this cowardly man, you feel that you're expected to go out to Ohio? Are you serious? Jill, this isn't your obligation. Why can't your brothers do it or how about his mom since he lived with her practically all his life. I just don't understand why you have to do this."

Every question Nick asked, his voice got louder filled with frustration for a man that used to mean nothing to him. Now, it was different. He got a glimpse of how ruthless and despicable people can be, he understood that this sperm donor of a father hurt his wife and there wasn't a damn thing he could do to change it.

As much as I hate to admit it, and I certainly wasn't going to right now, Nick was right. I shouldn't be responsible for all this. Fact is-I am. I am the oldest and must adhere to my responsibilities since my other siblings can't handle it. And I know they couldn't wipe down the walls or carry out the mattress that contained our father's blood.

Still, I felt like Nick didn't want me to do what I felt I needed to do. That angered me very much. It made me that much more defiant maintaining my plans. I was a woman true to my ancestry following in their footsteps filled of stubbornness.

Even though, I know in my heart Nick is only trying to protect me, but damn it, I am a grown woman and there are some things that I need to do that no one else can do for me nor would I let anyone stop me. *This* is one of those times.

"It's not like I asked for your help." Trying desperately to stay quiet, the gruffness of my tone came out with venom. I was on guard and wasn't going to be told I couldn't so, I became cruel like the man that helped create me.

I was so afraid that the kids might hear or worse, Gretchen. I hadn't mentioned it to Gretchen because I knew she would want to be there with me. I couldn't let her do that. It wasn't her place nor should she be subjected to such a morbid activity.

"What are you thinking? I mean, this is absurd. He did

nothing but cause you torment. You honestly think he would even be thankful you did this for him?" Nick was standing with desperation thick in his attitude. He was trying to ration his thoughts out loud to me trying to make me re-think my decision. Too bad, my pride got in the way and disregarded his pleas.

"It doesn't matter what he would think, Nick. I'm not doing this for him; I'm doing it because there isn't any other choice."

"Bullshit!" Nick fired from his baritone voice.

"And just what would you suggest? Having some stranger clean up my father's blood? You want me to carry this for the rest of my life feeling guilty because, I knew in my heart this is the right thing to do?" Standing right in front of my husband I felt exceptionally strong with confidence. I will win this argument because I knew this is what I needed to do.

"Alright Jillian, you win. I just don't want this to affect you negatively. God only knows the scene you're going to have to deal with. This isn't some challenge that you need to take on."

As much as I wanted to tell him he wasn't going to control me, I knew if I opened my mouth once more I would surely start a war and say things we both would regret. Instead, I mumbled a "Fine, but I'm doing this," through gritted teeth and clenched fists, as I turned and walked out of our bedroom. Slamming the door behind me was an instantaneous want however I refrained myself for fear of waking everyone in the house.

Clearly, I was taking my frustration and hurt out on my husband. I couldn't stop the cockiness that mounted within me, disregarding any reasoning that Nick could try to explain. I should have sought after the knowledge of the Lord and for Him to step in and control the situation, pounding me on the head with a walking stick. I needed the Holy Spirit to plant the seed of knowledge and reason, but most importantly, peace. Too bad I pushed Him away just like I did Nick.

The feeling of tiredness had escaped my body as the increased adrenaline surged through my physique dispersing its energy. I felt like I was on fire as the pulses of energy emerged through my pores. Knowing full well I couldn't sleep now, I grabbed some lemonade from the fridge and made my way through the dimly lit kitchen to the stairway. Old habits were hard to break since I always kept a dim night light on at night that was included under our microwave. Since the kids were little I have always kept a light on in case they woke during the night.

Flipping the switch and making my way down the familiar steps, Nick and my conversation was agitating me further. He came from a family that has never had to deal with suicide or abuse. Nor did he know about alcoholism or moving so frequently, becoming a loner was your only option to survive. How would he like to have his mother depend on him to parent his siblings? Or talking his mom through the loss of her own mom or the divorce of his father? How would he like the weight of an entire family on his juvenile shoulders? I pitied myself and I hated it.

Plopping down onto the padded blue chair, I felt like I had lost it. What was I doing? I completely bared my hidden world for all to see. Now, I have to travel the three hours to Ohio to scour the last predicament my father has left for me. "Way to go, Dad." I said aloud bitterly.

I scribbled on a scrap piece of paper that appeared to be expecting me. I found myself drawing a weeping willow with elongated delicate branches that had an ample amount of leaves. It camouflaged a silhouette of a slumped woman, shielding her from all of her reality as time passed by. Although my art work was quite child-like, the image portrayed exactly how I felt and what I wanted. To disappear and hide, crawling into my shell, protecting myself from any further harm.

"Faith," I thought, I need faith. It reminded me of a sermon my Pastor had one Sunday morning not too long ago. He said that faith enables you to experience deliverance. Without it, we would self-destruct, and destroy those we love the most. "Hebrews 11:1-3," was written on the church bulletin beside the page I was scribbling on. "*Now faith is assurance of things hoped for, proof of things not seen. For by this, the elders obtained testimony. By faith, we understand that the universe has been framed by the word of God, so that what is seen has not been made out of things which are visible.*"

I hadn't given it a thought as to why I even came downstairs.

I could have turned on the television and lost myself in a movie. Instead, I fumbled through a drawer and found some old pictures. Ironically, I found the one of my entire family that was taken before I ever had children. My father's uncle had passed away. During the time my biological parents were married, my great uncle always showed consideration for my mom and she loved him for that. I went out to pay my respects to a man that I cherished as a child. My mom and stepdad, Howie, had gone to Ohio for the funeral, as well.

Mom, in a thick red dress with a cardigan over top that contained a black vine with white screen printed flowers attached evenly as its vine descended down. Her short blonde hair curled and the same plastic smile on her face I recognized from childhood. Chris was in the back, tall, dark hair and his glasses seemed to shield his eyes a bit from the red eye of the camera flash. Andy was to Chris's right, just a tad shorter than Chris. His smile looked genuine as his hand was gently on Mom's shoulder. Chloe to the left of mom, looking extremely young however, her joy of having her parents in the same picture showed on her face. Me, standing next to Chloe, I noticed my style hasn't changed much. Black dress pants, button up collared shirt and a black vest. Then, there he was…Dad. His hair was receding then and still dark brown with little gray. Dad's Adam's apple noticeably protruding just as I remembered it to be. His lips were smiling yet his eyes were sad, worn, and looked as though he was remembering when it all was right in his life. At least, while he was sober. He was worn then, and as time passed I suppose he decided it just wasn't worth it anymore. He lost hope of Mom returning while his children were grown with their own families and lives. He only had his mother who constantly brought him down each and every day.

My bottom lip started to quiver as I tried to hold it all in. As my hands shook, my fingers suddenly lost feeling as I dropped the picture and landed on my desk. I just stared at him through the water. His face blurry, not able to see his hand on my shoulder, the drips started sliding as it reached the paper I drew on. Soon, the tree was smeared almost to the point of not being recognizable.

"You son of a bitch! Damn you! You did this! Now look, I have to clean up the mess again. Why couldn't you just pull it all together and be a man?! Why couldn't you just be a dad with honor and courage?" My questions went unanswered as the silence left me feeling unfulfilled. "You always said I was your rock. That doesn't give you the right to make me clean up your blood! This isn't what family does to one another! You piece of shit, I hope you're happy now!"

Falling to the hard floor my knees felt the resistance rumble through my spine as I covered my face in despair. I was pissed. Or was it the sheer emotion of being mortified to think what I had to do next? Whatever it was, everything came to light that it was all true. Traveling to Cleveland so that I can carry out a bloody mattress filled with my father's brains. Great- just great.

Safe Under the Willow

Gathering my limp defeated body, I pulled myself to the Queen Victorian. "Gram, oh how I miss you," I thought. Her chair was the only comfort I had left of her. I needed her right now yearning for her arms to wrap around me as if I were eight years old again. Her dark brown eyes burning into my soul telling me it was going to be okay. Somehow, she gave me strength with only her eyes. It was magical how our emotions reached one another even though no words were ever spoken.

Searching the room for the box of tissues I knew I had, I spotted the painting hanging in the corner above my craft table. Art had always been a love of mine. And I was lucky enough to have a few friends that dabbled in painting.

I was surprised Gretchen hadn't seen it before. I know she would have laughed remembering it was the first painting she had ever done. It may have just been a one star painting to her however, to me - it was perfect. For my thirty-second birthday she mailed it to me. Opening it, my breath was taken away just like the first time I had seen it when she texted me a picture of it. So simple yet, it had so much to offer in its expression.

Removing the art from its longtime hook, with delicate fingertips, I gently caressed the canvas with all its texture. The background was a warm gray that indicated no right or wrong, only pure acceptance. In the middle were two vibrant yellow puffy cotton looking seeds, demonstrating the white globes of the dandelions after they had transformed in their last stage of life for the season.

To the right above the orbs, Gretchen had included three scattered seeds flying above.

Recalling our conversation about her piece, I told her how it reminded me of Kevin. He was three years old then and picked a dandelion from the yard that was ready to pollinate the earth to reproduce. As he began to blow the air from his lungs, the seeds got stuck to his moist lips. He opened his mouth full of white spores that were fused to his tongue. I giggled remembering that was a tiny moment to cherish forever.

It also brought on another meaning to me, one far clearer to me now than the day I said it. I finally understood what I said so many years before. My words came out slow and steady, "The three seeds soaring in the air denote new life, new hope, and a new beginning."

This was my sign from above. My God, have I been lost. I've hid for so long, coming out has scared me to death. I thought I was doing the right thing, shielding my family from my previous sufferings. I shut them out when it wasn't necessary. Now, I have to do exactly as the painting tells me. Start new filled with hope and faith of a brighter beginning. Gretchen was right. This was going to change our entire lives forever.

Chapter 11

The Cleanup

The rest of the night I spent restlessly cuddled up in my chair downstairs. My emotions were extremely varied from sadden to peaceful, hatred to love and irate to calm. All forms of questions crammed my very existence with no real answers. The uncertainties almost made me feel as though I was suffocating on my own thoughts.

Glancing down at my watch the night hours seemed to slither along slowly. Ten minutes until three in the morning and I was downright exhausted. And knowing Gretchen would be up any minute, I decided to make my way back upstairs. I hoped my eyes weren't puffy from all of my crying. The bathroom was calling my name to freshen up before Gretchen caught on that something wasn't right.

Exiting the bathroom, I heard footsteps coming from above. Gretchen is up. "Thank God for cover up," I thought.

Craving for a triple shot of espresso, I decided to brew a cup of extra bold coffee.

"Well, good morning sunshine!" My tone was cheerful considering the night that I experienced and what I had to look forward to later today.

"Oh my goodness! I can't believe you're up Jill *and* before me? What did you do, stay up all night?" Gretchen of course, was joking. Little did she know she was right on track.

"I thought it would be nice to make my best friend some breakfast before she heads to the airport." Genuinely smiling at my comrade thinking of how much of an asset she has been to me over the years. We both sat down at the table with our fresh cups of morning fuel.

"You know, Gretch, God gave me the ultimate friend when he put you along my path. And for that, I am forever thankful."

Gretchen started shaking her head as to hold back her tears. Her emotions were extremely noticeable as she grabbed my free hand and said, "You are very welcome. Remember Jill, you have the courage, you have the heart, and you have the brains. I am only one of the few watching your journey sail the waters. With every ripple of wave, I see you high above the crest with grace."

"John Quincy Adams once said, '*If your actions inspire others to dream more, learn more, do more and become more, you are a leader.*' That leader is you, Gretchen. If not for you, I wouldn't have been able to come clean so easily. It really means the world to me that you came to visit and help me through all this. Seriously, I love you like my sister and you know you're my angel of inspiration."

By this time, we were both choked up on sentiments. "Okay,

enough of this mushy stuff how about some breakfast?" I tried to lighten the mood by turning our attention to food.

"Honestly, I would prefer a bagel. Do you have any cream cheese?" Gretchen asked as she sipped on her high octane coffee.

"Sure do," I answered as I retrieved the ingredients.

Gretchen and I kept it light in conversation throughout our breakfast. As we carried her belongings to her rental car I started to feel guilty for not telling her my plans for the day. We hugged and I made certain she understood how thankful I was for her trip.

"So, what's your plan for today? I suppose you will go back to sleep?" Chuckling, Gretchen found humor in her usually correct assumption.

Pushing out a laugh, I shook my head no.

"You're kidding me right? I would be snuggled up in bed next to the hunk of a husband you have in there."

"Nope," by then my loyalty and conscience was overwhelmingly bursting with shame.

I saw Gretchen's eye twitch which told me she knew something was going on that I hadn't disclosed.

"What are you up to now, Jillian Davenport?"

Sweaty palms told me that my nerves had kicked in high gear. Shifting the stone beneath my feet, I was rummaging for time, for words, for a reason. Honesty was the only possible solution with Gretchen.

"I'm driving out to Ohio today." My words were very direct

175

and to the point.

"Okay," Gretchen drawled out, "for?"

"Chloe called me yesterday."

Just then Gretchen threw her hand up to stop me as if she were a crossing guard halting the traffic. "I'm going with you."

"No! No way will I let that happen, Gretchen. You *do not* want to do that. I'll be fine. Please don't make me beg!"

"Give me one good reason?" Now her arms were crossed, back perfectly aligned while her lips were thin with fortitude and resilience to my pleas.

Now it was my time to prove to Gretchen I was ready for what's ahead. "Gretchen, you have *always* been there for me. This is different. A task I must complete alone. You have equipped me with strength, wisdom, self-esteem, and determination. You did your part, now let me do mine. Please."

I was desperate to have Gretchen understand this was an obligation I needed to do alone.

"Why alone? You don't need to do this alone. Hell, you have me, you have Nick. What are you thinking?"

"Actually, I don't have Nick. He doesn't think I should go. He and I were arguing about it last night. I was so furious that I was downstairs all night just thinking and recollecting. While I was down there I grasped the meaning of all this. I will explain it all to you once my job is done. But until then, trust in your dear friend that she knows what she is doing."

I wasn't sure if Gretchen would accept my request by her facial expression. Her teeth were clenched as her lips puckered. Her foot was tapping faster than I could run. Without warning she uncrossed her arms and I saw her aspect soften. Extending her arms, she grabbed me for a huge hug.

"I won't leave. I can stay here until you're back. I know you will need someone then."

"No Gretch, please, go home to Jake. I promise, I am a survivor. No worries."

Without another word, Gretchen got into her car. Unwillingly, I am sure. As I waved goodbye I saw the make-up running down her slim cheeks. I felt my heart ache. I should have just kept quiet. I think. Maybe. Maybe not.

"Oh my God, what am I about to do…alone?"

Five o'clock in the morning and I had packed and began my journey of a three hour drive. I had my travel mug filled to the brim and the radio blaring with rock. Music always affected my mood and this was no different trying to prep myself for what's about to unfold.

I contemplated calling Hailey over the next two hours. But what would I say? Where would I begin? And her secret…

Ultimately, I decided to wait.

Crossing the Ohio state line, the radio station faded out from the rock music that was playing and a Christian faith based station took its place. I instantly felt the Lord tugging on my heart. I ignored Him last night and I knew I better not again. The song that began to play was one I was familiar with from church but I always ignored the lyrics. Me, sorrowful? I pretended and played the part well of being a wife and mother all put together. Plastic and perfect to the outside world's perception. Suddenly, the hurt was there while the pain was exploding within me. And then, there was hope. His rest was available for the taking. And I knew that there was nothing on Earth that Heaven couldn't fix. Whatever brokenness we each may have, we weren't too far from the Lord's grace, mercy and love. I fell into His arms as the shame of my life disintegrated into tiny grains of sand. Forgiveness.

As the tears flowed yet again, I pulled over. The self-righteousness I had was imminent by me believing I knew better. The gentle reminder that I too have made some very poor decisions throughout my life weighed heavy as I thought about previous choices regarding the ones I love in this world. Scripture tells us that God sent His only son to die for our sins. Including my own. How can I possibly tell anyone what the rules to life are when I haven't even followed them myself? I'm not God. I don't have the power to condemn and bring forth a pointing finger. I don't study His Word like I should but if I did I might have figured that out a long time ago. Both, Mom and Hailey did something that according to my faith isn't right. But that doesn't make them enslaved to hell. Instead, Jesus came here to save us from our sins.

What's done is done and not one soul can time travel and transform the course of history. I can't change the details I left out about my past to Nick when he and I first got together, just like I can't alter someone else's decisions they've already made. We were different people in different places within our lifetimes. We each made decisions based on who we were at the time. Not who we are now. Learning and growing every day, we aren't to be ridiculed and condemned by other believers. When we repent from our wrong-doings Jesus cleanses us wiping away the dirtiness. That's why His grace and mercy is such an incredible act of love to His chosen ones.

Turning off the radio I reached for my phone. Speed dial - Hailey.

Her voice was groggy, still not fully awake, as she answered. "Hello?"

"Hey Hailey, it's Jill. I know it's incredibly early but I needed to talk to you."

"Jill, I'm glad you called. Are you okay, hun? You haven't been to work all week."

"I'm doing better than ever, honestly. I've done a lot of soul searching and you are part of that."

I went on to tell Hailey that I was sorry for not calling

sooner. A better friend would have checked in. Our conversation progressed and I told her I started talking to Nick about the truth of my family and where I came from. It was a huge ordeal telling him and my children but, I felt comfortable with how things had gone and decided Hailey deserved the same genuineness. Especially, after she confided in me with hers.

"Jill, I am honored to call you my friend. I truly appreciate your honesty. And about what we talked about earlier this week. I know it's hard for you to understand, but I pray God will help you."

That's when I told her about how the Lord had revealed some truth about the type of person I am. My Bible meant nothing if I didn't open it up over the course of each day reaching for more of a relationship with Him. I explained that the compassion and unconditional love was prominent now and it's the way of living I want to commit to.

Hearing the sniffles across the air waves, I wanted to somehow comfort her. Instead, she comforted me with her words.

"Jill, you've had a bumpy road along your journey. I know you shy away from letting anyone get too close. Everyone knows yet they never stop trying. You have a way about you that draws people in. They look for you when they need a pick me up. Making people's day seem brighter is what you're all about. My advice to you," Hailey hesitated for just an instant and then continued, "people love you, so let them."

Now my reality check kicked in. Wow, Hailey was right. I needed to stop shunning those who care. Not everybody is out to hurt me.

Hailey, being incredibly accepting and filled with as much love as Gretchen, had one more remarkable gesture. "Jillian, the scars are there to remind us of our past. No matter how much we may think we want to forget, our past is part of us. Every part of our history, either good or bad, is what makes us who we are today. In the end, when we have truly grown, we will come to love those scars, for we know without them, we wouldn't be the person we see in the mirror today." Sighing, Hailey added, "Jill, I wish I could gather up all your worries and put them in my pocket while giving you the serenity you deserve."

I'm uncertain of how I am so blessed to have such great friends. Blessings are joyful but in my case, totally undeserved.

Hailey and I ended our chat with her asking when I would be back to work. I informed her I would return on Monday however, I anticipated seeing her Friday at Mr. Hopkins funeral. "I wouldn't miss it, Jill." I felt her comfort reach through the phone.

We exchanged goodbyes and I was back on the highway to Cleveland.

Another forty-five minutes and I pulled in front of the senior citizens apartment complex. The dreary gray building was quite bland. It was in serious need of updating however, city life didn't care about looks. Their main concern was where to gain the next dollar.

Gram and Dad shared a one bedroom apartment on the second floor. Looks like I would be taking the steps with all my gear. I packed a bucket full of cleaning supplies and a duffel bag with old clothes and shoes to wear. My hair was tightly pulled back into a pony tail complete with a ball cap.

Without any idea of what to expect, I tried to prepare myself for the worst. My movement was swift through the main corridor and thankfully I found the stairwell quickly before I had been spotted by any other tenants. I wasn't comfortable explaining to them who I was and what I was doing there. Besides, as an afterthought, it's probably illegal. I couldn't think about that now, my challenge was only feet away. Pushing the fear of possible prison time to the farthest corner of my mind, I found myself in front of apartment two hundred thirteen. "This is it," I thought. Sucking all the clean oxygen into my lungs as I could, I reached into my pocket for the key Chloe had dropped off in my mailbox the day before.

"Okay, I can do this. Just go in, clean the walls, wrap the mattress and get the heck out." Just then, I could feel my body going into a whole different realm. It was like something clicked inside that made me feel inferior. The fright extinguished like a fire being doused with water. I was in control, not the gore. The blood was simply the remnants of weakness. I'm ready.

Quietness deafened the hallway as I heard the key slip into

the tiny hole with only a zipping noise. Turning the coldness of what obstructs me to it, my hand turned right and then the bolt slid left. Removing the key and placing it back into my pocket, I slowly turn the door handle.

Immediately, the stench of death flows through my nostrils, allowing my taste buds to acknowledge the experience of fatality. The stale air made it almost impossible to breath. It kind of reminded me of a possum that's been run over on the road during a hot summer day. Then again, it was sort of disgustingly sweet. I had no idea how the smell hadn't made it's way through the rest of the building. One thing I was certain of, the smell would stick with me forever.

Glancing around, trying to take in my surroundings, immediately to my right after a tiny closet was a small kitchen with only enough space for one person to prepare a small meal comfortably. Straight ahead was the living room. Collecting all the images of decor, it was an imitation of my childhood. Nothing has changed. Same photographs, identical red furniture, exact dishes, unchanged knick knacks. Unbelievable; it was chilling as I made my way through the shrine of history. Who clutches to yesteryear this much? There is no present time or even a hope for the future. Instead, they let the ashes hold them hostage.

Opening the windows in the living room, I turn my attention to the location of the bedroom. The door, just partially opened, shows no signs of death besides the disgusting odor.

183

I grabbed my bag and decided to quickly change my attire. Once I was in the old clothing, I gripped the tarp I brought, still sealed in its package. Placing the nitrile gloves over my hands to shield myself from the gore, I snatched the bucket I filled with water and cleaning agent.

No turning back now, I seemed robotic as I stepped in front of the bedroom door. Reactions iced over like the ground during a Pennsylvania winter and numbness tangled my brainwaves into silence.

Sometimes, my strength has proven to be a curse. It's times like this to use that asset once more as much as it was an absurd task.

The door creaked when I lightly pressed the hollow wood forward to get the full view. The bed was directly in front of me. Tiny hairs stood tall on the back of my neck to show their own disgust while a cold shiver ran up my spine. Goosebumps appeared yet felt like they wanted to retract to hide again. The image before me was disgusting and shocking. The only thing my eyes could focus on was the mattress for at least five minutes. Over analyzing every blood splatter, chunks of brain matter, and positioning of the pillows.

Most of the blood and skull tissue were contained in the pillow closest to me on the full size bed. That told me it was planned and he did it well. He had to hold the pillow with his left hand to the back of his head to contain the blood while he held the gun in his right hand as he pulled the trigger. Looking for the blood on the walls, there was only one trace of a drip directly behind the bed. All of a sudden, I observed a tiny shimmer from the sunlight beaming in from the window.

I stepped toward the wall to gain a closer look. I felt the wall where the sparkle was bright. "Oh my God," I said aloud. The police had neglected to check the wall for fragments. Most likely, they figured it was still inside Dad's head. They missed the one piece of crucial evidence. The bullet casing.

Grabbing a pen that was laying on the night stand, I shimmied out the metal cartridge from the drywall. Once out, I brought it close to my face and evaluated the once perfect piece of ammunition. Only now, it wasn't intact. The brass casing was dented around the sides while the end where the powder was once confined looked as though it was a flower in full bloom. "Incredible", I thought as I held the last thing that went through my dad's head. Gathering the magnitude of what I just discovered sent prickles from the nape of my neck to the tips of my toes.

Hesitant of what to do with the round, I made a quick decision and I slid it in the pocket of my jeans. I then grabbed the sponge out of the bucket and began washing down the wall behind the bed. Once I felt I had gotten the wall complete, I turned my attention to the main area of concern.

Wiping my brow with my forearm as the sweat began to drip

downward, my sense of smell kicked into high gear. Bodily fluids had a wretched odor that no person should ever have to deal with. Desperately trying to choke back my insides, I knew I had to work fast.

The sheet and comforter would have to come off first. So, I picked up the roll of black garbage bags, tore one off, and opened up the concealing container. Rolling the blanket up soaked with blood I was able to fit it in one bag. Next, I took the thin white, yet stained, sheet and rolled it up to the pillows. I stopped when I got to the pillow that left the only remnants of him. I didn't want to, I just couldn't help myself. I could only stare in disbelief. The blood so thick, almost purple, positioned there like demons laughing; taunting me. I heard, "We won," whispered… or did I?

Paranoid of evil spirits lurking, waiting to pounce on their chance, I finished rolling up the bedding and threw it all in another black bag faster than you can say 'freaky'.

Shaking with fear as my heart pounded violently, I picked up the bags and put them by the only outlet to the apartment. I headed back to the room and prepared the tarp to cover the mattress. Duct tape became my new best friend as I wrapped the blue plastic around until it came together underneath. Using the entire roll of tape, I was satisfied that nothing could be seen to give any signs of what I was going to carry.

Removing the gloves and slipping them in a trash bag, I

headed for the sink. I couldn't get the feeling of something crawling over my entire body off of me. Scrubbing until my skin was red, I finally gave up. I still had to carry all this out so there honestly was no point in showering just yet.

Making my way to the stairs with the bags was easy. At least those can be explained simply as garbage. Luckily, no one in site and I made my way to the truck with ease. Now, time to carry the mattress. At least there weren't any box springs.

Picking up the light mattress, I positioned it on its side to kind of push it out the door. The tarp made handling the bulky piece of furnishing difficult. For an instant, I wish I had someone here just to help me carry it. Then, I remembered Nick's words telling me I would regret it. Yeah, I probably will one day - but that day is *not* today. Determination entered every pore through my skin, adrenaline hit hastily and down the steps and to the door without hesitation.

Peeking through the window that separated the emergency stairwell to the main corridor, I couldn't see a soul in site. "This is my chance to go," I thought. Slowly opening the door I saw my opportunity. Halfway through the route an old man walked up, smiled, and held the door open for me. Whew, that was close. Why he didn't ask what I was doing was unknown. Nevertheless, I was extremely grateful. Finally, the mess was done inside. At least the part in Cleveland was completed. The only thing left to do now is lock up the apartment.

Climbing the course once more, I made my way to the

familiar numbers; two, one, three. All I had to do was lock the door. So why did I go back in? I knew I had already taken everything to the truck.

One final look around. My last thought before I turned and walked out was, "Alcohol and pills mixed with foolish pride listening to the same old songs made for a cold, lonely heart in need of love. I wish it would've found him in time."

The ride back to Pennsylvania was quiet until I received a text message from Nick. I was by a rest stop so I decided to pull over and stretch while I was there.

"Me and the kids will be at my parents until you're done with your thing." Short and to the point, I knew Nick was still upset.

Rolling my eyes, I gathered from his message that he had taken the day off work. Surprised by Nick, I was glad he did so the kids wouldn't be home when I got back. I had no problem telling them what I had to do but I certainly didn't want them to be a part of it.

Back on the road, the next hour and a half was spent remembering the gooey blood infiltrated pillow. The image was implanted firmly into my memory bank with no promise of disappearing anytime soon.

A little after two o'clock in the afternoon and my home was in sight. Pulling down into our yard, I glanced at the radio. The time on the display read two thirteen. Ironic.

I wanted to get the blaze started so I pulled the bed down to the far right of our property. It was open land that was barely used by the local wildlife as they scurried across the land to seek shelter.

Once the mattress was positioned I dumped lamp oil over it. I wanted to make sure it all incinerated with one shot and gasoline burned too quickly.

I picked up the largest bag that contained the blanket and threw it on top. Then I grabbed the smaller bag that had the pillow. Not paying attention, I felt the warmth of the blood underneath my fingers. Very slimy and slippery I dropped the bag as quick as I picked it up. A full body shiver overcame me and the feeling like I needed to vomit overpowered my want to continue. I instantly bent over trying to catch my breath while my stomach muscles contracted. Breaking out in a full sweat, I had to walk away for a moment. Two steps, one step, then three more and I bent down to my knees, freeing my stomach contents.

I have to continue. I can't stop now. I picked myself back up and threw the rest of the bags onto the pile and added more oil. As I lit the match, the sulfur helped dissipate the death smell that was permanently embedded into my nasal passage. Watching the flame burn I threw it on top of the remains of him. The snap of a whip and the four and a half feet by six and a quarter feet of space was totally engulfed in flames.

Backing away from the heat and horrible aroma, the flames came alive. I felt his presence next to me. This was no horror movie as I felt Dad enter my very existence. I knew his pain, his every thought, his vengeance towards life. It all came clear and I understood.

Chris Cochran was no man of honor in society's eyes or his own children's. He wasted his life away rejecting his future. No desire to find happiness because he destroyed that pleasure years ago. Beer was his best friend and anyone who tried to come between him and his can of alcohol was pushed away.

Demons screamed in agony from being scorched. My body trembled watching him disappear. Haunting crackles came up from the mattress until I felt him telling me it was her fault. She should have died; not him all those years ago. His dad was supposed to be his saving grace. Instead, Dad blamed God for leaving him in the arms of a deranged mother. Too weak with not enough will power to overcome her wickedness, Dad became her puppet on a string. She said, "Dance, son of a bitch, dance." So he danced until I heard his last scream. He's gone.

Never in my life have I ever experienced such a disturbing incident. My breathing had become intensely labored, my heart beating hastily; tears were streaming down into my mouth as I tasted their saltiness. Shaking uncontrollable, I collapsed. Everything inside of me shattered. Raw broken emotion clouded over until I lay limp. The last coherent conception before I passed out was, "I never want to be cremated."

Chapter 12

Those Wretched Springs

Fluttering my eyelashes, mimicking the Mourning Cloak butterfly in flight, dancing as the wind propels around its wings. Fast and systematic motion until it rests on the rugged bark of my beloved tree, showing its dark brownish, almost maroon wings with pale, cream colored edges that looked a bit tattered. Bright blue spots along the edges of each section, the beauty of this butterfly rests perfectly camouflaged on the outer surface of the willow tree.

Fully awakened, instead of seeing a butterfly eating its nectar as I had in my trance, I recollected the previous event looking around my right shoulder. My view focuses and I regain my senses. The mattress had entirely incinerated leaving only the metal springs.

"What happened?" I thought as I picked myself up from the ground. Scratching my head, I glanced at my watch, realizing I didn't recall the last hour. It was half passed three o'clock and I still had to cut the springs.

Positive that snipping all the small wires apart was going to be extremely time consuming, I headed to the shed to retrieve the tin snips and work gloves. Once I located both, I remembered I needed to get a dozen commercial heavy duty garbage bags. Rustling throughout the shed, I found everything but those. I knew we had them; I just needed to remember where Nick would have stashed them. I honestly didn't want to text and ask him. I was still perturbed with what happened last night. Thankfully, I remembered when he cleaned out his old hunting gear not too long ago he used the contractor bags in the basement.

Jackpot! I retrieved them and out the back door I scurried. Surveying how I wanted to start, I decided to dive in and start snipping from the top and work my way down each row of springs. The work was repetitious without much thought. Fifteen minutes into it and I had one small square cut. Sweat was already pouring off my brow and beads were dripping down my back. Wiping the perspiration off my face with the top of my shirt, I went back to work.

Before long, my mind traveled in reverse to twenty-six years prior. A year after I lost my gram and all hell broke loose medically.

I should have graduated a year before I actually did. The problem was when I was fourteen and after my father left for good, I ended up in the hospital with some major problems. At first the emergency room doctors thought I had the flu. Unfortunately, they were wrong twice before they realized there was an underlying reason why I was so sick. My kidneys had shut down and my organs decided they didn't like me anymore. My body filled with fluid while I leaked a tremendous amount of protein through my urine. If I remember the doctor telling me correctly, the type of disease I had

I should have been through all this when I was an infant or toddler. But that just wasn't the circumstance with me. God decided that I was to be unique and one of a kind. Going down in history books, my disease made me just that - unique.

Usually, with the disease I acquired the doctors would stabilize the patient and send them home on a very high dose of steroids. The patient would go in remission and life would go back to normal. Yet again, God decided that He had another plan. Yes life threw me some curve balls but I learned to swerve.

My first night in the hospital in Morgantown, West Virginia I had a dream. But it was more than a dream. It felt real and meant more than just a fluke. I lost my gram a year before my sickness and I missed her terribly. She came to me that night. I remember the trance as though I had it the night before this very day. We were in her home she passed away in and was sitting in her kitchen at the supper table. I remember the table was an off white with silver wrapping to its edges. My gram had her head on my lap as I was stroking her black colored hair. When she looked up to speak to me, I saw the oddest thing. Her eyes were not the same dark brown eyes as her and Della share. Instead they were a cool steel gray filled with mystery. When she spoke it was only one sentence yet that one sentence was all that I needed to hear. "Jillian, don't worry, you're going to be fine." Once I woke to reality I remember feeling a sense of peace. I knew that nothing detrimental was going to happen and I was going to be okay.

Seven months of medication and I was lucky enough to say I was in remission. The first two of the seven months were spent in and out of the hospital. My first release, I begged my doctor to let me out so that I could surprise Gretchen for her birthday party. I still have the photographs her mom sent me that I glance at once in a while. Her mom said I looked like an overstuffed chipmunk. Chuckling, recalling her portrayal, she was right. I packed on over twenty pounds of fluid and it really showed in my face. Since I was so slender, any weight gain was visible. It didn't matter to me; I just wanted to be there for Gretchen. Her eyes wide with astonishment, words caught in Gretchen's throat, leaving my friend's mouth wide open practically hitting the floor.

Instances like this happened regularly during the years of our friendship. Our relationship wasn't based on convenience but showing up when the rest of the world walked out. I don't see that ever changing either.

Regaining concentration on my task, only a third of the way done with the coils and my hands were becoming uncomfortable developing callouses with every squeeze of my device. I removed my gloves now filled with moisture from my hands. I should have taken the entire set of springs and discarded them in the dumpster at work. On the other hand, I'm sure I would have a lot of explaining to do with our maintenance director. Scratch that contemplation. Luckily for me, our garbage gets picked up early Friday morning so

I can take it up to the road tonight and be done with it.

Resuming the tedious constant movements, I couldn't help but thinking about my kidney disease and all the effects it had on me. While in the hospital, I actually felt relieved. I didn't have to be anyone there. I didn't have to be strong or try to smooth things over so there wasn't a fight. I was simply me. Alone with my thoughts.

My mom, Chloe and Andy came to visit every day during my stays. I enjoyed their visits however; I was also happy when it was quiet. No fights, no worries, nothing but silence. It was perfect.

After my third release from the hospital, my kidneys had begun to work again. I missed a total of two months of school due to my body deeming it necessary for a much needed break. When I went back to school, it was like a ghost entered the hallways. The looks were weird as if I had either died or moved away only to return and ruin their world again. In Spanish class, I remember one student telling me they thought I had died. Great, so I take it the principle didn't let anyone know that I was in the hospital like he promised to do. Even the teachers had no clue what had happened. It was just another sign to prove that I didn't matter to anyone. No one from school bothered to ask, no one visited, no one cared. I was another lost soul of the universe, quietly living each day without a notice.

There were a few that showed concern outside of school. Gretchen of course, sent a card from the whole gang that I knew and hung out with on occasion. Plus, my church pastor did a ton of praying for my recovery. For that, I am forever grateful for. Pastor Brenda has always been an inspiration in my life. She was aware of where I came from yet still genuinely loved me. She saw past the shyness that muted my words, anger that raged in my eyes, and wounds that I wore on my chest. I will always love and respect Pastor Brenda because she helped guide my walk with Jesus through her wisdom and teachings over the years. She showed me who Christ was and all His glory. You can't get any better than that.

Smiling to myself, remembering a mentor that will be forever etched in my soul, I realized that I was more than half done cutting up all the metal. I felt like I had sweat out an entire gallon of water. Needing to rehydrate I took a small break and grabbed a bottle of water from the fridge. I wanted to sit down for just a moment to rest. Unfortunately, I couldn't relax even for a moment. If I sat down, it was over and I would fall asleep within minutes, envisioning scenes that I wanted to permanently erase. I was determined to cut up the springs so that my family wouldn't have to see anything except black garbage bags with the contents unknown.

My body moved sluggish to my designated area. As I reached my destination, immediately a spell was casted making phases in my life fade in and out. As I boarded the train, faces of my past appeared like phantoms. The crystal ball pointed signs to Hell. The flickers of images stopped to show a man that I loathed almost as much as my father. Philip Henley.

Mom was always weak when it came to men. She was the type that needed a ring on her finger to know she wasn't alone. Reaching out to those who showed interest, she eventually met a man that treated her like a queen. He built up her confidence, showed an extreme amount of affection and most importantly, made her smile. I hadn't ever seen her that happy, as she introduce Philip to us. Things seemed to be going smoothly until I started picking up on some little comments he would make occasionally. I tried brushing it off hoping my gut feeling was wrong. Besides, I was only fifteen and quite honestly, I was leery of every man. A few months forward and my suspicions proved to be correct.

She constantly said I was her right hand so she asked for my opinion about Phil. Being so young, at first, I felt it to be a privilege. As time passed by I deemed it as more of a burden. Anytime she had a worry she would come crying to me about her concern. She looked to me for answers and advice. The problem was once I did give her advice she did the exact opposite. I felt betrayed and hurt.

Mom married her second husband, Philip, and I knew in my heart he was no good. Following the same pattern of a man as my father, Philip proved to be an alcoholic as well as an addict to marijuana. On my seventeenth birthday, after a year of hounding me, I finally caved to his pressuring and tried pot for the first time. I must admit, I felt a bit rebellious and my image of being the good girl diminished. Once I obtained the high I felt extremely tired so I went to sleep. My happy birthday went up in smoke like the joint disappeared into ashes. Needless to say, I was not impressed by the drug and refused it countless occasions afterwards.

Phil was, in numerous ways, a mirror of my father. In fact, I feel he had a slight edge to my father and potentially may have been worse. Yes he drank and got high. The real problem was his abusive habits. I can say as a fact that Dad never hit the kids vengefully with the exception of me. I made sure they were out of Dad's path and I would much rather me get it than them. Phil wasn't like Dad though. Phil would attack all of us.

Phil and my mom were fighting constantly usually about money or us kids. I remember one day they were arguing and yet again, I tried to protect the woman who gave me life.

She was taking a bath as he was screaming at her. As she got out of the tub and trying to dry off, Phil decided that he was going to knock her around. I, of course, got in the middle of it. Standing up to my mom's aggressor, I told him to leave her alone. Aggravating him even more, he took his arm, swinging it across my dresser filled with unicorns. They were always my cherished items that I collected from various places, usually yard sales. I heard my beloved knick knacks crash between his flesh and the hard exterior of my bedroom wall. I saw red, my face furious with anger. "You asshole," I yelled! I lunged forward and propelled him in to the adjacent bedroom where my youngest brother slept. As I went full force with adrenaline pumping my veins, one swift turn from Phil and I got karate chopped full force down across my nose. Bam! I felt the warm ooze flow down as the pain violently surged throughout my head.

I went to school the following day and my computer class teacher asked me why my nose was bruised. Being the headstrong adolescent that I was, I told him the truth. Not caring about the potential consequences that could be done to my youngest brother and I. Children and Youth were contacted, and wanted me to press charges. My mom literally begged me to let the matter go. Phil's parents were irate with me saying I should have kept my mouth shut. Me, feeling guilty and sorry for my mother, I obliged my mom's request and the whole ordeal was forgotten.

That wasn't the only time Phil made himself out to be a jerk. At the time, Chloe and Chris were out in Ohio living with our father. Andy and I were with our mom and Phil. It was Christmas Eve and Phil had been drinking all day. He was angry because we had no money so that he could buy more weed. Fighting with Mom about it, Andy and I decided we would make the best out of our situation and be happy on the eve of the birth of our Lord. We laughed at each other's jokes and sang Christmas carols. Mom, noticing our good spirits, joined in. Besides hearing Phil in the kitchen grumbling, we were enjoying ourselves. As an hour passed of us sharing a rare special family commemoration, that set off Mr. grouchy pants. Not to be outdone, he went to the breaker box and turned off the power to the house. Us, being in high spirits and refusing to let him ruin it, kept singing and laughing. Infuriating him beyond words he finally gave up and went to bed. He made sure he told us not to flip the breakers back on since he pays the bills. Man, what a joke.

It was because of him *not* paying bills, that I got made fun of and ridiculed in school. During that period, we were renting a small two bedroom house right across from Phil's parents' home. The house happened to belong to the grandfather of a cousin on my mom's side. Being their intrusive selves, they stuck their noses in our business.

My cousin went to the same school as I was attending that year so my vindictive family would tell the entire junior class about my home life. Most of it being true, I had no defense. Again, I was criticized for what was out of my control. Every year, every school, every student, looked down on me, made fun of me, and tortured me because of my parents' choices.

Nobody felt my pain, saw my tears, answered my prayers. I felt alone with a house full of people. My defeated soul only made me want out even more. It made me that more determined to make a better life for myself knowing that I deserved happiness. Even with that determination, I had many nights where my light was diminished. I'd lay awake as the minutes ticked by well after two o'clock in the morning knowing I had school in the morning. The demons would visit then planting ideas of suicide in my mind. Grabbing a knife and slicing my wrists seemed like the thing to do. I felt like no one really cared if I lived or died. My father's words would loop in my head over and over. "If you're going to do it, do it right. Don't slice across but down the center of your vein." I don't know why God spared my life when I could have so easily given up completely. Only thing I know for sure is- He sustained me.

I needed acceptance and stability. Thankfully, a few years later, God answered those prayers with Nick.

I felt the motion of my hands still moving simultaneously as I smiled thinking of Nick. Yes, he may get on my nerves at times but I love him more than he realizes. I am definitely guilty of letting daily events capture my attention and filling my day with unwritten lists of tasks. Thanks to Gretchen taking the kids, the day under the willow will always remain cherished in my heart. We rekindled that spark that seems to dim at times. I'm thankful to her for allowing us time to seize the rare occasion of only the two of us.

I contemplated calling Nick and apologizing for getting so temperamental with him last night. He was only trying to protect me. Our fight was one that could have been avoided had I not gotten so irritated and prayed first. Honestly, I think I took my frustration out on him instead of my family. Unfortunately, I can't change that now, so I kept clipping away at the metal since I was so close to being finished. Truthfully, I believe if I talked to him in person there would be a better understanding between the two of us.

Nearing the last row I felt a wave of relief wash over me.

I've almost completed the outlandish feat. The snipping became faster as the minutes quickly rushed by as my memory relapsed into the forgotten world of yesteryear.

Mom moved her, Phil, Chloe and Andy back to a school we had attended the year before. I had moved out right before that during my senior year of high school. I'm not sure what all happened between Mom and Phil but things ended between the two of them. Once Mom left Phil permanently, she moved her and the kids to a low income housing plan. From the stories Chloe and Andy have told me over the years, things went from bad to worse. Both of them got into drugs including marijuana along with any other mind altering substance they could get their hands on. Andy was deeper into the drug abuse than Chloe. Both suffered in school due to all their partying. Neither wanted to get up early and they usually opted for sleeping all day and up all night. Failing grades and an extensive amount of days missed at school lead to both kids being taken off of Mom and placed in foster care.

Luckily, Chloe and Andy were able to be in the same foster house since the judge decided Mom had lost control of her children. They were placed together in one home and then they went to another that was better than the first but not exactly their cup of tea. Rules and accountability wasn't part of their thought process and they rebelled regularly. They remained there until our father came out from Ohio to gain custody of them. Mom once said he did that to hurt her. The kids say she turned her back on them. She said she tried her best. I wasn't there and refuse to choose a side. Unless I live through it myself, I don't think it's fair to say what I would have done or what should have happened. Instead, I told them hard feelings were within each of themselves, excluding me.

Recalling my thoughts of Mom and Phil, it brought an ache in my heart knowing who Mom was then. She was incredibly different throughout the years of my childhood. I haven't seen another woman as feeble since. Once she finally divorced Phil, things started looking up for her.

Mom worked at a local restaurant when she met Howie. Visiting from North Carolina, he stopped in to visit his sister who cooked at the same restaurant as my mom waitressed. Howie's sister introduced him to Mom and the relationship blossomed.

Howie courted Mom for a few months, traveling back and forth from North Carolina to Pennsylvania. I didn't realize she was falling for him until I found out she had elected to move to North Carolina with him. It all happened relatively quick since it was the same time the kids left foster care and went with our father. Their plan was to move back with her once they were out of the system. She didn't know that though because she didn't talk to them about anything. Communication is really essential in families but we always seemed to lack that in ours. At least not the right kind of communication. Screaming and yelling were typical but after all the battles, the words fell on deaf ears. They had no meaning, no love.

Instead, hate hardened all of our hearts. When she moved to North Carolina Chloe and Andy felt she gave up on them, leaving them to the wolves in Ohio.

Howie was different from Dad and Phil. He wasn't an alcoholic or a drug abuser. His posture was impeccably straight just like the Marine Corp taught so many years prior. Howie's a man of pride and self-worth. Thriving on honor, Howie taught Mom many new ways of life. Self-confidence being one of which she desperately needed. Exploring the world and all it has to offer is another. Howie has helped my mom find how open up to a different lifestyle, teaching and loving her all along the way. Sure, he has his faults but nothing like she was used to. They have both grown together.

In the beginning of their relationship, I was preoccupied with my own new marriage and start at life. I see now how I didn't make any time for them early on. Most importantly, I neglected my siblings. Since then, there has always been a distance between all of us, including my relationship with my mom. To me, it's more of a friendship than anything else.

I left home right before I turned eighteen while Mom was still with Phil and I barely kept in contact. I clung towards the future because I wanted to move forward and never desired to look back in my rear view mirror. I was on the fast track to somewhere, anywhere but where I was. During my process of finding myself, I always felt like I abandoned the kids. I know it's due to the role I played while I lived at home. I reminded myself I wasn't their parent; I shouldn't have had to worry about making sure they were taken care of. It wasn't my place to protect them. Still, I felt responsible for my younger siblings. Lying in bed at night, I thought of them often, wondering what they were doing. Agonizing if I shouldn't have left as the ache in my heart became heavier until it felt like an elephant had sat on my chest. Insomnia was a constant battle every night during the early years of me leaving home. I left my little sister and brother to contend with the battles and hardships brought on by our mom and step-dad.

Now, twenty years later, my siblings and I have made do with what we had. Mom is happy with Howie living south while my brothers each have places in Ohio. My sister and I are in Pennsylvania away from the city life unlike our brothers. Considering where we came from, most of us came out pretty good. Until I'm reminded of surface feelings. We put on this display for others but what's hidden in the chambers of our hearts that we refuse to unbind? I can't help but wonder how much they each hold in.

Then I started to allow myself to really think about my relationship with my mom even in more recent years. I've focused so much on all that my father has done; it took the spotlight off her. Until now and I began to allow the truth of how I really felt be exposed to the light.

She has always turned to me for guidance and support. I was

her 'right hand' as she likes to put it. I helped her like a mother would help her daughter through tough times. Maybe it was because of that, we never built a true mother-daughter relationship. It was more of a daughter-friend relationship. I never felt as though I could turn to her for support because I was always supporting her. We didn't have that bond where I could talk to her about things and she would coddle me in her arms telling me it'd be okay. It just felt weird and out of place. Instead, it was the other way around. I was strong, she was weak. Then being a mother figure to the kids put me in a dominate role. I was their boss. Not their sister. I tended to their needs; I shielded them from the violence. I protected their eyes and ears. And because I couldn't love my mom like a daughter should, I never really created a sister-sister bond with Chloe cause I didn't know how until we were older. I felt like I was my mom's mom so the love was different. I only knew how to take control of a relationship and almost dictate what should and shouldn't be done. So, because of that sort of upbringing I was petrified of having a daughter because I didn't think I could love her the 'right way'. When I found out Della was a girl I was devastated but never told anyone. I kept it hidden and smashed it to the deepest pocket of my soul. And now that I remembered the let down when I first found out about Della, I hated myself. How foolish I was. Truth is, I was so afraid of the mother I'd be to her. That's when God stepped in and allowed her to teach me so many wonderful gifts, so much wisdom and knowledge. Most importantly, how a mother-daughter love really should be.

In life, we are given choices. We are also given free will. Mom chose hers and these are the effects from her choices. And these are my feelings from those effects. When Mom and Howie visit or every time we talk on the phone, I get this slight anger that grows a bit each time. And I know it's not healthy. It's not right. So I have to make it right. In the end I hope it makes our relationship stronger and her stronger too. Children need their mothers. Their fathers too... but really I had neither.

Something is telling me my childhood has a purpose. God will make it right. There's someone out there that can learn from this. That can heal faster than me. That can mend from the brokenness of hurt, shame, anger and pain. It's those souls I need to reach and I can only reach them with truth.

Allowing me to be completely open and raw with myself is something I'm not comfortable with. My mind is heavy with guilt and pain. Instead trying to digest these newest revelations, I went back to what I was doing.

It was quite a feat lugging the last of the bags up to the front of our property. Thankfully, I was finally done! I had no idea it would take so long to cut up full size mattress springs. Regardless, I was done and could now get a much needed shower.

I know Dad didn't think of what was left to do after he was gone. He couldn't have. I hope. Pap rolled into my mind and I knew better. Shivers once again started from the roots of my hair down to the tips of my toes. The same eerie feeling crept back into my frame and the darkness seemed to enter my mind once more. One man, lonely and filled with despair, took a gun to his head and pulled the trigger. I know how low you have to feel to get to that point. The misery pushes you beyond logical thinking making suicide your only option. There isn't an inner voice telling you someone cares, that you're not alone. The secrets bound tight from speaking them aloud. Instead, they swirl around whispering in your ear, giggling, taunting you that they know the truth.

The monster inside of Chris Cochran chanted over and over, "You're a loser, nobody cares, you ruined your life, pull that trigger. Go ahead, pull it you coward, pull it. You don't have the guts, pull it you son of a bitch, pull it... I'll meet you in hell. Pull it!" POW!

Chapter 13

One of Two

I scrubbed my body almost raw to the bone, desperately trying to rid the revolting stench from my skin. I called Nick to let him know that he and the kids were safe to come home. His tone sounded annoyed with me. I was sure he was still hurt from my words the previous night.

Dinner time had approached as I heard our old grandfather clock stationed in our living room chime six times. I wasn't in the mood to eat. In fact, my stomach felt quite queasy from the day's events. Food was the last thing I wanted at the moment. Instead, I opted for an ice cold drink and headed downstairs.

My sanctuary had become a regular refuge for me lately. I was thankful I had the area to myself. Plopping myself in the arms of my beloved grandmother's chair, I seen Friday circled on my calendar. It might as well be Doom's Day. Two funerals for two men that shared the same sort of past. Alcoholism ruined both men and their lives. With respect to Mr. Hopkins, I knew he went with the hope of someone still caring. Dad, however, gave up all hope and ended his life with a bang.

Thinking of the funerals I remembered to call Chloe to find

out what time she set the service up for.

"Hey Chloe, how are you doing?" I began.

"I answered my phone, does that count?"

I knew Chloe was taking Dad's death the hardest. She looked past his faults and loved him unconditionally. I wish I could say the same.

"Yes, I guess so. Um, I was calling to see what time you had planned the service?" I tried to be as delicate as I could because I knew her tears would choke her words within seconds.

"Four o'clock, is that okay with you?" Just then I heard the water works start as she inhaled deeply.

"Yes, that's fine. Call me later if you can. I love you, Sis." All I heard was whimpering on the other end.

As I ended our call I felt sadness for my only sister. She was hurting and I couldn't comfort her. What are you supposed to say to someone who just lost their dad? And why didn't I feel the same as her? He was my father too.

I felt like the willow tree standing strong out my back door. I should want to cry like the branches dangling down to the ground. I needed to let it all out however just as the bark protected the tree; the wall I kept built up sheltered me from pain.

This isn't right. How can I be so cold hearted towards my own father? He was the man that helped create me. I felt like I was acting exactly like him. Holding onto the past that never seemed to loosen its grip to try and let go. I thought I forgave him a long time ago. In fact, I know I did. Didn't I? What else looms over me that loiter around waiting to ultimately be put to rest?

The shuffling of feet above interrupted my thought process.

"Mom, we're home!" Della shouted.

I ran up the steps to greet my kids with a huge hug for each of them. As my heart swelled full of affection with the love I had for them, I knew I wasn't my father. I had emotions that outpoured to everyone around me. My fear of being like him quickly dissipated as I clung to my children.

"Oh, I missed you guys," I exclaimed! "Did you have fun at Grandma and Pap's?"

"Yeah, Pap took me for a ride on his motorcycle!" Kevin had always loved riding with Everett on his Harley since he was three years old.

Della chimed in and added, "I saddled up Tucker and took a trail ride with Daddy." Her smile beamed from ear to ear with shear happiness.

Glancing up at Nick I spotted the particular twinkle in his eye that he always had with his children. Loving them was one of his top priorities in life. And taking an hour for a horse-back ride was one way they had their special father-daughter time together. It helped them have their talks about everything and anything. Della would catch Nick up about her friends, he explained electricity, and the two of them would even talk about what Nick did when he was younger.

Field parties were popular when he grew up in the countryside. He warned her couple of times about drinking and driving. He lost a friend right after graduation because of it. Nick told the kids that if they were drinking or ever had friends drinking to call us and we would pick them up regardless of the time of day or night. He stressed that we certainly didn't agree with underage drinking however, we realize that kids will experiment. Together, we knew we couldn't turn our heads, pretending it didn't happen.

Nick met my stare and gave me a wink. The small gesture helped calm my bubbling stomach, wondering how I was to start and apologize for the previous evening. I mouthed a silent, "I'm sorry."

Taking my attention from the kids to my husband, we embraced for a hug. He quickly whispered, "It's okay, Della and I had a nice talk."

I was completely puzzled by how the conversation between him and Della could make everything alright. Raising my brow he knew I wouldn't let this go. I planned to talk to Nick when we had a spare moment together.

"So, did you all eat and your grandparents?" I questioned them.

"Yes," Nick confirmed.

Happy not to have to cook, I said a thankful, "Good!"

"What about you, Jill? Did you eat today?" Nick knew that

when I was overly anxious I never had an appetite.

Not wanting to lie but not hungry either, I simply told him, "I'll get something later. I'm exhausted to be honest."

"Go take a nap. I can tend to the kids," Nick stated as he stroked the middle of my back.

"I better not. I have to get things ready for tomorrow. Mr. Hopkins's funeral is at one o'clock and then Dad's is at four o'clock. Oh, and I need to talk to Chloe to see if there is any other planning that needs done. Then, I have to call Hailey."

"If you insist, honey." There wasn't any negotiating when I had an agenda. Twenty years of marriage taught him that.

Retreating back downstairs after making sure the kids were busy with a project, I refocused on my list of things to do. I decided to text Chloe and asked if there was anything else that needed done for tomorrow. I didn't want her getting upset again like the last time we talked. Her message back was brief only saying that since I took care of the clean-up she handled everything else. That was certainly a load off my shoulders, thank God.

Next on the docket was to call Hailey.

"Hey girlie, are you busy?" I asked when she answered.

"Nope, we just got threw dinner and the kids are going to start doing dishes for me." Her voice grew louder as a sign to her children to start cleaning up. Groans were heard in the background and I had to chuckle.

"Yeah, sounds like they are ecstatic about it," I concluded as I could barely contain an outburst of laughter.

"They'll be fine," Hailey assured with a groan. "So, what's up, Jill?"

"I just wanted to confirm meeting at the funeral home tomorrow around twelve thirty."

"Yes, that sounds good to me. Are you taking the kids?" Hailey asked.

"No, they will have enough of the funeral home for my dad tomorrow evening," I replied.

"Oh, Jillian. Are you sure you can handle all that? One funeral is hard enough but two and the second being your dad! Maybe you should reconsider going to Mr. Hopkins." Hailey was trying to save me from added stress but I knew I was able to handle it all.

"I promise, I can handle it. The hardest part for my dad is over. After tomorrow I hope to be able to finally move on and put to rest all these skeletons that have been lurking around for twenty years."

"Alright then, see you tomorrow," Hailey promised.

Once we hung up, a wave of sleepiness surged throughout my cells. Since Chloe had tomorrow's events planned and ready, my to-do list was all scratched off.

I headed back upstairs and almost hit Nick with the basement door as I swung it open to gain entrance to the kitchen. "Oh my, sorry Nick," I blurted out being startled.

"No problem. What are you up to?" Nick inquired.

"I was going to lay down for a bit. I'm utterly exhausted. What are the kids up to?" I asked.

"They finished their project for you and went outside. I think they wanted to play a game of basketball. I can handle the kids, go get some rest." Nick was being incredibly sweet ensuring me that him and the kids are fine.

"Thanks, I am, but first I want to know what you and Della talked about during your trail ride." I know he knew the question was coming since Della and Kevin were outside as I seen the mischievous grin come across his face.

"It's been eating you alive, hasn't it?" Nicked probed with a diminutive chuckle.

"Maybe…" was all I could sheepishly reply.

Grasping my hand in his masculine grip, Nick looked deep into my brown eyes, uncovering all that I once hid. Secrets were a thing of the past now that I felt comfortable knowing that Nick wouldn't ever hold it against me. I felt him breath in all my thoughts of today from cleaning up the mess in Ohio to cutting up every spring from the mattress. God must have poured His grace over the Davenport home today, knowing I was in need of a break. To have to explain the last twelve hours would be incredibly difficult right now.

We sat down at the dining room table and Nick began

explaining to me how Della unexpectedly helped him learn more about his wife.

She started off by telling her dad how she couldn't sleep last night. Concerned, he asked why and Della confided that she was thinking of me. Putting all the stories together she came up with a synopsis of who her mother really is.

"I think Mom is someone that needs acceptance. All through school she was shy, not wanting anyone to know what she had to deal with at home. So, she built this wall that shielded her from pain. But, it didn't protect her like she thought it did. Instead, I think it may have hurt her."

Della paused as Nick began to consider the assumption. "That's an interesting concept, honey. Why do you think that?"

"Well, after all the years you two have been married, she never confided in you about her past because she was afraid you would judge her for all the stuff that happened. She must have been petrified at the thought of losing you. So, instead she kept quiet. I can see why she didn't want to tell Kevin and me until we were older, but I couldn't understand why she hid it from you until I realized that."

"You really thought this out, sweetie." Nick wasn't sure how to respond however he didn't have to because Della picked up where she left off.

"I think Mr. Hopkins was a sign from God, telling Mom it was okay to come clean to you. I tried to imagine what it must have felt like to carry the burden of hers for twenty years without breathing a word to the man she loves. I mean, if it was me, I don't think I could handle all the pressure. Then, trying to dodge questions as to why we never visit our grandfather and great grandmother when they weren't that far away. Didn't you ever wonder about that Dad?" Della's question was naïve but hit a nerve with Nick.

"When Della asked me why I never questioned some of your actions or responses, I realized I wasn't the husband I should have been."

"Nick, my goodness, you have been a wonderful husband!" I exclaimed. "How could you have known I was hiding anything? I would have denied any accusations anyway. This isn't your fault, I take full responsibility." I couldn't let Nick take any accountability for not knowing. Guilt washed over me while Nick poured his heart out.

"Jillian, I never took the time to ask questions. I figured if there was something, then you would tell me. I am usually so focused on work and making sure I provide for my family I neglected to appreciate you had a life prior to me, a parent besides your Mom and Howie, hell even your grandmother is still around. You never call or talk about her or your dad. I loved my grandmother and we always visited her and we see my parents regularly. It hadn't clicked that we never saw yours. That's when all the factors came together for me and I knew why you had to go out to Ohio."

I was unable to control my tears as I stood up and clenched my slender arms around Nick's frame. "Thank you, God, for giving me Nick," I prayed in a whisper.

Feeling incredibly appreciative, I told Nick that I loved him forever and always. I was extremely tired and had to lie down for a bit so I mentioned my need for a nap. He understood, promised to keep an eye on the kids, and I retreated to our bedroom. I curled up under the warmth of our comforter that I missed terribly the night before.

Drifting off into a deep slumber, my entire physique felt numb. Visions started to appear but hastily vanished as the darkness closed in. Soon after, all was still, everything was calm, and my form fell limp as sleep took the reins.

I didn't wake up until I heard Nick getting ready for work the next morning. Rolling over I let out a small groan. Our queen size pillow top mattress was just too cozy to get up out of just yet. Normally, I would be half awake packing Nick's lunch and sending him off to work with a tired smile and a quick peck on the cheek.

Mornings should be outlawed in my honest opinion nevertheless, I tried to be semi coherent and not act like a zombie even though that's how I felt inside. I stretched my five foot six frame until I felt like I was a full six feet tall helped to initiate the will power to get up.

My daybreak ritual began as I plugged in the coffee pot, inserted the coffee pod and turned it on to brew the deliciousness of caffeine. I shuffled into the bathroom to brush my teeth when Nick came in to ask when we needed to be at the funeral home for Dad.

Trying desperately to think clearly, I was still quite groggy without having anything to liven me up.

"I am going to be there early, of course. It starts at four so, can you get off work early to be there by four?"

"Yes, I already had it approved to leave early today. See you later, love ya, babe." Nick hesitated realizing his mistake but I shrugged it off knowing you can't break habits overnight.

"Love you too," I told him and headed to the kitchen.

Clutching the solid oak chair from our kitchen table, I pulled it out to sit and really think about what I wanted to say to Mr. Hopkins' son and daughter. Although, I knew that it wasn't my place to tell them how they should feel, I wanted to express to them how much he loved them, realized his mistakes and wished for forgiveness. I owed Mr. Hopkins that much for helping me.

As the morning wore on, my patience level proved to be thin with the kids. Kevin was bursting with restless energy. He began picking on Della causing minuscule fights between the two. After the sixth screaming match him and Della got into, I had finally had enough and told them I was calling Grandma and having her pick them up. I wanted to break the two up for a bit except, time was running short before I had to leave for the funeral home.

"But Mama, I wanted to go with you," pleaded Della.

I slumped my shoulders because I knew I had to be the unfair parent, and I told her no.

"Why? That's not fair, Mom! I want to go with you. Please Mama, I want to see who Mr. Hopkins was," Della begged with those deep chocolate eyes that melted the core of my body.

Still crabby, I asked sarcastically, "Why would you want to see an empty body? His soul went with him."

Della was hurt by my words. The expression on her face was forlorn and full of sorrow. I didn't mean for it to come out so brassy. "I'm sorry, sweetie. I didn't mean for it to come out so harsh. But, you will have to be with me at your grandfather's funeral tonight. I honestly believe two in one day would be too much for you and Kevin. Stay with Grandma for a couple hours and I will pick you and Kev up in a little while."

Della hung her head down looking at the ceramic tile that was beneath our feet in the kitchen. Half whispering her words were soft, "I just wanted to meet the man that helped you."

I stepped closer, and brought her close to my chest hugging her. "Sweetheart, I would much rather show you a picture. You can thank God for sending Mr. Hopkins along the path I have been taking. Think of it this way; Mr. Hopkins was a pawn used to help another pawn dodge an attack from the dark side. You love chess, so you understand what I'm saying?"

Della straightened her posture looking me in the eye. "Yeah, I get it Mom. I'm just a bit disappointed. But, I understand what you are saying."

Holding her hand, I lovingly squeezed it and thanked her for understanding. "Besides, I'm going to need a little support tonight," I confided in her with a wink.

Kevin pulled Della aside and retreated to his bedroom. I figured he wanted to make sure she was okay. Five minutes later, they came out with a tiny box wrapped in gold wrapping paper. Puzzled by the contents, I looked skeptical of what they were doing.

Stepping forward, together with the gift, they handed it to me without a word. I wasn't complaining about getting a present but I was a bit shocked by it. Then, I remembered when Gretchen and the kids went away for ice cream.

"Just what do you guys have up your sleeves?" I joked.

"Open it!" Della and Kevin said in unison.

Peeling the tape back and then the paper, the white box had the name of our local jewelry company. My anticipation was getting the best of me, so I quickly opened the lid to find a beautiful silver cross with a tree in the middle of it along with a new chain.

"Oh my goodness, this is gorgeous!" I exclaimed with enthusiasm. "I'm going to have to call Gretchen! Thank you guys very much! I love it!" I spoke while putting on my new chain and pendent. I hugged each of them extra tight enforcing to each of them how perfect it was.

After I left a message for Gretchen, Kathleen came over to the house and picked up Della and Kevin for me. She was always wonderful at helping me out especially when I needed it the most. I thanked her for taking the four mile drive from her house to mine. It saved me fifteen minutes.

Once they left, I retrieved the bullet that I found in the wall. I quickly slipped it into my pocket. I took one last look in the mirror and headed out the door. Hailey had texted and said she would meet me at the funeral home. I started getting a bit nervous, wondering what I was going to say, how I was going to say it. Working myself up tight as a ball of yarn, I decided to take a deep breath as I pulled in the parking lot to release all the what if's. Instead, I shoved my fears to the back of my mind and cleared the brainwaves for all the wonderful memories I had of Mr. Hopkins. I remembered his smile that lit up the room when he saw me walk in. His laugh lines were prominent even with the short gray mustache that he was diligent at up-keeping.

Looking up to the sky, I saw the blueness that pumped its peace right into my veins allowing the warmth of the summer to keep my attitude beaming. Remaining focused on the positives, I saw Hailey pull into the parking lot. I felt relieved knowing she was here with me.

Greeting one another with a hug, we walked to the door of the funeral home. I paused to take one more deep breath, poised my stature and took the first step into the unknown. Finding my way to the guest book, I signed myself in. Hailey did the same and I began scanning the room for Mr. Hopkins son or daughter. The mood was light with laughter here and there. I saw more smiling here at the funeral home than at a wedding. I couldn't believe my eyesight.

The area wasn't what I expected to see. The chairs weren't in rows like the usual funeral. Instead, the seating was set up in a circle around the circumference of the room. There was only one flower arrangement setting in the far corner to my right. No wreaths or displays saying husband, father or grandfather. I felt a wave of guilt wash over me as I remembered I hadn't called ahead to send flowers. Seeing my surroundings, it made me feel even worse. Poor Mr. Hopkins, after all these years my instincts were right - nobody cared.

My heart ached for the man, now seeing it being put forth in front of my face. Only a hand full of people was in front of me, all middle aged and was there simply to support their friends in their loss. Not to give condolences for the rugged old man that was portrayed as a merciless brute.

Sensing Hailey by my side, skimming the gathering as well, I looked over with my eyebrows raised and asked, "Are you ready?"

Hailey nodded with a supportive smile and we headed to the

front of the room. I hadn't noticed the casket until now looking ahead of the few bodies that filled the small space. The brown vault set up in the middle was opened with only the shell of a life. Witnessing Mr. Hopkins lying there, completely still instead of seeing him sit up and smile was heartbreaking. The huge ball of tears was lodged in the back of my throat as I tried to swallow them down to the floor.

The siblings stood smiling and chatting with a friend as Hailey and I approached them. Noticing our presence, their friend quietly slipped away to the rear of the room. I extended my hand to greet the son and then his sister. Hailey followed my lead as we reminded them of who we were from the nursing home.

"Thanks for coming," the short plump redhead stated rather dry. Her brown eyes were merely a reflection of a blank paper bag.

"You ladies honestly didn't have to come. I mean, I appreciate it but it wasn't necessary," came from the tall and lanky dark haired son of Mr. Hopkins.

Looking at the two of them, it was hard to see the resemblances that confirmed they were brother and sister. I could see Mr. Hopkins a great deal in his son. And remembering a photograph he showed me a few years ago of his wife, I could tell that his daughter was a carbon copy of her mother. Had you not known their parents, their features mimicked nothing of each other's.

"We came to pay our respects," Hailey confirmed to the two.

I wasn't sure why I had lost my voice. I suppose I was in shock of how nonchalant the mood was for a funeral.

They turned their attention to a couple to the left of us so; Hailey and I went near the casket to have some privacy.

"I can't help but be upset with this entire setting, Hailey," I confided in a whisper.

"I know me too, Jill. Just try not to belittle your character because of someone else's actions. Let them be the fool, not you. Plus, we are here for Mr. Hopkins and not to make a mockery of his life." Hailey tried to rein me in as she knew I would have a hard time not saying that there *was* good to this man.

"I know you're right, Hailey, I just can't get over the love this man had to offer and not one of his children could see it. Now, it's too late."

"It's a sad situation. Nobody should have to but we all have choices in life. We pave our own road as the years turn into chapters of each of our own books. The pages written make us who we are. It sets the pace for what others think about us. Making mistakes can have a detrimental effect on others. They remember all the negatives instead of the positives or changes. Think about it Jill, you remember all the horrible things your dad did. But do you remember one good thing?" Hailey's question hit a core nerve provoking me to think about my own personal battle.

Switching my weight from my right leg to my left, I started

to recall back all the conversations I have had with my family about my past. Not one good thing came out of my mouth about Dad. It made me wonder if he really was the monster I have created him to be. Grunting with frustration, "I don't know, my friend, I'm so confused now."

Hailey once again, showed me a real friend. One to not throw the first stone but make you ponder your own actions, someone to share a different opinion and still be someone you trust. She has been there for me when things were great, now that things are up in the air, Hailey has shown me that she will try to pick me up to make things a bit better and if she can't help me achieve that, she will fall to her knees with me and be there to support me no matter what. Friendship has proven to be imperative to survive in this world. We need the closeness of others like Hailey and Gretchen for comfort, to offer support, to rest our head on their shoulder, and give advice when we ask for it.

Finally, it hit me that walking this earth with my head buried in the sand, afraid to want real friends wasn't the answer. We each need those that we can turn to, can laugh with. Hailey brought a whole new perspective and I couldn't have been any more thankful.

Hailey and I exchanged a hug as I told her how grateful I was to have her. "Let's pay our respects to Mr. Hopkins, shall we?" Hailey asked.

Agreeing with her, we walked the few feet over to the casket that held my favorite old man. Taking in every feature of his face, the white dress shirt that covered his chest, his hair combed to the left just as he had done for so many years. I will surely miss the man that lived right next to my office.

I held his cold hand in the warmth of mine desperately wishing for one last squeeze, a wink, something, anything but silence. Unable to control the river from flowing, I let my tears go freely without holding back. I loved him more than I should have. He opened me up like no other person has on this earth.

Kissing his forehead, I forced myself to tear away from the casket. Hailey handed me a couple tissues and guided me to the restroom. It was quite an intense moment and I desperately needed to regain my composure. The blur of all the others staring at me hadn't troubled me until I regained my poise a few minutes later. I heard the whispering as they were all confused as to why I cared so much.

Hailey and I returned to the room that was arranged for Mr. Hopkins' service. People had begun to sit around as the funeral home director stood in the front clearing his throat to get everyone's attention. Hailey and I quickly took our seats in the far corner.

"Can I have your attention please? The son and daughter have decided on a non-traditional service and wishes to go around the room to talk about the life of the late Mr. Hopkins." Looking at Mr. Hopkins son, he said, "Would you like to begin now?"

Cupping his hand to his mouth, his son coughed, which

seemed like he was searching for something to say. "Well, Dad and I only saw one another from time to time. It was hard to find the time to visit him in the nursing home. I'll miss him."

His sister was next. "Dad made Mom miserable for years. I know Mom loved him more than I ever could. I cherished Mom so for her, I tolerated my father. We always had our ups and downs. I'm going to try and remember the good instead of the bad." The red head showed a bit of her temper as her words came out with venom instead of compassion.

As the rest of family and friends went around, most of them hardly knew the man that was laid out before us. My jaw dropped and stayed at the floor as I listened to the hatred that flowed like rapids from their mouths.

All of ten minutes of others speaking, it came close to Hailey and I. Now, I was getting nervous knowing I was the only one, besides Hailey, with fond memories. Building my courage to speak up for the man that I grew to love like a father figure, I knew what I needed to do so I wouldn't have any guilt afterwards.

I stood up from the wooden unpadded chair. I felt stiff from being so uncomfortable and I tried to secretly shake out the numbness through my hands.

"My name is Jillian Davenport and I was blessed to know Mr. Hopkins for the last seven years while he resided at Buckingham nursing facility. His room was located next door to my office so I routinely checked in on him. Through his time there, we shared many talks including his dreams and his sorrows. He made a sinners life for many years as most of you have previously stated. Then, he changed as his heart softened and became a man that realized his mistakes and asked his wife for forgiveness. Being the loyal beauty that she was, she accepted his apology. Unfortunately, their bliss was cut short after her death and a year after Mr. Hopkins broke his hip. I feel like he was an angel sent there for a reason.

Throughout the years, he always said he wished his children would reconsider and hear him out. He had hoped for acceptance from them so that he may go in peace. However, as it was evident today, we all know that never happened.

Last Friday, he and I had a chat that was quite eye opening for myself. He asked a simple question- why I cared for him so much especially, when his own family had such little interaction with him because of his past. I confided in him that he reminded me of a young girl I used to know. I told him that he helped me see parts of myself that I buried years ago. Acts that were done to me that I needed to let go of once and for all, grudges that must be forgiven in order to find peace within myself.

You see, I lived the life you did," looking back and forth at his son and daughter in their eyes. I was hoping to touch them in a way that can help them forgive.

"My father was an abusive alcoholic. He has done some terrible things and finally committed the ultimate disgrace. Your dad," I began as I pointed to the casket, "has shown me how to love and forgive. To accept others as they are without passing judgment for their actions. I owe your dad more than I could ever repay him." Waiting a moment to catch my breath I ended my speech, "Now, I have to go bury my own father. I'm sorry for your loss."

Hailey rose from her seat as she and I started walking out to exit the funeral home. While we strode passed all the lost souls in the room, silence deafened the room. I have no idea how or why I obtained the courage to say all that I did but it was over. I'm sure my words seemed hurtful to some but, I needed to defend the man that helped me see the light. God used Mr. Hopkins as my teacher and I the student. I hope I passed his test.

As we arrived at our vehicles, Hailey gave me a huge hug and beamed with pride. "I'm so proud of you, Jill! I would have never had the nerve to say all that!"

"I'm not sure where it all came from. I hope I wasn't too harsh. I was just trying to preserve Mr. Hopkins' memory. He deserved better than what they gave him." Honestly, I was shocked at myself for being so straight forward with strangers.

"I know hun, you did well. Maybe a bit bold, however, I wouldn't expect anything less from you," Hailey told me with a wink. "So, I will meet you in a bit," Hailey promised.

"Please, you don't have to go tonight. You came with me here. Two funerals are just too much for someone. You don't have to go, Hailey."

"Are you kidding me? I'm going to be there for support whether you like it or not," Hailey persisted.

"Okay, okay. But don't feel obligated to. I hate to keep you away from your family practically all day."

Pulling me in for a quick hug, "We are friends, Jill. This is what friends do. We are there for one another, regardless of the circumstances," she said in a soft voice.

Pulling away, I looked at her with such admiration. She really was my friend. And this is what friends do. I can trust others. Gretchen has tried to teach me that for years. Unfortunately, I never listened.

"I'll see you at four," Hailey assured as she climbed in her car and drove off.

I entered my vehicle and turned the key to turn over the engine. As I sat there with my vehicle running, I started to play back the scene that just occurred. Was I wrong? Did I say too much?

My heart felt heavy with guilt for being so blunt with Mr. Hopkins' children. Maybe I should go back in and apologize. Reaching my fingertips to the key I was startled with hearing a knock on my window. Shocked, I almost jumped out of my skin and my head turned to the window of my door.

Seeing the familiar face, that looked like he was Mr. Hopkins in his younger days, I rolled down my window to acknowledge his son.

Greeting him with a small smile, I said hello to him. He responded back, of course, and then silence for a few moments. His eyes were moving all around while his mouth twitched as they fought to find the words to say.

"Ah, I'm not sure how to start so; I will just let it out. At first, I was shocked at how honest you were. Then, I started thinking and realized you were right. Dad begged me to visit him but I never did. You know, you made a lot of sense in there and I appreciate you candidness. I should have made an effort to hear him out. Instead, I refused his apology. You then came here and started telling us how he helped you. And through you, he helped me. I just wanted to say thank you for explaining who Dad was for the last seven years. I may always have guilt for not being a better son, but like you said, I have to find forgiveness. Not just with Dad but within myself. I hope one day I can achieve that." Taking a breath between thoughts he then continued, "And I'm really sorry about your dad."

My heart was bursting with pride! Mr. Hopkins finally got his wish. Maybe only one child I had reached but I'm thankful the Lord used me to touch his son. I was sure he was smiling from Heaven as he heard our conversation.

"Your dad was a wise man. He helped me without recognizing it. But, I know he would be very proud of you Mr. Hopkins. Remember that. And thank you - about my dad."

"Have a blessed day Mrs. Davenport," as he waved goodbye.

I drove off with a clear conscience knowing that I did make

the right choice. Sometimes, tough love is the only way to make your point. I suppose, this was one of those times.

Chapter 14

How the Weak Survive

Pulling in the driveway of my in-laws, Della and Kevin ran out to greet me. It always felt great that my kids were so happy to see me.

Exiting my vehicle, I prepared myself for bear hugs. As expected, Della's embrace was delicate. Kevin thrust his weight into mine, sending me backward hitting the S.U.V.

Giggling with the force my son had, probably from playing football, I tickled them both to keep the mood light.

Still chuckling from hearing the sweet laughter of my precious children, I told them I was going to go see Grandma and Pap for a minute and asked them to go get changed. They scurried inside as I followed them. When I opened the door I smelled fresh baked apple pie. The aroma made my mouth water as the sweetness in the air captivated my taste buds wanting to taste the flaky crust that housed the warm, cinnamon apples that hid inside.

I spotted Kathleen at her oven with a spark in her eye. She always enjoyed making special treats for her family.

"Hey Kathleen, the house smells fantastic!" I exclaimed.

I waited a few moments for a response and when she hadn't turned her head, I knew she didn't hear me. Hard of hearing since I have known her, I decided to walk over and tap her on her shoulder.

"Oh, hey Jill, I made a couple apple pies," she said as she was pulling the second pie from the oven.

"Yes, I can smell the sweet cinnamon throughout the house!"

I could tell she was pleased with her hard work as our eyes locked. She kept busy, rustling around the kitchen, washing dishes, going from cabinet to cabinet. She usually did that when she was nervous and unsure of what to say next.

"Maw, you okay?" I questioned.

"Yeah, why?" she responded.

"Cause you're doing your nervous habit when you don't know what to say. It's me, Jill, remember? I know you too well. It's okay. What's on your mind?" I probed.

Hiding her eyes, knowing I did know her too well, she went back to washing dishes and not looking me in the face.

"How are you doing, Jillian?" she began.

"I'm holding my own, Maw. I promise." My words were sincere and I put my hand on her back to reassure her.

"You need anything?"

"Everything has been taken care of. Chloe was a huge help," I told her.

She stopped what she was doing, turned to face me, and her feelings were said aloud instead of holding it all in like usual. "Jill, I'm sorry about what your dad did. No one should have to do what you did."

"Thanks, but I did what I had to do, it's almost over now." I was touched by her thoughtfulness.

I looked at my watch and knew that I had to get moving. So, I called for the kids and hoped they were ready to go. They came into the kitchen, dressed; hair was done and ready to go. Incredible, now why can't they do this on a regular basis?!

"Wow, you two look great, good job guys!" I complimented Della and Kevin.

They each said their thank you's and I asked if they were ready for what was in store for them. Della was firm in her decision that she was prepared. Kevin, however, seemed a bit weary of what to expect. He hadn't really dealt with death before, so this was a new experience to him.

"Grover, if you have any questions or you just need to take a break, let me know and I will answer what I can and we can go outside if you need to get away for a bit."

"Thanks, Mom. I'll let you know," Kevin swore.

I gave Kathleen a hug and thanked her again for keeping an eye on the kids.

"We'll meet you there," Kathleen said and we were headed out the door.

The kids and I got in the vehicle and buckled up. I took a deep breath as I was about to head back to a place I haven't visited in years. During the seventies, Dad spent his teenage years making

237

his mark on the pavement and in school. He graduated in seventy-nine right about the time the small town lost its fizzle when the coal mining and mills shut down thanks to our government and all their politics.

The forty-five minute drive was quiet between the three of us. I was expecting some sort of questions or at the bare minimum, a minuscule conversation about their day at their grandparents. Instead, the mood was quite somber. Glancing in my rear view mirror from time to time, I witnessed my children gaze out of their windows taking in every sight that was brought before them. Unchartered territory, they were fascinated with the unfamiliar property.

We arrived in Satan's lot that I once called home. The one-way street looked like it did thirty years ago. Old, worn, tethered, and tired. The boarded up houses amongst the rows proved what this town had to offer- nothing.

The kids and I was a bit early so I contemplated staying in the car for a while. Before I could make a decision, Kevin and Della had unbuckled their belts and opened their doors. Following their lead, we looked both ways to cross the road that was in need of repair. The pot holes were absurd as we dodged the six inch deep cavity that I luckily missed pulling in.

Opening the door to yet another funeral home, I was greeted by the director. We had our formal introductions and he asked me to join him in his office to review the paperwork. Obliging to his request, I asked the kids to stay in the waiting area until I finalized the last minute preparations promising them I wouldn't be too long.

Reviewing the entirety of the plans that Chloe had organized, I was happy with the outcome. She did a terrific job preparing the memorial, leaving me only a few signatures to complete. I was just signing the last page when I heard rustling in the waiting area and voices chatting quietly. I was sure Chloe had arrived.

Emerging from the director's office, I found out I was right in my assumption. Chloe and Della were chatting while Kevin and his cousin Ethan were trying to arm wrestle on the small stand that sat beside the couch.

"Boys, please stop!" I begged them.

Chloe was humored by watching the two ignore me and try to see who was stronger.

"Seriously, sis, this *is* a funeral home." I pleaded her.

"Oh come on you stick in the mud! They're boys and they are fine. It's not like anyone is here and they aren't even being loud. Calm down Jill, geez!"

"I am calm, thank you, but I know how those two get and rowdy are both of their middle names!" Trying to get Chloe to see this wasn't the place for horseplay just wasn't working out.

"Fine, Ethan and Kev, you're not allowed to be boys so stop arm wrestling, please," Chloe tried to say sternly.

Throwing my hands up in the air in frustration, I shook my

head. "I'm going to check out the set up. Della, do you want to stay here with Aunt Chloe?" I asked.

"Sure Mama," she answered as she remained in the stiff upholstered flower covered chair she was seated in.

I wanted to make sure the seating was set up properly, unlike Mr. Hopkins, the flowers were arranged in an even manner and of course, the casket was to be closed. I spotted the director walking from one room to the next and I secretly nodded at him to join me for a private meeting.

I motioned him to the corner of the room that held the body of my father. Something inside of me needed to know. I was utterly entranced to see. I burned his blood, now I felt it necessary to see his body. To visualize all that I have been speculating from the scene that has been imprinted permanently in my memory.

I looked the mortician squarely in his face and asked, "Can I see his body please?"

Faltering with his response I knew he was wondering why I would ever want to see a man with half his head missing. Little did the director know that I cleaned up the mess Dad left behind.

"Well," he paused, "you do understand that it's not a sight most can endure."

"Sir, I am aware of what I am about to see. I am asking you if I can view the man I called Dad inside the casket. Are you able to open it?"

240

"Of course, I can unseal the casket. Give me a moment to go to my office and retrieve the casket crank please. Are you the daughter that asked for us to apply the make-up?"

"Yes I am and yes, I'll wait. Thank you."

While he was gone, I took my opportunity to make sure the arrangements were in their proper place. Scanning the parlor, everything looked to be in order. I was grateful that I didn't have to request any changes.

Arriving back to the area in seconds, the director and I made our way to the front of the room. I asked if there was some way to shield the view from my family from the scene. Luckily there was a heavy gold curtain that was able to be pulled so that privacy was maintained.

Gripping the casket key firmly within his left hand, the director asked one more time, "Ma'am, are you sure you want to do this?" His nervousness was evident as he rubbed the decorative metal grip that was attached to the five inch long Allen key.

"Sir, with all due respect, I am a big girl and can handle the sight I am about so see. I am fully aware of what is inside the casket. So, yes, I am positive that I want you to open it up."

Wiping his brow, whether there was sweat about to pour down his face or simply from his hesitance, I shook my head yes to assure him I was ready.

Clutching the tool with his right hand, he moved to the end of the casket. His plump fingers reach for the silver bolt that was on the bottom of the vault and loosens the anchor until it falls into his hand. Snatching the casket crank that dangled around his left wrist from a bracelet, he grasped it with his right hand taking it off from his wrist. Inserting the key where the bolt once was, the director turned it counter clock wise five times. Rounding the fifth turn, I heard the lock click and released the two piece cover.

Once the lid was clicked open, the director and I stepped to the front of the casket where Dad's face was soon to be revealed. The butterflies started to swirl around my stomach and the anticipation and nervousness set in. Recalling the scene that I had to clean up, I understood that his face had to be one hundred times worse. And yet, I still *had* to see it without any one true reason.

Lifting the lid that held his body, I closed my eyes momentarily. Inhaling the air deep into my lungs, I prepared myself for what I was about to see. One, two, three, open.

My eyes fluttered opened and my vision was blurred for a moment until I focused in on him. We were strangers with memories as I stood looking at his right side of his face. His skin had a tint of orange, just a bit different than the way I remembered him. His makeup wasn't too overdone, on his thinned skin in fact, he might have been able to pull off more and still look okay given the circumstances. I was happy that they hadn't overdone it with the makeup.

Then, my eyes traveled to his nose and left side of his face.

There wasn't much left except what looked like beta dine that was caked with makeup trying to conceal the raw flesh that was left. His eyes were completely gone as well as most of his nose. The empty cavity of his skull was quite gruesome as the dried blood peaked through all the concealer. I understood why the embalmer asked me so many times if I was positive about my decision. However, after seeing him, I knew I made the right choice. I had to see him to say goodbye.

I turned my head towards the director and asked if I could have a moment. Nodding, he quietly slipped behind the gold curtain.

I started to cry thinking of the man I wished him to be. Only, I knew he wasn't strong enough. His mother enabled him to be weak. She supplied him with his needs and wants. He made no money since he didn't have a job, no car to get around in, and no home he could call his own. What he did have was beer, cigarettes, music and memories. The four of those components created a pit of self-worthlessness.

"You know Dad; this isn't how it was supposed to be. I want this all to be a nightmare however, I have to accept the man you were. And sure, I can do that. I'm pretty sure I can honestly say I forgive you. You know Dad, I see things differently now. A special old man showed me a new way of thinking, Dad. He showed me that truth and acceptance can be possible. That even though someone has done wrong, doesn't mean you have to hate them for the rest of your life. If someone loves you, they accept you. I think I hated you more than I ever loved you. And that just isn't right. I grew up and moved on with my life and never gave you another chance. I'm sorry, Dad.

We were both wrong in many ways. You always chose that can over us. One time, just one time, I wanted you to choose me. But you couldn't. Now, it's over. All the pain, all the hurt can begin to dull while the memories remain in my heart as a reminder of all that I've been taught. So, I thank you for the lessons learned.

I should have been a better daughter and yeah you could have been a better dad. We each have our own conscience to deal with. I wish I could alter the way things ended and most importantly, the way they began. I would tell you how I wished I had you comfort me when I was little. I'd ask you to walk me down the aisle instead of Chris. I'd probably involve the kids with you a bit more. There are a number of things I would change. But mainly, Dad, I just wanted you to be my dad. I wanted you to try. I wanted you to be that hero that every little girl dreams of."

Reaching into my left pocket of my pin striped slacks; I felt the hard metal within my fingertips. Warm from my body heat, I guided it out to see it one last time. I was unsure last night what to do with the bullet that killed my father. Today, when a new day dawned, I knew I had to bury it with him to finalize the last disappointment he left me with. I knew that if I kept the fragment, it would only drudge up bad memories. I had to let go of my past for the good, nailing the coffin shut with him and all the heartache.

244

Grabbing a tissue from a nearby end table, I was certain that I had said all that I needed to. I ended our conversation and closed the lid to the casket. Patting my eyes so not to ruin the makeup I had applied earlier, I escaped through the heavy gold screen and found the funeral director nearby.

I cleared my throat and told him, "I'm done; you can lock it back up. Thank you for your cooperation," in the softest of voice possible before it was considered a whisper. He nodded and obliged, disappearing behind the golden drape.

I quietly slipped into the restroom to be certain that nobody could tell I had been crying. Why it mattered, I wasn't sure. This *is* a funeral home after all.

Straightening my pin striped black vest along with the collar of my lavender shirt, as I looked in the mirror, I noticed a glimpse of my eyes. They were indeed puffy and red. Knowing I needed eye drops, I reached for my purse and fumbled around for the saline and my compact. Adding a few drops to my eyes and a fresh coat of powder to my face, I felt confident I was ready to reappear.

I walked out to find my two brothers and my grandmother Cochran in the waiting area. Della and Kevin were quite reserved. They were talking to Andy since they knew him. Ethan was more open with Chris and Gram. Chloe had never hid our family to Ethan. Luckily for me, he never mentioned them in front of my kids. Gram was hugging Ethan, plastering his face with kisses while he was trying to have a conversation with his Uncle Chris.

I knew she was about to attack my children with affection so I hurriedly made my way over to all of them.

"Hi guys, glad you made it in." My words were dry due to Chris and Gram. Andy knew I meant nothing harsh to him.

I embraced my youngest brother, pleased to see him. It's been a little while since we last saw one another and I was always happy to spend time with him.

"How's it going little brother?" I asked Andy.

"Could be better, you know," his voice trailed off thinking of why he was in Pennsylvania. "Good to see you though," Andy added.

"Likewise," I said smiling.

Gram took the open opportunity to hug me as I stood there wide open without anything to block my body from her. Of course, I'd rather her hug me insanely than my children. I knew I was still working on that forgiving thing. "Let it go," I said to myself.

"Oh baby, I missed you! Why didn't you visit me and Daddy?" she asked.

Half stunned by her question, I was unsure how to answer. Not wanting to start a fight but didn't want to lie to her either. Dammit.

"Well Gram, you know how life takes over and time slips by without notice." What else was I supposed to say?

She stepped back to give herself some room. Evidently,

mentioning my father made her think of him. Her right hand reached for her lips, a familiar motion she had always done. As the waterworks filled her eyes her voice turned harsh.

"You see what that asshole did? I couldn't believe the son of a bitch did that!"

"Gram," Chloe interrupted, "please, your language!"

"Oh, sorry babe, I forgot," she apologized.

I looked at my children and I saw how wide their eyes opened as they listened to their great grandmother use foul language towards her son. I placed my hand over my mouth as my heart felt heavy knowing this was going to be a long evening.

"Why don't we all take a seat in the viewing room," I said to everyone.

As the train of people walked through the area, I felt a bit annoyed. Chris was completely ignoring me although I could tell he had been crying. Gram was being overly affectionate and mean all at the same time. Andy was emotional, which was to be expected.

I felt compelled to at least say hello to Chris so I watched as he sat down in the chair next to Gram. "Nice to see you, Chris," I began trying to be civil.

"You too. Kids are big," he replied.

"Yeah, Della is fifteen and Kevin is eleven."

"Damn, didn't think they were that old," Chris said seeming stunned. Considering he only seen Della the night she was born and never returned, I was still bitter at him for all the opportunities he had to see the kids yet he turned them down each chance.

My blood pressure was rising as I felt my face redden. Chris had always been different than me. Quite honestly, he mimicked our dad and grandmother's habits a bit too much. We would talk every few years with nothing in common. He always did most of the talking about either racing his car or his volunteer firefighter experiences. He would nonchalantly ask about the kids but when I tried to tell him about them, he would go off on another tangent concerning him instead of listening to me about the kids. Infuriated with his selfishness, I usually ended the conversation on a sour note and I wouldn't hear from him in a year or two. His famous last words were always, "You're dead to me."

I headed back to where the kids were sitting. Smiling at them, I gave them a warm smile to comfort their shy faces. I was sure they had to feel uneasy with the two additional family members they had never really gotten to know. Bending down in front of them, I took a hand from each of them and asked if they were doing alright. Both kids shook their heads yes which eased my weariness. Just then, I heard chatter coming from the main entrance. I glanced at my watch and saw that it was almost four o'clock. As I looked up, I met the eyes of the man I fell in love with so many years before. "Thank God," I thought to myself.

Everett and Kathleen followed Nick into the viewing room. I stood up to greet the three of them with a hug.

"Hey sweetie," I conversed softly. "Did you find the place without difficulty?"

"It was a piece of cake thanks to our g.p.s.," he said proudly.

I expressed my gratitude to Kathleen and Everett for coming as well. They surely didn't have to since they never met the man. However, out of respect, they wanted to come.

Nick and his parents took their seats next to the kids. Once they sat down, I heard the floor creek, signaling more family to pay their respects. I only expected a handful of people to come because Dad ended up making more enemies than friends.

Within the next fifteen minutes, my cousin Sarah had shown up as well as Mom and Howie, Hailey, a couple cousins that I barely remembered from my childhood. Fred and Emma came as well as Isabelle and her children. Having these familiar faces sure eased my mind. Finally, the one person I never expected to see- Gretchen.

My heart soared when I saw her face. I couldn't believe she made yet another trip back home in such a short time. Gretchen was one person I knew would never let me down. Knowing I had her and Hailey there for support made this easier to endure.

"Gretch, I can't believe you're here! I told you that you didn't have to come back but I'm so thankful you did! I love ya girl," I said as I wrapped my arms around her neck.

"Now you know full well I wouldn't let you to the wolves alone," she confided quietly nodding at my grandmother and Chris.

"You're an amazing friend. I'm a lucky girl. And, I finally

took some of your advice from long ago. I started to trust people a little more. I know not everyone is out to hurt me and Hailey is one of the ones I began to trust recently. I want you to meet her, she's so awesome. I know you will love her too!"

I introduced the two and they started chatting with ease. They shared many interests and hobbies so I knew they would have plenty to talk about.

Skimming the room to ensure everyone was at ease and no fights were about to break out, I felt comfortable as I heard laughter and conversations emerge between long lost relatives. Everyone seemed to completely ignore the fact as to why we were here. It kind of made me sad to think most of these people were here for me and not Dad. And although the casket was closed, not one person made their way to the front of the room yet. It sure reminded me of Mr. Hopkins. Maybe I was just being overly sensitive. Or maybe, I realized I loved the man I called my father. But how after all he put me through? Maybe it was our talk we had when I had the funeral director open the casket.

The clock in the office began to chime loudly a total of five times. I couldn't believe how fast time was passing. The funeral director emerged from his office that contained the piercing clock. I caught his gesture that it was time to start the service. I shook my head okay as he made his way to the front near the casket. There was a wooden pulpit in the far left corner that remained hidden behind the gold curtain until now as I watched him pull it out.

All the conversations started to simmer down as the director cleared his throat to obtain the attention of the small crowd.

I heard shushing sounds from my brother Chris, trying to steal the limelight as if he had authority. I rolled my eyes in disgust wondering if he honestly thought he was making that much of a difference in an already quiet room.

"Good evening fellow family and friends. We are here to celebrate the life of Chris Cochran," he began as he stood in front of us in his poorly tailored navy blue suit.

He went on with his speech, as I am sure he does with every other ceremony. His words felt meaningless and unemotional. He never knew my father. He could only go by what my sister had previously told him. His message was empty and dry. As he closed with his final words, I knew my turn would be next. No one else wanted to stand in front and talk because they didn't want to cry in front of others. Chloe and Andy both asked me earlier if I would be willing to speak of him. It surprised me when they asked since they knew the relationship I have had with him over the years. Nil. However, they knew I wouldn't condemn him and would voice my thoughts in a more intricate way than they would. Being the "professional" as they liked to call me had its pro's and con's. I wasn't sure if that was an honor or not but I knew I had to do this for them.

"And now, Chris's daughter Jillian has a few things to share with us," the director ended as he cued for me.

I stood up from the padded burgundy chair. Last night before I laid down, I pondered writing down what I wanted to say. Instead, I decided to wing it and hope my message came across without getting tongue tied or not making any sense. Suddenly, I wished I had prepared at least some key points. Too late now, as the butterflies started to flutter and my stomach was knotted up like the old pine I felt at work days before.

I made my way to the old but sturdy pulpit. Fidgeting with my vest and collared shirt, I made eye contact with Nick, then to Hailey and eventually Gretchen. Warmth flowed from each of them and into my heart. I took a deep breath and felt my courage mount.

"Good evening. As you all know, I am Jillian, the first daughter to Chris Cochran." I felt a bit silly saying that but, there was my professionalism shining through.

Deciding to alter my line of thinking, I wanted to be honest instead of politically correct. I stopped for a minute, trying to collect my thoughts.

"Okay, so we all know who I am. The reason we are here is to pay our respects to a man that touched us each in different ways. Some were good while others were not so great.

I can't stand up here and tell you all lies that my dad was this wonderful person with great characteristics. I wish I could say he offered the world a magnitude of greatness. At one time, I know he had the potential. Unfortunately, Satan paved his path with fool's gold promising him the ability to revisit the past and have a chance at altering all of his mistakes.

One thing is for sure, the man loved his beer. And no disrespect to Howie, but I know he loved Mom until he died. Clearly, the can of alcohol took precedence over anything or anyone else including his marriage and children. He escaped his reality, hiding from life and all that it had to offer. His weakness, his fear, and his actions haunted him more than anyone could fathom."

I stopped to take a breath and quickly decide where I wanted to go from here. I scanned the crowd as a few shifted in their seats waiting for me to continue. I noticed Gram sitting there, almost gray in color. She had to feel broken inside, as the one thing she had in life was now gone, her son.

"Two weeks ago, I was a different woman. I hid my past from my husband and children trying to protect them from a man I despised. I realize now, I should have climbed out of my shell and been honest with those that accept me for who I am and where I came from. Now, I ask you for your patience and just listen to my story.

I have a willow tree behind our home, thanks to my husband, Nick. I visit my sacred ground for many reasons. It's a place I go to think, reflect, and find peace. To me, it represents God and all His glory. I find strength to go on. With the beauty of divine intervention, I leave with an altered philosophy, knowing that I am a better person.

Dad had no place of his own. He lived with his mother for most of his life, relying solely on her to tend to his needs and wants. He lost the word of God and signs of hope. He knew he screwed up his life in more ways than one. So, he plummeted until he hit the lowest point he has ever felt.

When he pulled the trigger, he ended all of his pain, his guilt, and ultimately his life. I don't pity him, instead, I forgive him. I now see that sometimes people just don't have the drive to do any better especially, when you have someone else to take the lead for you.

So, Dad," I turned to look at the casket, "I'm sorry I wasn't there for you at your weakest hour. I'm not sure I would have been able to change your mind, but I could have at least told you I forgive you. To hopefully put your mind at ease knowing I became a better person through your mistakes. May our Lord have mercy on your soul," I touched the casket, meaning every word.

"Amen," Gram hoarsely stated with tears running down her face. I looked at her straight in the eye as she wiped her nose with her hanky. We locked visual contact and she mouthed, "I love you." Before I could manage any sort of action, she took her last breath and slouched in her chair.

My heart stopped and the air caught in my throat.

"Oh my God," I exclaimed out loud.

Chaos was about to break out, so I quickly reacted and

summoned the director, asking him to have everyone remain in their seats.

I made my way over to where Gram was sitting. I tried to shake her hoping she might have just fallen asleep. Nothing. I felt for a pulse. None. "Dammit, she's gone," I declared looking at Gretchen and Nick. I hung my head knowing this makes three. I didn't understand why God chose now to take the third soul, nevertheless, she was gone.

Chris was quick to lower her to the floor and try to save her. He was glaring at me as though I had killed her. He began mouth to mouth and chest compressions on Gram.

"Chris, please, let her go, she's gone. Chris! Stop! She's gone," I yelled.

I tried to pull Chris off of her but he was too strong for me. "Don't touch me, bitch," he defied.

"Don't talk to my wife like that," Nick defended.

"Fuck you and your wife. You think you're better than me with all your fancy shit. I'm trying to save my grandmother so, shut the fuck up." Chris was displaying quite a scene.

By this time, people began building a circle around the location, witnessing Chris act like a fool. I spotted Nick balling up his fists ready to fight.

"Nick, I will handle this," Andy broke through the crowd declaring.

Andy bent down and touched Chris's shoulder.

"Dude, let her go. She's with Dad. Let them be together." His words were kind and soft.

"No, I can't. I can't lose both of them at once," Chris began to cry harder than I have ever seen before. Ceasing his efforts to resuscitate her, he laid his head on her chest. "God, no. Why? Why?" he whimpered like a child.

The next half hour was mostly a blur. Everyone was in shock of her death at her son's funeral. There were many apologies and hugs. The police came to confirm the death and her body was taken out of sight.

Gretchen and Hailey noticed that I wasn't coherent to my surroundings so they walked me outside for some air.

"Jill, are you alright?" Gretchen asked.

I could only stare with nothing in sight but blurriness.

I felt Hailey shake me a bit trying to bring me to out of my trance.

A sense of panic stuck in Hailey's tone, "Jill, please focus." She clicked her fingers in front of my eyes and I forced myself to regain my composure.

"Yeah," I started to say.

"Jillian Davenport!" Gretchen yelled. "Talk to us!"

"Yeah, I'm here now. I'm sorry. I must have zoned out."

"Oh, thank God," they said in unison.

"You had me worried girlie," Hailey confided.

"Me too," Gretchen added and then asked, "Are you sure you're okay?"

"Yes, I will be fine. This has been quite a day. I'm sorry girls. I guess my mind just needed a getaway."

The girls each gave me a hug and asked another four times if I was sure I was alright. Adamant that I was able to go back in, they finally believed me and we joined the rest of my family.

I found Nick and my children saying goodbye to people they met tonight for the first time at the door. I joined in and hugged and thanked each person that was leaving. I heard "I'm sorry" and "if you need anything" with each person, knowing only a select few would actually come through with their promise.

Soon, the funeral home was left with me, my family and two best friends, my siblings, Mom and Howie and Nick's parents.

"Well, everyone can follow us to my place for dinner if you'd like," announced Chloe.

"Nick, I can drive your truck home if you want to ride with Jill and the kids," Everett offered and subtlety saying thanks but no thanks for the invitation.

"Sure Dad, thanks. I will get my truck after we are done at Chloe's. Do you remember how to get home?" Nick asked.

"It shouldn't be a problem," Everett promised.

They shook hands and I hugged each of them, thanking them for their support.

Looking at Gretchen and Hailey, I questioned if they were

going to Chloe's for dinner. Gretchen was an affirmative yes and Hailey said as long as Chloe doesn't mind she would love to join us.

"Of course," Chloe answered.

"Great! Chloe, do you guys want to lead the pack and we will take the back so we don't lose anyone?" I asked.

"Sounds like a plan."

Everyone grabbed their belongings and headed out the door. I took my time and took one last look at the casket.

"Goodbye, Dad," and I closed the door behind me with the question lingering in the back of my mind. How do the weak survive?

The old beaten town hasn't changed much since the last time I visited years ago. Houses falling in with grass about a foot high in multiple yards. Coming to one of the few stop lights in town, it turned red requiring me to stop and take in all the brokenness this town had on display. Looking up, I had seen my two naive children amazed of all the bleak scenery. To my right, is my husband with a look of pity for a town that seen its glory days when the steel mills were at their peak.

I was fortunate; I vanished from the poverty-stricken countryside never to look back. I didn't let fear hold me in place, pretending to be content, that the rest of the population seemed to be doing. I knew in my heart I had more self-worth, a surplus of wisdom to give back to the world. I wasn't going to settle for a meager sliver of pie when I was worthy of the whole thing. I knew God had blessed me infinitely.

Breaking the cycle is probably one of the toughest things a person can do. It changes your direction, it sways your thoughts, you realize life can and will be better. And most importantly, it changes *YOU* as a person…for the better.

The traffic signal turned green and I heard yet another horn blaring as if I hadn't noticed. Creeping past the light, I pulled over to an empty lot. Without a word, I leaned over and kissed Nick. "I'm a lucky girl because of you, Nick Davenport." Unconditional love and acceptance is the ultimate blessing one can have.

I looked back to Della and Kevin smiling with tears streaming down, knowing how incredible our journey has been. That's when it all clicked together and made sense. I finally had the answer to the one question that has probed me for decades. The final piece of the puzzle was added and serenity was found.

I used to wonder how the weak survived. Now, I realize I was weak due to my fear of being judged by others because of whom and what I came from instead of who I am today. I'm *not* my parents; I am Jillian Davenport. I understand now that only *I* can break the cycle of abuse and fear. I have learned that life does get better when you have faith, courage, love, and most of all, hope.

Those choices have enabled me to better myself. I shouldn't disregard my past but instead embrace it and yell from the rooftop, "I made it!"

Epilogue

Two Years Later

The room remains silent immediately after the video ends. The screams from the little girl echoed thunderously throughout my entire being. The child was filled with fear for her mother's life. It left the audience aching to reach out and help the girl. I knew the clip was going to be played. I listened to it ten times before the event. And yet, as I sat at the round table centered in the front of the church, it brought out every emotion I tried to contain. The lump positioned in the middle of my throat was not budging until I allowed myself to release a tear. A moment of terror surged throughout my body as I realized I was about to go up on stage and give my testimony. How on Earth was I going to talk to a group of people I never met? And to further my anxiety, my mother in law, Kathleen and sister in law, Emma were sitting in direct view from the podium.

"How did I get here?" I quietly ask myself before standing up.

Two and a half weeks ago I would have never thought I'd be embarking on a new adventure such as this. Public speaking was never something I felt I could do, nor did I think an opportunity would ever arise.

261

I had heard about a local ministry trying to start up to help women in domestic violent situations. It was a great cause and I agreed that more help was needed. After all, I knew how it felt to grow up in such a home. I contemplated trying to help out with it but never got around to contacting the president of the ministry. Then, I heard about the kickoff fundraiser dinner they had scheduled. That's when God's hands began to intertwine me and ministry together. I contacted the president of the ministry asking if she needed a speaker. I couldn't believe what I was doing. I didn't understand why I was even asking. I just felt like I needed to ask. A force had overcome my shaking fingers as I typed the question: "do you have any speakers for your event?"

"I have one," she began, "but I'd love to have another. Are you interested?"

Talking to a crowd of people about my childhood? I couldn't do it. I *won't* do it. My thoughts were yelling "No! Are you crazy? No!" but my fingers typed, "yes..."

And there I was, heart beating faster than a cheetah can run. I made a vow to speak at a dinner to raise funds to help battered women. Me, speaking to a crowd of people, about a childhood I kept secret for twenty years. At that moment, I handed the keys over to God and said, "You're driving. I don't know the way of your will so I'll buckle up and hold on tight."

Feeling the rush of reality slam me in the face, the memory

of the little girl from the video pulsates my eardrums, "Mommy! Mommy!" The video might have just ended but the flashback of me calling 911 kept playing over and over.

I felt my legs rise in the upright position and I am walking to the podium with a microphone in my right hand. I totally missed the host introducing me to the attendees of the benefit dinner. I felt the tiny beads of sweat along my forehead threatening to roll down the sides of my cheeks. My heart beats like a set of drums at a rock concert. Stepping in front at the very center of the room, I'm facing my lion. The moment of truth when I discover who is actually in control. I close my eyes and inhale deeply.

"Dear Lord, be with me as I deliver a message of hope. Amen." I pray silently.

My vision restores as my eyes flutter open and I scan the room. I had everything written out as to what I planned on saying. But the clip that was shown, I knew I had to address it with the crowd. Clearing my throat and choking back tears, my voice begins to speak.

"The video that just played brings back many memories for me. You see, I was like that girl. My father had thrown my mom against the refrigerator and I was scared. I called 911 just as that little girl did. Only my call was quickly ended as my grandmother, my father's mom, hung up the phone. The emergency dispatcher called back and my grandmother answered reassuring them that I had made a mistake and there wasn't an emergency." I shook my head desperately trying to rid the memory so that I could begin what I had intended. But as I did that, a peace poured over me like I was just washed in water and made clean again.

"I'm not sure why but I feel like self-destruction is closing in on me." My voice was steady without cracking holding strong with the passion I felt inside about to be conveyed.

"I'd like for each of you to imagine yourself with these thoughts: I'm not good enough. I'm so weak how can I manage on my own with my kids? I haven't had the courage to get out because I find every excuse to stay. I feel like giving up but I can't because I keep holding onto a bare thread that dangles me in the air like a puppet. Maybe it's the books I read, the songs that loiter in my thoughts, the television that conditions us to become numb of emotion. This heaviness on my heart is more than I can bear. I just want to shut out the world and not look ahead of me. I only have myself to blame for the way he treats me. It's my fault he did this. Welcome to hopelessness. " As I spoke the last sentence, I scanned the room and one woman in particular caught my attention. She was probably around mid-thirties and about to deliver her child at any moment.

"Who all feels that way? Do you have thoughts like these? Or do you know a friend or family member in this same situation? The fear of everything, creating doubt and worry that succumbs your entire body until you feel nothing but weakness. Nothing but," and I pause for just a fraction of time, "hopelessness," annunciating the word as though every bit of life was taken out of my soul.

"Now, imagine you're ten years old with similar thoughts, fears, and worries. The only difference is you can't put your emotions into words because if you do, it makes it real."

Here's the hardest part. This is when I know who is in control of my life because I know I can't do this alone. "Father, help me," I beg in silent prayer.

"Hello, my name is Jillian Davenport and I am a survivor of domestic abuse." I did it! Praise God, I said the words out loud! A smile crept across my face. I can't help it honestly. It's a new chapter of my life, a clean page to start fresh. I have been washed in the blood of Jesus. This moment, right now, begins a brand new journey.

My words are filled with truth and conviction as I continue. "I was the oldest of four children who attempted to protect my brothers and sister as well as my mom from the man us kids called 'Daddy'. We grew up in a home that was filled with fear, physical and mental abuse, and a raging anger that lashed out anytime a beer can filled his ego enough with liquid courage.

"You see, children watch adults as their wondering eyes catch the smallest of clues. Their young ears hear the harsh words spoken, despite their mother's best efforts at keeping him quiet. Their hearts feel the pain watching you go through this battle. Their minds begin to resent circumstances that, in their opinion, could be changed. And in my case, I felt all of those. I hurt for my mother; I felt the need to protect her and my siblings from the monster that made my nightmares seem pleasant." My eyes dance from face to face until I find the pregnant lady sitting there, crying. Her tears pierced my heart and I thought, "Please don't cry, please."

The fire in my heart was dominate. I felt the Holy Spirit within me and I knew I had to fulfill His will. I was about to dig deep into my childhood and put on display just how I grew up. There was no room for fear of judgment or criticism. So I continue.

"I distinctly remember second grade. At the time, we lived in the projects as the stench of stale beer and cigarette smoke danced around my nostrils on a daily basis. Almost every morning I'd wake up and complain of a stomach ache. Other times I'd say I had a headache. I made excuse after excuse as to why I shouldn't go to school. I wasn't lying, I always felt ill. But why?" I stopped for a moment to let the audience ponder. "One fear- I'd come home to find my mother dead. Seven years old, petrified I'd lose the one woman that I tried to protect day after day."

Looking over to the right of the room my vision captures Hailey. Over the last two years our friendship underwent a dramatic turn. We were more than mere acquaintances that only saw one another at work and an occasional dinner. We started to integrate ourselves and our families together more so than ever before. Dinners, movies, boating, and a tremendous amount of talking became the routine for all of us. And her smiling as I look at her now gives me a reassurance that I'm doing the right thing. Not that I doubted, but it's certainly nice to have her here tonight.

"His control over us was a death grip filled with vengeance. He rarely let my mom out of his sight, listened in on phone calls, and accused her of cheating. Calling her names, telling her how worthless she was, and no man would ever want her with 'baggage'. Baggage meaning us four kids that he helped create." The hurt I felt for years stung a bit as I recall my father calling me baggage. "It was his way of keeping her filled with fear so that she didn't leave. I recall begging her during private moments to whisk us away from a man I viewed as one of the devils workers. She worked up the courage to leave a few times and each time she returned the abuse got worse."

"I witnessed my mother being thrown from one end of a room to the next. Every yank on her arm, each slap to the face was observed by my young eyes. I saw how she was rammed into the television sending her body doubled over in pain. And I saw her limp body slide down the front of the refrigerator door because his fit of rage hit its peak with his mother and me standing right there. During my fourth grade year, I walked into the bedroom that my parents shared in my maternal grandmother's home. With my grandmother standing behind me, we witnessed my father with the cold barrel of a shotgun hugging my mother's nose. 'Don't make me pull the trigger,' he said to my mom. Out of the corner of his eye, he

267

then noticed me and my gram. He laughed to try to ease the terror in our eyes and said, 'it's not loaded,' as if that made it all better. I pleaded with the Lord for His refuge because I knew that was the only way we'd survive."

I heard a gasp exhale out of woman directly in front of me. I look up to find my mother-in-law Kathleen shaking her head. A tear had escaped as our eyes became deadlocked on one another. Over the last two years, I had shared only a handful of stories of my childhood with her. It wasn't easy and I usually ended up choking on my words and leaving the room. I didn't understand how I could be so strong when I spoke to my husband and children and even with Hailey but it was incredibly difficult when it was to anyone else. And here I am now, telling my story in front of a hundred people.

"Like branches on a willow flapping aimlessly, we moved from place to place regularly. I attended ten different schools throughout my education. When this piece of information is leaked out, I usually get asked if my father was in the military. I used to shake my head no and change the subject. Who wants to say, 'No, my father doesn't work and we live off the system. Usually we move because my parents can't pay the bills. Either we get kicked out or they find a cheaper place to rent.' New place usually meant new school district. So practically every year, I met a new set of faces. And every year, it became easier for me to mask my pain, essentially hiding my home life from society's *fantasy* world." The word fantasy rolled off my tongue quite bitter and I wanted to take it back but I couldn't. I wasn't angry with the world or even this room of people but their hearts needed to be taught. Domestic violence is very much real, happens daily, and it hurts more than they realize. So, I proceed.

"I was petrified of their judgment because I was different. Quiet as a church mouse, I would sit in the back of the class whenever possible. Passing each grade level with C's and D's, putting forth as little effort as possible because I was too worried about what was going to happen when the lights went out. I had only one friend that I trusted and she went to a different school. Everyone else…well there really was no point in even attempting to make a friend. I'd just be gone next year and I had to worry about if someone found out and reported us. What if a teacher would look in my eyes and see the torture within myself I desperately tried to conceal. What if… Children and Youth services took me and my siblings away from my parents and then I'd have absolute no way to protect my mom."

The threat of CYS taking us off our mom weighed heavy on my heart for many years. That was a constant worry growing up. It's one thing I wanted the audience to know. A life filled of domestic violence had its consequences. It carried many burdens on the shoulders of the one being abused, but it also affected the children in more ways than one.

"I can stand in front of all of you and recap my entire life for hours. Chapter after chapter my words filling blank pages supplying much needed details and reasoning's. They would include the divorce of my parents that I cried out in joy for. How I refused to let my father walk me down the aisle when I married my husband." A deep gasp from the very back of the room snagged my attention. I didn't know who it was but it must have astounded the man. I refocused and went on.

"That dark cloud wasn't lifted for long because a new step dad brought on more abuse. I got a broken nose from the hands of that new man my mother loved as I defended her honor. I remember when I was fifteen and he laid on top of me and ask if I liked the weight of a man on me. When I said 'No, get off me,' he laughed and said 'Oh, one day you will honey.' He was a man I hated just as much as my father. Maybe even more. He drank, he smoked weed regularly and he hardly worked. Women tend to go after the same type of men. My mom was no different than the statistics. So, the cycle continued. I was miserable filled with anger and resentment. Finally, I couldn't go on living in such an abusive realm, I moved out my senior year of high school. I went to school and worked as many hours as possible until I graduated high school. The only thing I regret was leaving behind my two youngest siblings. I felt like I abandoned both of them as I saw the fear in their eyes, pleading with me to stay. But I had to get out for my own sanity. My heart aches as I think of my siblings faces when I said I was moving out. My gosh it was a horrible feeling. All of the fear, all of the pain, all of the abuse. And I left them there. I've questioned myself for years always living with that guilt on my shoulders."

Taking a deep breath, I stare straight into the eyes of the crying pregnant lady. Her delicate slender fingers find another tissue. I just want to go and hug her. 'Just wait and dry your tears,' I think to myself, 'because the story has a victory!'

"I harbored resentment towards my mom for the choices she had made over time even up until the last couple years of my life. I blamed her for a portion of who I had become because of the pressure that was placed upon my shoulders. 'You're my right hand' she'd say. At first being so young I felt like it was almost an honor to be *that* needed. *That* wanted. But as time marched on it was more of a curse. Building a true mother-daughter relationship wasn't something we did. It was more of a mother-friend kind of thing. At fifteen years old I didn't need a friend, I needed a mom. I carried that with me for many years, hiding from myself and my mom the resentment I concealed. And as I kept the feelings at bay for all that time, I've never opened up to her about it releasing the truth of how I actually felt. I allowed the anger and frustration to build up for far too long. When I asked myself why I never told her, the answer was plain to see. I never wanted to hurt her because I already knew what it felt like. I held a grudge when in reality, she had no clue. There came a point where I had to stop placing blame on her choices and start taking accountability for my own. I've learned from it and it

271

was time to put to rest the emptiness of a relationship and begin building a new one."

Being very candid about my mom was one of the hardest parts of this. Especially, since I only recently had the courage to talk to her about it. As I wrote this days before the dinner, I heavily contemplated even adding it. But like I said in the very beginning, once you say it out loud, it makes it real and you are forced to deal with it. And there it all was, out in the open.

"For a long time, there were many moments when I felt that hopelessness that I mentioned earlier. According to various family members, we were destined for failure. The black sheep of the family had no means or knowledge to achieve great things. But you see here's what they didn't know. I had a faith inside that I drew strength from. I knew about God and I had heard his promises. He gave me a hope that I desperately needed. That doesn't mean I didn't stumble along the way. Sure, I said things I shouldn't have. I've done things I knew were wrong. I intentionally hurt others," I stopped and scanned the entire room, "because they hurt me." I need the audience to understand that I have done a lot of wrongdoings too. Regardless of any excuse, I sin just as everyone else and this is my way to try and teach others not to deliberately cause anguish to others.

"No, I'm not perfect. However, God had a plan so He placed particular people along my path to guide my way and they planted seeds. Those special individuals included my maternal grandmother that offered silent strength and security. The stability she offered was my only saving grace until she passed away when I was thirteen. She's been gone for over three decades and I still miss her terribly. When God blessed us with a daughter we named her after my gram. The moment I saw my daughter's eyes, I knew they were a carbon copy of my Grams. It gave me comfort knowing a part of my Gram will always be remembered through my daughter's eyes." My mind instantly goes to Della. What a soft soul she has that makes her so easy to love.

"I also had my best friend of thirty plus year that I was able to confide in with all of my secrets and who offered a shoulder to lean on. The miles have always been between us and yet we have remained as close as sisters. She's been a woman I've admired and trusted over the years.

"There was a pastor in my early teens that I listened to numerous sermons from, etching hope into my heart. She also taught me something that wasn't typical knowledge in my home- love. The love she showed to me was like Ephesians 5:2 *Walk in love, even as Christ also loved us and gave himself up for us, an offering and a sacrifice to God for a sweet-smelling fragrance.* A true Christian love that held no grudges or judgment. It was her compassion given by the Holy Spirit that got me to smile knowing one day my life would change." Smiling as I speak about her, I know I'll always treasure the lessons I have learned from her.

273

"At nineteen, I met a man that I knew I was going to marry. Two years later I took his hand in marriage. He taught me about a new life and he showed me the type of person I wanted to be." My voice rose in excitement as this is the turning point for my story.

"Those seeds took root and I began the very slow process of discovering my self-worth, my abilities, and what I wanted out of my life. Plus, I had the determination set forth from the pitiful whispers of family members predicting what failures we would be, that gave me the edge I needed for success." The words were flowing without hesitation or apprehension. It's as though it's second nature for me being in the center speaking. I think God is telling me something but I don't have time to think about that now because now is the time that defines the purpose of me speaking. This is the message that was meant to be conveyed to others so they will know that our Father provides for all of our needs. Hope, salvation, redemption, and mercy, yes our Lord provides. I smile as I am about to cross the finish line of my testimony.

"For as long as I can remember, I knew my upbringing wasn't what it was supposed to be in life. I knew that alcoholism and hitting women and children are wrong. We were a broken family and not just because my parents were divorced. Our souls were wounded and bleeding out. We were consumed with shame, guilt and broken heartedness. In abusive relationships neither love nor obedience to the Lord is carried out. So, I made difficult choices, I broke the cycle that so many think they have the inability to do. As I got older, I forgave those I needed to and learned to embrace my upbringing, using it as a tool to become better instead of using that as an excuse or to gain pity. There are three words I used to become the strong, independent and confident woman I am today: Faith, Hope, and Inspiration. With God and His love you will have hope. And with hope comes inspiration. Inspiration will not only open your heart but the doors to new possibilities, a chance at a life you deserve. And I stand here before you all tonight, to plant a seed of hope. If you're living a life filled with abuse, you have a support system right here to help you climb your way out of the ashes and scale that mountain and yell, "I made it!"

The audience quickly rose out of their seats and started clapping feverishly. I looked to my right to find Hailey only to find her crying and smiling at the same time clapping her hands together. Emma and Kathleen both teary eyed and clapping were right in front of me. I handed the microphone back to the host and met my family at the table. Emma quickly embraced me with an intense hug. "I'm so proud of you," she whispered. I nodded, and thanked her and took my seat as the others followed suit.

The president closed up the event with some final words and contact information. She thanked everyone for attending and clapping erupted once again.

"Wow," I thought, "wow." It's the only word that could sum up the entire night. I didn't have much time to reflect back on anything as audience members came over to me. There were numerous hugs and thank you's. The smiles, the tears, the hugs were very touching. I guess I didn't expect any of that. I simply told my story. I told the truth.

It is at this moment, when I fully understand the meaning of my preachers words when he said, "It's not what you can do for God, it's what God can do through you. But you have to be obedient enough to trust His will and not your own." For so many years I painted myself as though I was some plastic superhero of an ordinary person with super human capabilities. I wore my cape and mask in front of others while I portrayed as though I was complete and whole inside and out. I went to work, activities, school functions, and even church, hiding my brokenness to everyone including my own family. I was quick to paint a few brush strokes to cover any blemish and forge a smile to hide the pain. My arms moved with robotic nature while my legs only bent with force as my head was held together with a metal pin attaching itself to the rest of my body. The mask that covered my eyes was a shield to protect the tears I didn't want anyone to notice. The cape was tied too tight around my neck and often felt like a noose.

My life as an adult was good in comparison to others, but was it really perfect? No way. The secrets I locked deep within the chambers of my heart ate a whole into my soul. I've experienced shame and heartache. I know the guilt that builds within that manipulates you into believing you deserve this. That it's somehow your fault. That's when we must fight evil with good. It's knowing scripture, not to say we know it, but to actually live out what He asks of us. To apply every lesson we can learn into the world around us. And it's because of His love and grace, I have been set free of the bondage from the superhero image. There is nothing in this world that God can't handle. There's nothing in life that God can't turn to good for His glory.

My attention was brought back to the swarm of people around me. I wanted to find that pregnant lady and just give her a huge hug. But, it seemed every time I turned there was someone else ready to talk to me. One woman said she felt like I was up there telling her exact same story. I thank her for her willingness to share and finally close in on the teary pregnant lady.

"Hi there," I began.

She greets me with a halfhearted smile and thanked me for speaking. I was sensing some story was behind the emotion but I also knew with pregnancy hormones are raging with many highs and lows.

I return the smile and say, "I appreciate you coming tonight. I kept glancing your way when I was speaking. I'm sorry you were crying so much. As I was talking I wanted to tell you that it all turns out okay just give me a few minutes to get to that part!."

We both chuckle but my attention is diverted to yet another lady. So, I shake the pregnant ladies hand and the other lady and I take a few steps away from the crowd. "I can't help but feel overwhelmed with your words. In a good way though. You have helped me to understand how my daughter has felt over the years. I really needed to know that. Thank you." She squeezed my frame extremely tight. Her words catch me off guard at first. I think to myself how I got to this point in the first place. I know that healing was needed and admitting I had a problem was the first step. The second is having the courage to say it out loud because once I did, it made the issues real. It was at that point when I began speaking about my imperfections, my family's shortcomings and hidden sins that the superhero mask was lifted and truth prevailed. I feel incredibly blessed she appreciated my story because I know my testimony helped someone. It's not necessarily the fact that it's *my* story, but a voice. A compassionate voice that was bold enough to speak the truth about a subject that so many fall victim to. I'm serving others just as Jesus served us. And that, I believe, is the entire point of it all.

Because of You

I feel like I'm suffocating
Because of you, I am able to breathe

Noise fills my ears with destructive criticize
Because of you, I have silence

My heart stumbles and falls almost flat
Because of you, I am able to feel my heart beat

The darkness surrounds my vision
Because of you, light peeks through

Pride swells my ego like a balloon
Because of you, I am humbled

My emotions are in turmoil
Because of you, I have peace

Malice pummels my core
Because of you, I know who's in control

The invisible wounds pour out toxins

Shannon Bibby

But because of you, I have scars

My greatest weaknesses haunt me
Because of you, they are my greatest attributes

Swirling thoughts fog my eyes
Because of you, I find joy

I carry around a rock in my chest
Because of you, my heart is softened

Shame and guilt curdles my stomach
Because of you, I'm offered redemption

I'm brought to my knees
But because of you, I have strength

Difficult words from a trusted ally
Because of you, I find Truth

When the storm just won't stop
Because of you, I rejoice

Safe Under the Willow

The puzzle is scattered in a million pieces
Because of you, it's completed into a masterpiece

The path I'm faced with splits
Because of you, I see the direction

When I think I don't have enough
Because of you, my needs are met

Tears pour down my cheeks
But because of you they wash me clean

I can't seem to take another step forward
Because of you, I take two

Perfection isn't humanly attainable
Because of you, I'm given your perfect love

Because of you, I'm granted life
Because of you, I'm offered grace
Because of you, I'm given a purpose
Because of you Lord, I am me

Shannon Bibby

Note from the Author

I'd like to take a moment to reflect upon the story you have just read. Although this book is considered fiction, it includes situations that I have personally found myself in. Initially, I wanted this story to go out to the general public under the assumption that it's completely made up. But if I had chosen that route, God wouldn't receive His glory. Dear Reader, understand that the world is filled of evil that lurks around every corner and slips in unnoticed. Whether it's in our schools, our government, our churches, or our homes including our daily lives, we must acknowledge when it's our duty to take a stand against the evil forces of Satan. This was one of those times in my life that I knew I had to be courageous enough to latch onto the Lords hand and go into battle.

This book isn't perfect. This book isn't grammatically correct nor has it been edited. I've been told on numerous occasions that the literary world of readers and writers can and will bring attention to those mistakes found throughout this book and will post poor reviews because of those errors. I have contemplated heavily for a long time whether or not to release this book as it's written or have it professionally edited before its debut. The defining moment was when this revelation came about: My life wasn't edited. In fact, it was quite messy filled with blunders and wrong turns. So, I prayed. And then prayed some more. And here's what God revealed to me:

"This book may not be perfectly written, but it will be the perfect message for those who God calls to hear it."

This is more about reaching for truth. It's extending a hand to those left hopeless in a world filled of self-righteousness and judgment. It's *not* about shaming anyone. The message is about picking those up who need a boost. For years, I hid the truth of my childhood to various family members and friends. It was over and done with, why would I revisit old wounds? Opening up and revealing the truth was scarier than actually living in the abuse. I thought to myself, "I broke the cycle, what does it matter anymore?" Yes, the anger and resentment still lingered. My pain and hurt lashed out at times. Simply put, I needed a physician. And that great healer was Jesus Christ. One day everything clicked together and I knew I was supposed to start writing. I found out later that God had a plan in mind. And that plan began with this book. A valuable lesson He taught me was that the Lord has a divine plan for each of us. However, that plan isn't in your future- it's here and now. In everyday life with all those you interact with. With all that you feel, all that you breathe. He is in YOU living through YOU Every. Single. Day. His plan for you is now. Not twenty years from now- not a year from now. But *today*. And every day you are given. Listen to His guidance. He'll take you where you need to go.

There were years where I was foolish enough to believe I could carry the heavy load upon my shoulders all by myself. We have flaws and blemishes that we'd like to bury under a giant willow tree praying no one tries to dig up our demons. Our whispers usually go unnoticed. Our silent tears flow at night when no one is looking. The wounds that scab over never truly turn into scars because the littlest scratch will start the blood flowing again. I've found that scars don't hurt but wounds do. And because we shove all the pain and hurt deep within the chambers of our hearts, we don't allow God to work miracles in our lives. Sometimes He sends us a person to glue together the tiny particles of the ashes left in the wake of the fire. Because of Him, they help mend the brokenness of our heart, mind, and soul. The secret is to know when to allow the person He sends in and permit them to get close enough to the rawness of truth that we shield from society. Those that He sends will listen and accept you for exactly who you are. They take the time to care. They take the time to be your friend. They take the time to love you unconditional. And because of all they show you, the walls that you've built so sturdy will tumble down into a pile of rubble. Other times He sends us items such as books. It will bring a new light, a new hope-like I pray this book will do for you. And often, there's times where we solely have Him. Remember dear friend, you are never truly alone because we have the Holy Spirit within us. I remember many nights as I prayed I felt our Lord holding me tightly in His arms. I sought after His refuge and it sustained me. I felt the comfort He delivered as I cried asking how I can mend. I just wanted to feel normal, if there even is such a thing. What He gave was more than the feeling of normalcy. He gave peace and a much needed rest. You can have that too. Know that I am praying for you with whatever your need may be. We have a powerful God who sees and hears our cries. When we hit our knees, He's bending down to help us up. There's nothing, no nothing, He can't fix. So regardless of what you've done in your life, it doesn't change the fact that God loves _you_ for exactly who you are. And He's ready to help if you allow Him. If you're looking for a change, He's ready to transform your heart and offer wisdom and discernment covering your sins with His son's blood. He extends His grace and love offering us eternal life by us simply believing Jesus Christ is our Lord and asking Him to be our personal Savior! If you don't personally have Him as your savior, you can pray this simple prayer asking Him in. If you're ready to make a commitment, if you're ready to give up your will and follow His path He has planned for you, if you're ready for a life filled with so much love from our almighty God repeat this prayer:

Dear God, I am now ready to believe in You and accept Jesus Christ as my personal Lord and Savior. I don't know all there is to know, but I understand that you love me and want to give me eternal life. I place all my sins at the foot of the cross and I ask for forgiveness for each and every single one. Father, I know I have done wrong and I ask that you help me become a better servant to

You. Thank you for sending your only son to die on the cross so that I may be redeemed. Please direct my path from this day forward. In Jesus' precious name I pray. Amen.

Congrats! I'm incredibly proud of you to take that leap of faith! You may be wondering what's next. The biggest thing to do is pray. Pray often, pray hard, out loud or silent. God hears you either way, but PRAY! It's a crucial way to build a relationship with Him. Don't forget, He extends His grace to you forgiving you of all your wrong doings. He'll show you how to offer grace to others through prayer and scripture. He'll also fill your heart with unconditional love. We are all sinners and fall short of His glory. Unconditional is the key word. Study it. Learn it. Believe it. Live it. Another is reading the Bible. I recommend buying a study bible to help understand all that it entails. If you're unsure where to start, John, Matthew, Mark, and Luke will explain the story of Jesus as He walked this earth with us. By studying His Word, you will be able to get to know Him better enhancing your relationship with Him. Jesus was the only man alive to be completely sinless. And it was due to that reason that He was the ultimate sacrifice delivering us from our sin and giving us salvation. Glorify His name because He was ridiculed, beaten, hung on a cross, and died for *you*! You also may want to find a church. But find one that fits you and your style whether it's traditional or contemporary or somewhere in between. This is where learning the Scripture comes into play at. There are plenty of wolves that have infiltrated our churches. If you know the Truth, you'll spot the wolves. Oh, and pray for those false teachers, the ones left in darkness, and anyone who does you wrong. They need it most, my friend. Lastly, when just starting your walk with the Lord, you are to serve. Serve others with love just as Jesus had done. This life isn't about me, or you, your significant other, your mom, your dad, your child, your extended family member, or your friend. It's about our Creator, our Heavenly Father, and the One who was, who is, and who will always be. Focus on the Him and you'll share in His glory. One thing Jesus didn't do was go pick out the best of the best -the ones who followed all the 'rules'. Instead, He hung out with the sinners. He healed the sick- the great Physician of all time- and dear Reader, *we* are the sick! Don't fret though because He offers hope! Healing and restoration are to be had! Allow Him in and you'll be blessed with miracles beyond your imagination.

I'll leave you with this to ponder. Build a home within your heart that you would want to have. But remember to center God in the middle. Branch out from room to room and fill it with what you feel is right. Visualize it daily; hoping God will answer your prayers. Just remember, be thoughtful for what you place in each room. And as time passes see if those items you place in each room change. You may be surprised because at the end of your journey, you'll see that it's not the home you live in, in the material world-it's the home you have built in your heart that completes you.

Safe Under the Willow

About the Author

Shannon Bibby, wife and mother of two children, lives with her family in a small rural community in Pennsylvania. After living through a childhood dominated by domestic violence, she was able to break the cycle of abuse. Building a sturdy foundation of faith in Jesus Christ, she devotes her extra time to ministry helping others look to the Lord to heal from their brokenness. Outside of church, she enjoys spending time with her family creating memories filled with laughter and love.

You may contact Mrs. Bibby by emailing her at safeunderthewillow@gmail.com

Closing

The author has been asked on numerous occasions if she wished her childhood was different. Here's her response:

"It's not about wishing for me. God provides for every need we have. Even when our days look meek or scary, when we as mortals, feel like we've been given the short end of the stick, we must trust the Lord knowing He will provide regardless of the need. So, for me to wish for better parents, more money, a bigger house, a different childhood is like telling God He screwed up. No- He didn't. Those are earthly things. Possessions and people are temporary. They have no lasting qualities. However, once you accept Jesus as your Savior, you will have everlasting life and that makes all the trials and hardships you may experience here on Earth worth it as He teaches us what it means to be a child of God. So, to answer the question no, I wouldn't want a different childhood. In fact, I'm thankful for the life I've been given. Without my past, I wouldn't have a story. Without the story there wouldn't be this book, and without the book I couldn't convey the message God has placed within my heart to all who will listen."

Made in the USA
Columbia, SC
12 March 2020